Every Tir
 า

Every Time I
Talk to Liston

A Novel

Brian DeVido

BLOOMSBURY

Published by Bloomsbury Publishing, New York and London
Distributed to the trade by Holtzbrinck Publishers

All papers used by Bloomsbury Publishing are natural, recyclable products made from
wood grown in well-managed forests. The manufacturing processes conform to
the environmental regulations of the country of origin.

The Library of Congress has cataloged the hardcover edition as follows:

DeVido, Brian.
Every time I talk to Liston: a novel / Brian DeVido.—1st U.S. ed.
p. cm.
ISBN 1–58234–458–2
1. Boxers (Sports)—Fiction. 2. Male friendship—Fiction. 3. Las
Vegas (Nev.)—Fiction. 4. Trenton (N.J.)—Fiction. I. Title.

PS3604.E886E94 2004
813'.6—dc22
2003021810

First published in the U.S. by Bloomsbury in 2004
This paperback edition published in 2005

Paperback ISBN 1–58234–577–5
ISBN–13 978–1–58234–577–2

1 3 5 7 9 10 8 6 4 2

Typeset by Palimpsest Book Production Limited, Polmont, Stirlingshire, Scotland
Printed in the United States of America by Quebecor World Fairfield

To my family

Someday they're gonna write a blues song just for fighters. It'll be for slow guitar, soft trumpet, and a bell.

—*Charles (Sonny) Liston,*
former heavyweight champion of the world

Round One

Diggs throws a quick right at me, but I beat him to the punch with a hard right of my own, twisting my fist at the moment of impact. Diggs's jaw contorts. He'd feinted first with a jab, trying to set me up. But I don't get set up easy. Diggs does this often—feints a jab and throws a right instead. He's not very imaginative with his offense, and that's why if the two of us ever fight for real, I'll knock Diggs's ass on out.

But Diggs, and his management, know this. They know a real fight between me and him would be a war. So instead of a real bout, they use me as a sparring partner, which happens to be my stock-in-trade these days.

I slip another right. Diggs always loops it a little wide anyway, and I counter with a short left hook that snaps Diggs's head back and sends him into a corner. All Diggs can do here is one of two things: tie me up or fight back.

The smart move for Diggs would be to tie me up, so he can clear his head. But nobody ever accused Diggs of being smart. He's a stubborn son of a bitch, and I know he wants to brawl, so I keep my hands high and move toward him.

"Time, fellas, time!" yells De La Rosa, his trainer. "Enough sparrin' for today."

I know this hasn't been a full round yet—not as long as the previous rounds we sparred today—but De La Rosa probably thinks Diggs is getting his ass worked. Which he is. He's getting his ass worked just six days before he's about to fight for the heavyweight championship of the world. This is going to be the last heavyweight title fight of 1999, and if Diggs is going to have a prayer of winning the belt, he'd better be sharper than *this*.

De La Rosa comes up to the ring apron, moving slowly, like his bones are tired. Diggs spits his mouthpiece into De La Rosa's weathered hands. De La Rosa gives the mouthpiece a quick rinse with a cold bottle of water, something he's done a million times. The man has been training fighters longer than I've been alive.

Diggs is breathing hard and seems glad for the rounds to be over. Not a good sign for a man about to fight for the title, considering he only did five rounds with me today and the fight with the champ is scheduled for twelve.

If this were a fair and just world, it'd be me fighting the champ next week, not Diggs. If this were a fair and just world, I wouldn't have a record of 32–11, most of the losses coming in fights I took on short notice just to pick up a payday.

If this were a fair and just world, I'd wear a suit and tie to work every day, instead of a leather protective headgear that's supposed to protect my brain cells—but I know damned well doesn't— sixteen-ounce boxing gloves, a mouthpiece that tastes like dried spit, a T-shirt soaked with sweat from the day before, always moldy gym shorts, dusty black-and-red training shoes, and a hard plastic protective cup that just had its sixth birthday.

But this isn't a fair and just world. I found that out long ago.

What does it take to get to Vegas? As a fighter, I mean. A regular person can just call up any old travel agent, get a plane ticket, a hotel reservation, and get on out to Vegas. Gamble. Drink too much. Buy overpriced clothes if they happen to win some money.

But what does it take for a professional fighter to get to Vegas? It takes this: one part guts, two parts luck, and three parts connections. I've got the guts, but not the other two. At least not yet.

Funny thing is, I'm *in* Vegas *now*. But not as a fighter. Not really. I'm here as a sparring partner for Diggs. After the rounds, Diggs asks me what I'm doing tonight. There's casinos aplenty and the nightlife—a million ways to get into trouble—but it's training camp, and if I want to keep my job, I've got to behave myself. Diggs knows as much, but asks what I'm doing anyway. It's another one of the reasons I don't like Diggs. He asks the obvious way too damn much.

"Maybe I'll catch a movie," I tell him. There's a theater just down the street where a Van Damme action flick is showing. I might just drop on in for a while.

"Then what?" Diggs asks. He's an inquisitive bastard. Does this with all the sparring partners. Does it with Machine Gun Jackson and TNT, guys who hit harder than Chinese arithmetic and who I'm grateful I don't have to spar with.

"Then I'll probably read for a while, then go to bed. You wanna know what I'm gonna dream about, too?" I can only take so much of Diggs. He's annoying as hell and shouldn't be fighting for the title. He's got good management and a suspect chin. TNT actually dropped him last week in sparring, but we can't tell the media that. They'd eat it up. But then the title fight wouldn't draw as much on pay-per-view. This is all stuff that's not in the job description when you sign up as a sparring partner: Make the guy you're sparring with look good at all times. Screw that up, you'll likely find yourself out of work real quick.

Diggs winces a bit and looks hurt. "Hey, man, I was just kidding," I say, and give him a quick slap on the back. For all his bad qualities, Diggs does have a good jab. A beautiful jab. It's quick and whipcord fast and he can double on it—even triple sometimes. He can make it look effortless.

If I don't ask Diggs to come with me to the movies, I know he'll sulk. And the bitch of it is this: I need Diggs to like me. If he wins the belt, he'll need sparring partners. And champions usually pay well. I can't afford to burn any bridges. "You wanna come?" I ask him.

Diggs gives me a small smile. In lots of ways he's just like a little kid. His eyes get real wide when you scold him. He laughs at every stupid joke you tell. And he loves candy. Just last week I saw him sneak a Butterfinger into his room after sparring. He's not supposed to eat any candy during training and neither are the sparring partners, but I saw that yellow paper wrapper hanging out of Diggs's pocket, and his mouth moving furiously, munching on the candy.

About that time, I spotted De La Rosa walking by Diggs's room, looking for him. I stalled De La Rosa a bit while Diggs stood inside the room, chomping on some damned candy bar.

I stalled De La Rosa because as much as I don't like Diggs, I've got a job to do. Which is make Diggs look good. And De La Rosa seeing his fighter hiding behind a door and devouring a candy bar just a few nights before the biggest fight of his life would *most definitely* not make Diggs look good.

There's lots of fight history here in Vegas. There's a graveyard directly under the flight path for planes approaching McCarran

International Airport. Go into that graveyard and see a guy working—maybe a groundskeeper. Chat for a minute and tell him you're a fan of the fight game, he'll probably direct you to a grave that has an old metal urn atop the headstone, broken plastic flowers inside. The grave of Charles "Sonny" Liston, former heavyweight champion of the world.

It's funny, but most people remember Liston for the fights he lost rather than the fights he won. He's the guy Cassius Clay beat for the title. Clay beat Liston twice, once to win the belt, then again in a rematch. Clay, of course, would later become Muhammad Ali. And after the second Ali fight, just like that, Liston faded away.

But people don't remember Liston the way he was in his prime. Big and surly. Attitude of a drunken sailor. Mean as piss. Strong as hell. There were rumors that he actually knocked the stuffing out of heavy bags, tore speed bags off their hinges when he hit them. He knocked people down in fights with his jab. His jab!

In his prime, Sonny Liston, in my estimation, could've handled just about anybody. But people don't remember that. Instead, they remember the man who was twice humbled by Clay.

I come out here—to Liston's grave—every time I come to Vegas. It gives me a sense of perspective, I think. See, Liston came to this town when his career was over. He retired here. Then one day, he died here. People aren't sure to this day, but many say he crossed the mob and they killed him. It's possible. Hell, in this game, *anything's* possible. So in a sense, Liston will *always* be in Vegas. It may have taken his death to make it happen, but he's here. He's here for eternity.

I've often wondered what it would be like to make it to Vegas as a fighter. Not as a sparring partner, a fighter. Names like Leonard,

Hearns, Tyson, and Holyfield. They've all fought in Vegas. Just once, I tell myself, I'd like to fight here. Be part of that select group, if only for one night.

It wouldn't have to be a title fight, either. Just a regular old under-card bout would suit me just fine. I'm not picky. Just give me an opponent and let us go at it, under those bright lights in the hot desert night, and I think I'd feel whole for once. Like I'd tried real hard and finally, for once, got what I wanted.

Vegas is the pinnacle for most fighters. It's where you go when you've made it. There's a saying among some of the old-time Vegas fight trainers: "When you're fighting in Vegas, brother, you've arrived."

Diggs and I see a movie with Van Damme in it, and it gets him riled up.

"I'm gonna work that motherfucker," Diggs tells me after the movie. We're walking down The Strip, back to the hotel, two black men enjoying the dry desert heat. Diggs is jabbering about what he's going to do to the champ. "I'm gonna stab him with my jab all night long and knock him out in ten."

"Easy, boss," I say. "He's never been *knocked down,* let alone out." I should know. I've sparred with Taylor—the champ—before. He's got a chin of granite. Never been on the canvas as an amateur or pro. I swear, God must have put solid marble in Taylor's skull.

"Shit," Diggs says, shaking his head in disgust. "He's never been tested with *these* mambo jambo's, now has he?" Diggs holds his fists in front of his face and gives me a goofy grin.

Diggs has that good jab, but what he lacks is pure power to back it up. In thirty fights he only has fifteen knockouts. Not a bad percentage of kayos, but not a great one, either. He has fair power, at best. The job requires I keep Diggs's spirits up, but I don't want to see the boy get slaughtered, thinking he can go toe-to-toe with Taylor. Diggs goes in all cocky like this and he'll get killed.

"Just use that jab of yours," I tell him as we walk back to the hotel. "You can win this fight on your jab alone."

Back in the room, I'm staring in the mirror. Diggs's camp has put us up in the Riviera, right on the main Vegas strip. I've got to admit, they've done us sparring partners right. Usually they put us in dumpier hotels, but the Riviera is nice. Not a Caesars or anything, but, hell, it'll do. Two queen-size beds, huge tub in the bathroom, and a casino downstairs. No complaints here. I take a quick look at myself and rub my head. I shave it every day, with one of those old-fashioned barber razors. My old-school haircut. Keeps me feeling solid. Like a fighter.

I'm sharing a room with TNT. He can fight a bit but isn't too smart with his money. He's downstairs now, no doubt on a blackjack table, pissing his money away. They pay us six hundred a week here for sparring—good money—and that could go all the way up to two grand a week if Diggs wins the title. Hell, I heard Tyson, in his prime, paid as much as twenty-five hundred a week for good sparring.

The mirror is my ally right now. It's where I practice my other stock-in-trade. When I'm finished with the ring, I've got a plan to get into television. Be a boxing announcer. If George Foreman can do it, so can I.

I give a great big smile, like I'm on camera. I smile real wide and just stare at the mirror, like I'm a stranger to myself. I hold the gaze for a good twenty seconds.

This is useful to do because sometimes when you do a fade-out from a fight, the camera tends to stick on the announcer's face while the station is trying to cut back to the studio. If the announcer doesn't have a good smile that can hold the viewers to the television, the station is likely to lose viewers. See, I understand this kind of shit.

I practice the smile a few more times and, satisfied, notice there's a voice mail blinking on the telephone. I check it. Sure enough, it's Al Bradley. He's covering the Diggs fight for ESPN this week and has asked me to appear on a fight preview show with him the night before the bout.

Since I've sparred with both Taylor and Diggs, Bradley and his crew want to get me on camera for a couple of minutes. Get my opinions on both fighters. It's a good break for me. I've helped Al out before with insider tips about goings-on in the fight business. I'm a "source," and he knows my ambitions once my career is over. Al has always said if he could get me on air, he would. And he's delivered.

It's midnight. I'm in bed and the television is on. I'm watching CNN but not really paying attention to the content. I'm paying attention to the newscasters. I always do this just before going to sleep at night. I watch the anchors' facial expressions and how they pronounce words. I notice the girl that's on now, a brunette, probably in her mid-forties, as she distinctly separates President Clinton's last name like this: Clin-ton.

Me, I'm from Jersey. Tren-ton. It's where I live when I'm not on the road sparring or fighting, four months out of the year, all told. People in Jersey say Clinton's name this way: Clin-in. But I've been practicing, just in case a boxing report ever presents the situation for me to say Clinton's name. It's doubtful that it will, but you never know.

"Clin-ton," I say out loud, putting the channel on mute. "Clin-ton. President Bill Clin-ton." Before I can say another name, the door opens. It's TNT, all six foot five inches of him.

"Whassup?" TNT says. He flips the lights on and rubs his head, which is covered with dreadlocks badly in need of washing. His eyes are red and swollen, most likely from all the smoke down in the casino.

"Not much." My eyes squint from the sudden burst of light. TNT isn't the most considerate roommate I've ever had. And besides that, he's breaking camp rules. "Man, you know damn well they catch you gambling, you're gone from camp. They want us in the room by eleven. You got to spar tomorrow."

"Man, shit" is all TNT offers. It's his favorite thing to say when you ask him where he's been. Another is "Man, fuck." TNT takes his shirt off and reveals a massively developed upper body. If TNT took his career more seriously, he could go places. He can hit hard and is quick for a big man. Problem is, he's dumb as a brick and has no direction.

"You blow this week's money already?"

"Tables were a bitch tonight," TNT says as he gets into bed. "Loan me a hundred. I can win it all back, man."

"Forget it." I don't loan money to other fighters. It's like putting your cash into the toilet. "I told you to stay out of that damn casino. Don't bitch to me when you lose your money and when they fire your ass."

"Man, fuck."

"Turn the damned light off."

"Nah, man. I'm tired." He says it in a lazy voice like this: ta-hed.

I get up and turn the light off, not wanting to argue.

The funny thing is, TNT's fighting on the undercard of Diggs's title fight. And TNT's in no kind of shape. He stays up late most nights, gambling whatever little money he has left, then drags ass in the morning when all of Diggs's training camp goes for a six-mile run.

TNT's lazy, pure and simple. But he's got that body. And he's a good interview. The public likes him. He's big and says silly shit after fights, like "I was just trying my best to knock his head on out to Jupiter." He wins fights he shouldn't, and loses fights he should win, which always keeps him just out of reach of a title bout.

Of course, I was never asked to be on the undercard, even though the promoters know I'm Diggs's chief sparring partner and in good shape. I'm older, have an unattractive record, and even though people who know boxing know I can fight, guys like me don't sell tickets. Guys like TNT, with dreads, magnificent bodies, and funny quotes, do.

TNT told me himself that he's getting twenty-five grand to fight some undefeated kid from California, a white heavyweight who's been carefully managed. Word is some bigwigs want to move this kid up a notch in class and they see TNT as a way to do it. A dangerous bout for the young fighter, sure, but if he beats TNT, he suddenly becomes a hot commodity. I'm skeptical of the kid because I know he hasn't fought anybody yet, and even though TNT is in no kind of shape, I figure he'll knock this California kid out in about four rounds, maybe five.

I shake my head in disgust. TNT probably has that twenty-five grand all spent by now. Probably owes the casino at least that much.

Not me. I try to save a little here and there. I take 10 percent of whatever I get and throw it into a mutual fund. This white-collar guy who used to train in my uncle's gym in Newark told me it was a "smart investment," so I send the company a check every month.

It grew 41 percent last year. As of now, I've got $8,344 invested. The fund specializes in large, blue-chip companies like IBM, GE, and Wal-Mart. Something about them makes me feel secure.

I stay away from casinos and make sure that check gets sent out each month. That's what I do. And TNT, the interplanetary scholar—he gets the big fight.

It's two nights before the fight. Sparring has stopped. Diggs's camp wants to taper off his training now, to make sure he's in the best possible condition. Now it's nearly midnight, and I'm watching CNN again. Tomorrow afternoon is when I go on the ESPN set with Al and company. I'm nervous but at the same time excited about it. I'm thinking of how I'm going to respond to Al's questions and conjure up an image of him in my mind.

"Scrap Iron, you've sparred with both men, and given those sessions, what can you tell us about the fight?"

"Well, Al, I'll tell you this much: Both men can fight." This will allow me to make both men feel good about themselves, leaving me in the good graces of each, and hopefully, let me be a sparring partner for the winner in the near future. *"Everybody knows about Diggs's jab and about Taylor's great power. It comes down to a classic boxer versus slugger match, and it's a great mix of styles."*

"So who are you predicting?"

Smiling—the key is to smile real wide, so my teeth show. I have real white teeth and I think they'll show up well on camera. *"Al, as a member of Diggs's camp, I couldn't make a prediction against him. And a prediction for Diggs would be too obvious. So I'm neutral on this one, my man. I'm Switzerland!"* We both laugh heartily over this, and I get the chance to further show my white teeth. *"But I can tell you that I predict a great fight between these two men."*

"You heard it, folks. Amos 'Scrap Iron' Fletcher, who has sparred with both men, is predicting a barn burner. Make sure to tune in to ESPN for all your pre- and postfight coverage."

A knock at the door. I check the clock. It's nearly one A.M.

11

I go to the door. TNT probably forgot his room key.

"Man, I told you a million times, bring your damn key with you." At the door, however, is De La Rosa. He's doing a bedroom check.

"Where is that motherfucker?" De La Rosa demands.

"He went to the bathroom," I say, quickly sticking my head out the door and looking both ways down the hall. No TNT. That idiot. I knew he'd get caught sooner or later.

De La Rosa stares at me skeptically. "He goin' to the bathroom in *here*?"

"No," I say. "Our toilet is stopped up. He went downstairs to the bathroom." I move closer to the door so De La Rosa won't get a fancy idea like stepping inside. TNT is stupid, sure, but I don't want the kid to get fired.

"I'm coming back in ten minutes. He'd better be here."

I nod and close the door. Then I walk over to my duffel bag and throw on some sweats and shoes. I've got to find that dumb son of a bitch or he's history.

When I visit Liston's grave, the last thing I usually look at is the epitaph on his headstone. "Charles 'Sonny' Liston," it says, along with the dates of his birth and death, "1932–1970." Underneath, it says, "A MAN." That's all.

When it's all said and done, isn't that the easiest way to break it down? When it's all said and done, isn't that the way a person should be remembered?

Despite the late hour, the Riviera casino is crowded. My search isn't as hard as it could be because I know TNT's game of choice is blackjack. A quick scan of the tables here, however, doesn't show any TNT. I check all of them: the ten-dollar minimums, the twenty-five, the fifty, and the hundred. Leave it to TNT, a man no doubt in debt, to be seated at a hundred-dollar-minimum table—one-on-one with the dealer—betting his dreadlocked ass off.

But there's no TNT to be found. I scratch my head and decide to go back to the room. TNT is a grown man, after all, and I can't live his life for him.

A couple middle-aged blondes walk by, wearing tight skirts and pink lipstick. I like pink lipstick. Something about it—maybe the glossiness—makes me smile. I'd go up and say something to the ladies, maybe hello, how are you, or what do you think of the Riviera, but I got business to take care of.

A familiar voice calls me before I can head upstairs.

"Scrap Iron, what the hell you doing up this late?" I turn around and see that it's the champ, Terrence "T-Bone" Taylor himself. Forty-two and zero, thirty-six of those wins coming by knockout. Count me as one of his forty-two wins, but not among the thirty-six knockout victims. He beat me on a decision, in Atlantic City, before he was champ.

I've never been knocked out. Not by Taylor, not by nobody. That's why they call me Scrap Iron. I hang around, a bit rusty, but hard and sharp and still useful, ready to go the distance.

"I'm looking for TNT," I say. Taylor knows of TNT, but hasn't ever met him, far as I can tell. It's not altogether surprising to see Taylor here, at a lesser casino like the Riviera, by himself, late at night. Everybody knows Taylor likes to gamble alone, so he waits till later in the evening, usually, and goes to one of the less popular places like this.

Taylor's seated at the hundred-dollar-minimum table. The ten grand in black chips sitting to his right looks like a miniature version of the Vegas skyline. He's playing at least five hundred a hand, but since I've come in late, it's hard to tell if he's up or down.

"Haven't seen TNT," Taylor says. I watch him pick up about ten chips and place them on the table's cool green velvet. Taylor has huge hands, the size and color of steaks. That's how he got his nickname. And it's why he hits so hard.

"Yeah, TNT's supposed to be working. But if I can't find his ass, he's gonna get fired." I notice Taylor's face looks thinner than usual. I suspect he's gotten lighter for this fight for a reason. He's concerned with Diggs's ability to move around the ring and likely wants to be quicker to catch him.

"Sorry," Taylor says, and turns to the dealer momentarily. It's the kind of blackjack where both cards for the player are faceup. Taylor has a five and a six showing. The dealer shows a six. "Double down," Taylor says, making his five-hundred-dollar wager a thousand. The dealer gives Taylor a six, then flips his card over. It's a queen. Hits again. A five. Taylor's out a thousand bucks, just like that.

"Can't win 'em all," Taylor says, shrugging his shoulders at me. His head's shaved neatly, just like mine. "But in the ring, I sure as hell can win 'em all." He gives me a wide grin. "How you been keepin' these days, Scrap Iron?"

"Good," I say. I remember my fight with Taylor. He was ranked number one in the world at the time, and he won nine of the ten rounds. After he won the belt, I sparred with him for two weeks. Gave him good work. But I haven't sparred with him since. I hear he has two or three guys who work with him real well on a regular basis, so he doesn't have the need for more people just yet.

"So you been getting Diggs ready for me?" The dealer, no doubt knowing who is playing at his table, patiently waits while Taylor continues his conversation.

"As much as possible," I say. "Doing what I can."

Taylor, wearing a black leather trench coat, leans into me. "Anything I should worry about, in particular?"

I shrug my shoulders. "Not really."

But Taylor leans into me again. I can smell his aftershave, something like the ocean air, mixed with peaches. He thumbs a stack of the chips in his right hand. There must be about fifteen of them in there. "Of course, I'd be willing to make it worth your while," he says, giving me a little wink. "Just in case you had anything in particular to tell me."

I back away. "Naw, Champ. You know your way around the ring. I've got a feeling you'll be okay."

"I know I'll be okay," Taylor says, giving me a hard glare. His voice is more serious now. The blackjack dealer looks the other way, pretending not to notice our conversation. Probably a healthy decision for him. "Where's he weak?" Taylor demands.

"No can do, Champ. I don't work that way."

Taylor shakes his head and lets the chips fall back onto the table. He wagers a thousand and looks back at me. "You must be the stupidest man I ever did see."

Turns out TNT's gone and gotten himself arrested. He was walking down The Strip with a couple hundred bucks that Mike Renetti, Diggs's manager, advanced him and solicited an undercover cop posing as a prostitute. To make matters worse, TNT had some marijuana on him, too. He's in the downtown jail now. TNT's gone and fucked himself—he's not going to fight and his future as a sparring partner for Diggs has been terminated.

Since TNT can't fight, they need somebody to fill in. A break for me, right? Not so. Instead, they sign up Machine Gun Jackson

15

to fight the kid from California. Machine Gun is more responsible than TNT, for sure, but he's not as good a fighter. A spell ago he took Taylor the distance in a title fight. I did the same thing, but I fought Taylor before he was champ. Machine Gun fought him more recently, and he's younger than me, to boot. Such are the breaks of boxing. Getting to Vegas, I mean *really* Getting to Vegas, remains far away.

But I'm almost too excited about the upcoming interview to worry about not getting the fight. It's the night before the title bout, we're in front of the Thomas & Mack Center, where the fight is taking place, and I'm sitting on set with Al and Jon Stellato, who writes for *USA Today* and serves as the paper's sports columnist and boxing scribe.

Al is on the latter side of fifty with a bushy mustache and a nice, conversational voice. Jon is about forty and all facial hair—black beard and mustache plastered across his thin face, ponytail tied neatly in back. He could be a regular fashion model. At thirty-six, I'm easily the youngest in the group.

"Now we're just gonna ask you a couple questions about the fight, mainly about your experiences sparring with both men," Al says. "It's going to be taped for broadcast later tonight, so don't be nervous about getting it perfect."

"I can't give any insider info about Diggs," I tell Al, figuring he should know this in advance. "You know, me being his sparring partner and all. It wouldn't be right."

Al considers this for a moment. He looks sharp, dressed in his black tuxedo, as does Jon. It's something ESPN usually does for boxing coverage, dressing up their onsite reporters in tuxes. I came here dressed in a navy blazer and khaki slacks, but they had a tux waiting for me to try on, too. What a touch it gives to the program. Al shakes his head. "No big deal. In fact, I'll probably ask you exactly that question, and you can tell me the same thing. It'll be good material for the broadcast. Now just relax and be yourself."

The taping begins.

I get back to the room around seven. Diggs is down at the gym with De La Rosa, no doubt going through some last-minute fight plans. They've given the sparring partners—now just me and Machine Gun—the night off. Machine Gun went for a run, his last before his bout with the California kid. I hope Machine Gun wins because he's an okay guy, even if he's the one fighting in Vegas and not me.

The boxing segment will be shown on *SportsCenter* at eleven. I can't wait to see it. I think I did well. When Al asked me what I thought of each fighter, I made sure to smile widely and enunciate my words.

I told him, "Well, Al, as a sparring partner for Diggs, I can't give you any inside information as to what we're doing in training camp. But anybody who has seen Diggs fight before knows he has a great jab, and that jab is going to be the key weapon for him in this bout. He wants to utilize the ring—it's a big ring and I even measured it before we went on air—and pump that jab in Taylor's face. Taylor's forte is power, and he wants to trap Diggs on the ropes and pound the body. By doing this, he'll take away that speedy jab of Diggs's and wear him down."

I knew I did well because I noticed Jon smiling at me when I was done. Afterward, Al shook my hand and said, "Nice job. Tune in at eleven."

"Great," I said. Then I asked Al if he could mail me a tape of the broadcast. He was busy undoing the tux and yelling to somebody offstage to bring him a glass of water. I don't think he heard me.

I asked him again about the tape.

"Sure, sure," Al mumbled. He got the water and took a long sip.

"Here's my address," I said, slipping him a business card I had made up not long ago. It has my name, address in Trenton, and the words "Boxing Consultant" written on it.

"Gotcha," Al said. He stuffed it in the breast pocket of his tux.

I'm reading the *USA Today* weather section, something I do almost every day. I like taking looks at the weather of exotic cities—places I never been but would like to visit. San Juan, Puerto Rico; Kingston, Jamaica; Istanbul, Turkey.

Some fighters travel overseas to fight. I never have. But I like to look at some of the cities I know some of the great fighters fought in, see what the weather's like there on any given day.

Foreman, the former heavyweight champ, fought in San Juan and Kingston. Muhammad Ali fought all over the world, too. Places like Munich, London, and Manila. Knocked Foreman out in Zaire.

The weather's partly cloudy in Istanbul today, with a high of seventy-two. Low of fifty-two. Good weather. Wouldn't be a bad place to fight. I wonder if they got big outdoor rings in Istanbul?

Madrid. That would be a cool place to fight. It'd look good on my record, to see it written down that I fought in Madrid. Or Stockholm. Or Ho Chi Minh City. That would look real cool. Ho Chi Minh City. "Now, for the main event, here in Ho Chi Minh City . . . ," I could hear the announcer say before he cries my name and record. Hell, yeah. I wonder if they'd cheer for me there, if I'd be a fan favorite in Ho Chi Minh City?

There's a hard knock at my door. I open it, half expecting to see De La Rosa again. But it's Renetti.

"Hey, boss," I say. I'm surprised to see him here.

Renetti gives me a good looking over. "Go downstairs," he says. "There's a cab waiting for you. Machine Gun's out for tomorrow

18

night. He broke his ankle this afternoon while he was coming down the stairs. Some sort of freak accident. Gene Davis, the promoter, wants to talk to you."

"He wants to talk to *me*?"

"Yeah, you. You're the only fucking heavyweight left in town that has a heartbeat, aren't you?"

I say nothing to this. Sometimes Renetti lacks people skills. "There's a cab downstairs?"

"Yeah," Renetti says. "You need me to come with you? Help you negotiate your purse?"

"I don't think so." I know what Renetti's up to. He knows I don't have a manager, and he knows if he comes with me and negotiates my purse, he'll get the usual manager's cut of one third. I don't have a manager for exactly this reason.

"Your loss," Renetti says.

The cab takes me over to Davis's office. I sit down in a comfortable red leather chair. Davis looks like a lawyer, and for all I know he could be one. Boxing is more big business these days than it used to be. Back in the forties and fifties mob guys had control over certain fighters and you did business their way, or else.

Now, everybody involved in boxing, outside of Don King, of course, has a law degree and more knowledge of legal contracts than a Supreme Court justice. It's the way the game has moved, I guess.

Davis is dressed in a sharply pressed navy suit, and thin bifocals frame his tired eyes. Promoting fights can be a draining business. Davis tries to smile a lot. "Well, well," he says, staring at me for a moment. "I guess it's true when they say timing is everything, isn't it? I've been told this will be your first time fighting in Vegas."

"Yes," I say, trying to enunciate each word as well as I can. "That's true."

19

"Well, that's great," he says, still grinning, giving me the buddy approach. My pal, the promoter. This can mean only one thing: He's going to try and lowball me on the purse.

Davis carefully looks over the contract and slowly hands it to me. "What we have here is a standard State of Nevada boxing contract." He looks me in the eyes and says, "And your purse for this bout will be seventeen thousand, five hundred dollars."

I figured Davis would throw something between fifteen and twenty at me. TNT was getting twenty-five grand for the same fight, so anything Davis pays me lower than that goes directly into his pocket. Don't get me wrong, seventeen-five is good money—it'd be the second-largest purse I've ever gotten. But I've negotiated my own purses before. I know there's room to haggle.

I stare at the contract for a few seconds and shake my head. "I know for a fact that you were giving TNT twenty-five grand." This could get TNT in trouble, but, hell, I did all I could for the guy and he's in jail now, so it really doesn't matter.

"He tell you that?" Davis demands.

"We were roommates for the past three weeks."

He takes his glasses off. No longer my buddy, he's now Mr. Hard-Core Negotiator. "What *he* made is not the issue. What *you're* making *is!*"

I don't like Davis as Mr. Hard-Core Negotiator, so I do my best to bring these proceedings to a quick close. "Listen, now," I say. "I don't want to be difficult here. But I know for a fact that I'm the last guy available who'll take this thing on short notice that you don't have to fly in and check to make sure he's in shape. I've been sparring with Diggs for months, and my record speaks for itself. I've never been knocked down and never dogged it in the ring. You know that. I don't want twenty-five grand, either. Just give me twenty for this fight and I'll sign right now. Twenty is a fair purse for both parties."

Davis puts his bifocals back on and seems more at peace now that we've gotten some of the nastiness out of the way. I can't blame him for trying to make as much as possible, but he can't blame me either. "Eighteen guaranteed," he says. "And two more if you win."

"Eighteen guaranteed," I say. "And two if I go the distance. You don't care if I win." He knows I'm right. Even though he doesn't promote the kid from California, he's more of a hot prospect than I am, surely more marketable and useful to him down the road.

Davis nods. He slowly scratches out the seventeen-five and writes in the new figures. He puts his initials by them. I sign.

It's quarter past eleven and I'm back in my room. I've watched stories on college football, the baseball playoffs, and a brief preview of Sunday's NFL matchups. There's a commercial break on right now, and the boxing segment should be next.

I'm nervous—probably more about this than I am about the fight. Maybe HBO will be watching—perhaps they'll be impressed and ask me to be a guest analyst for their next big fight. Anything, it seems, anything at all, is possible.

I pick up the telephone and dial. There's no answer on the other end, just a machine with a familiar voice that says, "Can't come to the phone right now. Please leave your name, number, and the time you called and I'll get back to you." Then there's a long beep.

"Unc," I say. "This is Amos. Listen, I was hoping to get you on the phone but I guess you're out. Anyway, I just wanted to let you know that I'm fightin' in Vegas tomorrow night. Can you believe it, Unc?" My voice rises at the sound of the words. "I'm fightin' in *Vegas*." I almost let out a whoop. "I'm on the undercard of Taylor and Diggs—

TNT was supposed to fight Randall 'Rocket' Richards, but he got himself into some trouble. Then Machine Gun Jackson was supposed to replace him, but he messed up his ankle. So it's me and Richards tomorrow night, Unc. Ten rounds. I feel like I'm in good shape, too. Think I can take him. I hope you can catch it on pay-per-view."

I take a breath because I've just said a mouthful. Telling good news is tiring work.

"I was also hoping to catch you because I'm gonna be on ESPN tonight. I filmed with Al Bradley and Jon Stellato earlier. We talked about tomorrow night's title fight and I should be on there in a few minutes. I think I did all right. Don't worry if you don't catch it, though. I'll just have Al get me a copy of the tape." The message machine beeps again. I've run out of time.

The commercial finishes, and *SportsCenter* cuts to outside of the Thomas & Mack Center. I see Al and Jon, dressed to the nines in their tuxes, and they talk about the fight.

Al: "Jon, a lot of people have said Terrence 'T-Bone' Taylor is ready to be taken, that he's looked a bit slow in his past couple outings. What do you say to that?"

Jon: "Al, people have been saying that for the past two years. And yet Taylor has knocked out his last three opponents. He may be getting slower, but Taylor still has tremendous power in each hand."

Al: "People are also wondering about David 'Dynamite' Diggs, a master boxer with a razor-sharp jab from the old school of boxing. Can his elusive style give Taylor trouble tomorrow night?"

Jon: "Most definitely. Diggs moves well in the ring, has good range, and his jab is the best in the division. It's a big ring he's in, and if he can move effectively, then Diggs has more than a decent chance of perhaps pulling the upset."

Al: "Be sure to tune in tomorrow night for postfight coverage on

ESPN. For Jon Stellato, I'm Al Bradley, reporting from Las Vegas. Now, back to the studio."

I throw the remote across the room. "Motherfucker!" I yell. I can't believe it! They've cut me out. Not only did they not use any of my interview with Al, but they didn't show me on the set. To top it all off, Jon took my line. It was my idea that the ring was big. Not his.

But why? My heart is racing. I want to storm down to that set first thing in the morning and figure out why it happened the way it did—why Al, after he said I did so well—didn't use me.

My chance. My fucking chance.

I look in the mirror. Surely, I spoke well enough. Jon smiled, after all, when I was through. I swallow and notice my Adam's apple move.

After he won the title from Floyd Patterson, back in '62, Liston and a friend were flying back to Liston's hometown of Philadelphia. He was the city's first heavyweight champ and figured the hometown fans would be on the runway to greet him.

Liston was eager to begin his reign as champ. But since he was an ex-con, most people viewed Liston as an undesirable person to hold the belt. Still, Liston told his friend he was excited about his opportunities to reach out to people in his new role.

"I want to go to a lot of places," Liston, who was the twenty-fourth of twenty-five kids, said. "Like orphan homes and reform schools. I'll be able to say, 'Kid, I know it's tough for you and it might even get tougher. But don't give up on the world. Good things can happen if you let them.'"

But when Liston got off the plane, there was no large crowd of hometown fans waiting. No reception. Nothing. Just a few airline workers and reporters. "I watched Sonny," his friend said. "His eyes swept the whole scene. He was extremely intelligent, and he understood immediately what it meant. His Adam's apple moved slightly. You could feel the deflation, the look of hurt in his eyes. It was almost like a silent shudder went through him. He'd been deliberately snubbed. Sonny felt that after he won the title, that the past was forgiven. He was devastated."

I swore to myself if I was ever in a similar situation, there was no way anybody would ever see my Adam's apple move. Not like Liston's.

I pick the remote up off the floor. It's still working, so I quickly turn on something else and look away from the mirror. I try not to swallow for a long, long time.

Though he was an uneducated man, Liston could, at times, make a whole lot of sense.

"Someday they're gonna write a blues song just for fighters," he once said. "It'll be for slow guitar, soft trumpet, and a bell."

Fight time. I'm standing here, gloves on my hands, mouthpiece firmly in, breathing deeply through my nose, inhaling the thin desert air. The bell's about to ring. I look across the ring and see the face of a man I'll soon be trading blows with. His face is much like mine. Nervous with anticipation, eyes filled with both hate and fear, fists compact and ready to trade concussive blows. Such is the nature of my job.

It's going to ring any second. And I'm here. In Vegas. The Land of Opportunity. Who knows? This fight will be on pay-per-view, and if I win and look impressive, big things could happen. A fight with a contender? A purse for a hundred grand? A million?

I try not to think about Al and Jon and the whole ESPN thing.

I'm a man, I keep telling myself as I stand in the ring, hot lights overhead, crowd wild, yelling, wanting to see blood. I punch my gloves together, bite down hard on my mouthpiece, and raise my arms, partly to loosen up, partly to let this California kid know who he's dealing with on this night. A man. That's who.

Machine Gun, on crutches, is working as my chief second. I'm giving him the trainer's usual ten percent cut of my purse to work my corner. He'll rinse my mouthpiece, give me water, watch the fight, and offer strategy in between rounds. Machine Gun has only one good foot, sure, but he knows the game of boxing. That much, I reason, is worth ten percent.

My body glistens with sweat. This is good. I'm going to start quick. Pump my jab in the California kid's face, work his body with both hands. I'm going to tattoo his rib cage with my left until he's sucking for air, work him over and leave him gasping. We'll see how bad he really wants to be in Vegas. I know, without a shadow of a doubt, it can't be as much as I do.

That bell. I'm waiting for that bell. Any moment now it's going to ring. And I'll be here, in Vegas, stepping toward the center of the ring, ready to make it happen.

Round Two

Machine Gun's in the corner, yelling to me above the deafening crowd noise.

"Okay, keep the jab in his face early! Double up on it, then slide to his left, away from his power! And remember, be the boss!" He slaps me hard on the back and hobbles away. The bell sounds. Me and the California kid—Randall "Rocket" Richards—meet at ring center.

Rocket stands six feet five, weighs about 235. He's got four inches and fifteen pounds on me. White skin, but looks like he's been to the tanning bed. All these white heavyweights these days, they look like they want to be in the movies instead of the fight game, the way they keep themselves up.

I fire a quick jab and pivot. Rocket has his hands up high and picks my jab off with his gloves. No big deal. I figure he's gonna do this the first few rounds, fight textbook style. All young fighters do. They fight like they're *supposed* to the first couple rounds, hands held high, punches straight and down the center of their body, bending their knees to slip a punch—all the stuff they've learned to do in the gym.

But let 'em get hit a few dozen times, I always say. Let 'em go a hard four, five rounds against a man who's been in there a bit, then let's see how they do. Let's see then, in rounds six through ten, if their hands don't come down a little, if their punches don't get a little wider, if they stop bending those knees and start getting hit with shots that wouldn't even have touched them earlier on.

Rocket bends his knees a little. I feint with the jab and throw a right hand instead. It lands on the top of his head but doesn't do much damage. He responds with a short left hook. Rocket's quicker than he looks. The punch lands on my jaw and sends me into the ropes. Damn. Maybe that's how the kid got his nickname. I see a flash, like a picture being taken, and there's a moment of blackness. It's what happens when a man gets caught with a good one to the head. All you can do is hope the darkness clears as fast as possible.

Didn't expect this kind of speed. I cover up, chin tucked in tight to my chest, hands high on my temples, elbows hard against my ribs. The posture I'm in now, Rocket's gonna have a hard time nailing me clean. I can roll my body with whatever he throws, take some of the steam off his shots. I've done this many a time before.

He offers a basic one-two-three: jab, right hand, hook. None land cleanly. He comes in a little too close and I grab him. We clinch and the ref breaks us. I stick out a couple more jabs. He deflects the first one but the second lands and snaps his head back. He smiles as the bell rings and says something to me, but through his mouthpiece I can't understand what. Rocket's cocky and wants to let me know it was his round.

Machine Gun wipes the back of my neck with a cold sponge as I sit on the stool in my corner.

"You're doing all right," he says. "The kid's got a decent left hand, so keep your right up when you're jabbing. That's how he nailed you last time. Your right was down at your side."

I'm breathing hard, trying to get in air. Suck a lungful and hold it for a second.

"Double the jab, now," Machine Gun says. He puts a fresh glob of Vaseline on my face, which will help to make Rocket's punches slide off. "When you're doubling the jab, it's landing. Don't just give me one jab at a time, now." I nod, suck in some more air. I like it that Machine Gun said to "give me" more than one jab at a time, like I'm fighting for *him*. He's a man that takes charge when put in a situation. I like that. It inspires confidence.

"You okay?" he asks, just before the bell's about to ring for round two. He gives me a look and I remember that I'm on television. A guy like TNT would say something crazy right now. People watching would hear TNT say something absolutely nuts, and they'd love it.

But I'm not TNT.

"Yeah," I say. Machine Gun feeds me my mouthpiece, which he's given a cold-water rinse. No blood on it, yet. "Never been better."

Rounds two and three are better rounds. I like to win the first round of every fight because it sets the tone for the rest of the bout. Lets your opponent know right away that you're a man to be reckoned with.

But failing to win round one, a man needs to go out and win round two. Needs to let his opponent know that he just got plain lucky, that things are gonna be different. And in round two, that's just what I set out to do.

I double the jab throughout the round. Rocket catches the first jab I throw on his gloves, but the second jab is getting through to him more often than not. He doesn't seem to have much of a jab himself. Instead, he's looking to counter me, mainly with left hooks to the body and straight rights to the head. He hits me a couple times with some little hooks to the ribs that I feel, but my jab's doing most of the scoring, knocking his head back each time it lands. I've got a good hard jab that can bust a man up over the course of a fight.

Rocket shakes his head a few times after my jabs land, like they haven't hurt him. Lots of young fighters do this. They think that when they smile, it tells their opponent they're not hurt. But the funny thing is, older fighters like myself know when you get your opponent smiling, it usually means he's frustrated.

Yeah, man. Taste my jab. That's right. Taste it. Tastes good, don't it. You want another? Here, I'll give it to you. There you go. Right in the mouth. Right on your lips. I see blood, man. Your blood. It's running down your lips now. I just sliced you, motherfucker. Yeah, I did. Sliced your mouth open. You gonna be drinkin' blood the rest of the fight. Come on. Make a move, man. Make a move. You in here with a man tonight. That's right. A man, motherfucker. Sure, man, cock your right. Throw it. I'm gonna slip it anyways. Throw it, man. I'm gonna slip it. There you go. There you go. Missed. My turn. Gonna nail you. Gonna knock you. Gonna hurt you. Left hook. Follow with right. This here's my fight. My fight.

Machine Gun wipes me down good again between rounds five and six. I didn't do much in round four. Trying to conserve energy. Round five was even, with me landing some jabs early, then Rocket taking me to the ropes and pounding my body later in the round.

Didn't think the kid had it in him to push me around at this point in the fight, but he's craftier than he looks and is pacing himself well. He's got a small silver-dollar knot under his right eye, where my jab's been landing, but I'm starting to swell a bit under both eyes myself. And my legs are feeling heavier each round.

"You got to get off the ropes, baby," Machine Gun says, smearing Vaseline under and over both my eyes. I can still see okay, but if Rocket lands a couple more counterrights, things could change. My right eye could look something like fried bacon fat, and then I'd be screwed. "Get off them ropes and keep that jab in his face. You got to jab and slide away, baby, can you do that?"

I'm trying to get a load of air in. Shit, this kid hits hard to the body. He hit me with a hook to the solar plexus last round that would've deflated a tire. Where'd he learn to go to the body like that? It's a lost art, bodywork. Most kids coming up in the ranks, they're all headhunters. Want to get those quick knockouts by landing those hellacious shots to the jaw, the ones that make highlight films. But few fighters learn the craft of going to the body anymore. Damn shame, too, because it's effective as hell.

"I can do that," I say, mainly to let Machine Gun know I'm not too far gone to stick to some sort of fight plan. I know what I got to do. I've got to keep the jab in Rocket's face. Just keep it coming. Jab him till my arm falls off.

Only problem is, my arm's already dead. I know it don't have but one round more of hard jabs in it. After that, I'm gonna have to retreat to the ropes, let the kid bang on me, hope he gets careless. Hope he drops his hands and I can land a clean one on his chin.

"All right then, Scrap. Now go out there and be the boss for me. Take this kid apart!"

I think of Diggs, warming up for his title fight. He's probably in the dressing room right now, his black satin robe on, working the hand pads. He's probably jabbing the hell out of those hand pads—

stabbing 'em with his left, occasionally hooking off the jab. I wish I had Diggs's left hand right now. Sure as hell could use it.

Arm's tired. Real tired. Got to throw the jab. There. Shit, it's slow. This kid ain't slowin' down none. He in shape. He gonna keep bangin' my body, sticking it with hooks and crosses. He ain't gonna let up on my body. Got to slow this kid down. Got to pace myself. Feel like I might vomit. Got to jab. Arm about dead but got to jab. Got to keep it in his face. Got to.

Halfway through the sixth, my left arm goes. Rocket's being patient, content to let me peck away at his high guard. I jab him twice and the second one lands. Rocket's head snaps back and he tries to counter with a hook. I step away from the punch and jab him again. But this time, my arm's slow coming back. My shoulder muscle's exhausted. Feels like there's acid boiling up in there, feels like nothing will help it but having it drained.

Rocket lands a wicked right on my unprotected jaw and my knees bend without my wanting them to. I see the flash again, sag into the ropes, and Rocket bangs away at my body. I tuck my chin in, let him whack away. He mixes a furious volley of punches to my midsection, but I cover up well. I've got enough left to go the distance, but that's about it. There's not gonna be a knockout, and chances are I'm not gonna win on points.

Before the ninth, Machine Gun tells me I need a knockout in order to win. But I'm battered. Rocket's body attack has gone and left me weak. My legs feel like a chemical burn and my ribs feel like they're about to collapse in some places, looking for a place to die. My body can't take in oxygen fast enough.

There's a point in every fight where a man realizes that's it, he's done all he can do. The only thing left is to survive.

With Liston, it all ended with one fight. After he'd lost his title, Liston made a comeback of sorts, winning a string of fights over in Europe and back in the States. A few of those fights were over in Sweden, home of former heavyweight champ Ingemar Johansson. I don't know why Liston fought in Sweden, of all places, but the Swedes seemed to like Sonny. He always drew pretty good crowds over there.

His opponents during this comeback were mainly no-name fighters, guys with no track record that he was supposed to beat. At times, Sonny talked of regaining the title. Other times, he said nothing of getting back the belt. Around this time, he moved from Denver to Vegas.

Then, in 1969, on a fourteen-fight win streak, Liston met up with one of his old sparring partners, Leotis Martin. They'd sparred together back when Liston was champ. Sonny figured to win the bout without too much trouble.

But Martin was more of a problem than Sonny thought. In the ninth round, Liston pumped out several of his trademark jabs. They weren't as quick as they used to be. The punches didn't have any snap or zing, and they came from the ex-champ a hair slower than they used to. All the jabs missed. Martin countered over the top of one of those jabs, poleaxing Sonny with a right hand. Liston's knees bent awkwardly. Martin landed a left hook and another right that put Sonny face-first on the canvas. The ref counted to ten. Just like that, any dream Liston had of regaining the title was over.

In a year, Sonny would be dead.

* * *

"Ladies and gentlemen, we have a unanimous decision," says Jimmy Brandon, the ring announcer. Jimmy could be a flyweight, he's so small, but hell if he doesn't have a great voice. It's rich and deep for a guy so tiny, and it carries well.

I know who the decision is going to. This is just a formality. Rocket stands next to me, white towel with splotches of blood spread across it draped over his shoulder. He's sweating pretty heavy and so am I. At least I made him work for the win. There's the lump that used to be his right eye, and I hit him with a couple of body shots that he'll feel over the next week when he laughs or coughs.

"Judge Tina Kasmarick scores the bout 99–91. Judge Lou Dibell scores it 98–92, and Jack Leonardo scores the fight 97–92, for the winner, and still undefeated, Randall 'Rocket' Richards."

Rocket comes over and hugs me. "Good fight," he whispers in my ear.

"Same to you," I say. Then he's whisked away by his manager. Television cameras are all in the ring, wanting to interview him. I stand alone. Look over to Machine Gun in the corner, hobbled on one foot. He shrugs at me and I shrug back.

After a fight is when reality sets in. It's when you take stock of where your life has been, where it is, where it's going.

I've just lost my first fight in Vegas, on pay-per-view, and my body is battered like a heavy bag Liston just got through pounding. My head's throbbing. Machine Gun's talking to the doctor, who's come in for the postfight examination.

The doc's slightly overweight and bald, and I wonder what they pay docs like this to check out guys like me after fights. I wonder if there's a long line of docs trying to get to Vegas, to work the big bouts, or if it's something they get assigned to—something that's looked upon as a chore.

"How you feeling, young man?" Doc asks, holding a small penlight to my eyes. He's checking my burned-out pupils for dilation, to make sure my vitals are all in order.

"Never better," I lie. My head is pounding and Machine Gun comes over and gives me a couple of aspirin to kill the headache. After every bout—and every headache—I always wonder: How much damage has been done?

Liston had a simple way of putting it. He said the different parts of the brain were set in little cups, and that when a man got hit with a terrible shot, the brain flops out of the cups, knocking you out. He said when you come to, the brain has settled back into the cups.

"But after this happens enough times," Liston said, "or sometimes even once if the shot's hard enough, the brain don't settle back right in them cups, and that's when you start needin' other people to help you get around."

Doc's checking my pulse, and I hear the crowd start to go wild as Diggs's name is announced over the loudspeaker. He's in the ring now. The title fight's about to start. Machine Gun and I need to get out there quick so we can watch.

I hope my cups are still in working order.

"Stick the jab, Diggs!" I yell. Machine Gun and I have gotten hooked up well—fifth row, a great view for the title fight. It's the first round, and Diggs is doing what we planned so far: sticking the jab and dancing. His jab can be a beauty at times, thrown straight from the hip, quick as a whip, and with a terrific snap. Diggs was blessed with naturally catlike reflexes and can move his head a fraction of an inch to either side just when a punch is gonna hit him.

For the first minute of round one, Diggs is doing just like we planned. Taylor's picking off some of Diggs's jabs with his right, parrying them away, but many are getting through, landing right on Taylor's face. Taylor tries to jab himself, but whenever he throws, Diggs, who's using the ring well by bouncing on his toes, is nowhere to be found.

"Kick the jab out, baby! Stick it all night long!" Machine Gun offers. I have a pair of sunglasses on that Machine Gun went out and bought today, so I can cover up my swollen eyes. It was a hell of an idea on Machine Gun's part. What insight. He's going to make a great trainer.

I'm sipping a tall glass of ice water to replenish lost fluids. Doc gave me a clean bill of health, said that outside of some muscle fatigue, I should be okay. The water tastes good, so I'm drinking lots of it. And even though my head still hurts like hell from the pounding I took, I'm getting into the fight. Diggs may act like a kid and all, but it would be really something if he won the belt. I start feeling like *I'm* in the ring and my ailments go away momentarily. In my mind, *I'm* in the ring, sticking the jab out at Taylor, trying to win the title.

Halfway through the round and Diggs is still sticking and moving. He jabs twice, lands both, feints a right, and spins around Taylor, who has to reset his feet. Diggs fires a three-punch combo and lands them all: right hand, left, right. Taylor's head sprays sweat. Diggs is on the move again. Taylor smiles and shakes his head. Machine Gun nudges me with one of his crutches.

"Looks good, don't he, baby?"

"Damn straight."

Diggs jabs, lands, pulls the left back to his head, trying to turn it over to a hook. Taylor sees this and plants his feet, throws a straight

36

right of his own. Just as Diggs's hook leaves his chin, Taylor's right meets Diggs's temple. The punch lands with a thudding, devastating impact.

Diggs's knees dip and his mouthpiece flies out. In a delayed reaction, his legs wobble and he stumbles backward, into the ropes. They hold him up for a second, then he falls on his ass to the canvas.

Most of the crowd stands up, especially those in media row, up in front. They'd love for it to end quick, because it'll be easier for them to make deadline. I spot Al and Jon and shake my head.

"Attaboy, T-Bone!" I hear a guy a few rows in back of me holler. "Helluva right hand!"

"One," the ref counts, waving Taylor to a neutral corner.

"Shit!" Machine Gun says, shaking his head. I grimace and shake mine, too.

"Two."

Diggs, on the canvas and looking baffled, shakes his head. He's been down in the gym several times, but never in a fight. This worries me. You never know how a man is going to react when knocked down in a fight. It's different in the gym, where the man you're sparring might lighten up if he decks you.

"Three."

"Get up, Diggs!" Machine Gun yells. Diggs, thankfully, gets off his ass and puts his weight on one knee, shaking his head to clear what I know must be serious cobwebs. That was some right Taylor landed.

"Four."

De La Rosa stands just outside the ring, behind Diggs, talking to his fallen fighter. Diggs nods like he understands. A good sign.

"Five."

Diggs gets up. Bounces up and down on his toes, trying to revitalize his legs, to shake the sleepy feeling he probably has in them. Since I've never been knocked down, I can't say what it feels like to get decked. But I've been hit hard before—damned hard—and know the first thing that gets messed up is equilibrium. Balance. Usually, it's a mixture between the head and legs. It's like there's a thin wire that runs from your brain to your feet, and when you get hit with a good one, the transmission of that wire gets stopped somewhere.

The ref gives Diggs a mandatory eight count, then waves Taylor back in. Taylor has his gloves up high, and his eyes are blackjack serious. He's a fine finisher. Knows how to take a man out once he's got him in trouble.

"Tie him up, Diggs!" I yell. I want to take the sunglasses off to get a better view, but don't want people to see how swollen my eyes are, especially my right, which I can't even see out of.

"Finish him, T-Bone!" I hear another voice yell. "Knock his ass dead!"

Machine Gun hits me on the shoulder with a crutch. He's sweating hard and his voice is animated, spit forming in the sides of his mouth. "He needs to grab Taylor and hold on till the ref breaks 'em. Then he needs to step in and jab, 'cause it'll get him close to Taylor, where he can tie him up again. I worked on this with him in camp. Hope the bastard remembers."

Machine Gun's been down a couple times as a pro and is an expert at getting up after a knockdown and coming back. His knowledge on the subject, in my opinion, should be taken as the gospel truth.

Taylor, as I expected, throws a right to the body. Most good pros do this—when they get a man hurt, they go to the body right away, to take away their opponents' legs. This'll allow them to wear their opponent down, allow them to focus on the head in later rounds.

Diggs ducks under Taylor, though, deflecting the right, and ties up the champ with his left hand. Just like Machine Gun said.

"Good job, Diggs!" Machine Gun yells. He smiles and looks over at me like a proud father.

The ref breaks them apart. Diggs tries to dance for a moment, but his legs are still rubbery. Taylor advances. Diggs plants his feet and, his weight coming off his back foot, steps into Taylor with his jab. A power jab, it's called. Something Muhammad Ali used in the old days. Diggs is in close again and ties Taylor back up.

"He fucking listened!" Machine Gun is beaming now.

"Kid's got half a brain, after all."

Taylor tries to whack to the body with his free left, but he's in too close for anything to be effective.

The bell rings. Diggs, that candy-eating sucker, is still alive.

Diggs begins the second round by trying to dance again, but his legs still aren't under him. It can sometimes take a while to get your legs back when you've been hit hard. I wonder if Diggs can regain the spring in them. If he doesn't, he's a goner. Flat-footed, Diggs is no match for Taylor.

It's not pretty to watch. Diggs moves around a bit, but the movement isn't effective. When he tries to go side to side, Taylor just steps in with his own heavy, plodding jab, then bangs to the body, mixing the shots with short uppercuts on the inside. Diggs's head sails upward after each uppercut, and Taylor, who's an expert at putting punches together, adds whistling left hooks that intensify the damage.

It's like artwork, watching Taylor throw leather. There's a beautiful brutality to it all.

"He's not moving, man," Machine Gun says, shaking his head.

"The boy has got to move." He sticks his head out toward the next row, as if being a row closer will allow Diggs to hear him better. "You got to move your head, Diggs!" he yells. But he's got to know that Diggs can't hear him.

"Doesn't have his legs back yet," I say.

"I know that! You don't think I know that?"

"Don't get mad at me."

"Shit, man. I know the boy has legs. He ran like Mercury in training camp."

I need to calm Machine Gun down. He's getting really worked up. "His legs'll come back. Just give him a round or two."

"In a round or two, Diggs might be DOA."

"Dead on arrival?"

Machine Gun shifts his weight on the crutches and looks at his bad ankle. "Nah, man. Dead on his ass."

Round five, and Diggs is getting his ass worked. His legs haven't come back. Outside of an occasional jab, he's got nothing to offer Taylor, who's doing what he does best: giving another hotshot contender an old-fashioned beating. Machine Gun's been quiet the past round or so. I have, too. There's not much to say when a man you've trained for a big fight is getting pounded right before your eyes.

Liston won the title from Floyd Patterson, a quick but small fighter who probably had too nice a personality to be in boxing. Patterson was fighting a guy once and he knocked his opponent's mouthpiece out. The guy, in a daze, went looking for it on the canvas. Instead of taking advantage of the opportunity and knocking his opponent cold, Patterson bent over and helped the guy find it.

Patterson dodged Liston for two years before finally signing to fight him in Chicago's Comiskey Park. Most boxing experts figured Liston would win the belt easily; he was simply too powerful for most fighters of his day.

The experts were right. Liston knocked Patterson out in two minutes and six seconds. Hit Patterson with a left hook that would have given God a headache.

The two men fought the rematch in Vegas less than a year later. The fight had originally been scheduled for Miami, but was moved to Vegas when Liston twisted a knee playing golf.

Liston's manager at the time wanted him to train away from Vegas, in isolation. Liston said no way. He wanted to be in the middle of where the action was.

The truth of the matter was this: It didn't really matter how much Liston trained. Patterson didn't have a chance no matter what shape Liston showed up in.

The fight did go longer this time—Patterson lasted two minutes and ten seconds, four seconds more than the first fight. But the result was the same—Liston left Patterson a battered heap on the canvas.

After the fight, a reporter asked Patterson for his assessment of the brief, violent bout.

"I felt good" was Patterson's explanation. "Until I got hit."

Round eight, and Diggs's face is starting to show the effects of Taylor's fists. His right eye is swelling badly, looking something like a hard-boiled egg ready to explode. Diggs's cheekbones are puffed out, too. Blood is streaming steadily from Diggs's lower lip, and his nose has been bloodied since the second round.

Machine Gun occasionally throws out a comment like "Jab, Diggs! You got to jab, baby!" But for the most part, he's funeral quiet, sitting back like me, watching the carnage continue.

"He's got to get into a groove. That's what he needs to do." I'm trying to get Machine Gun back into it. Nothing I hate worse than to see a man like Machine Gun lose spirit.

"He ain't been in a groove all night long, man." Machine Gun's voice is softer than I've heard it in a while.

"You don't think he can get back into one?"

"He ain't doing nothing right."

"He jabbed well in the first."

"Yeah? Well, it's the *eighth* now," Machine Gun mutters. "The first was a long damn time ago. Long damn time."

"C'mon, Diggs, use the jab!" I yell, hoping to inspire some sort of confidence. I look over to De La Rosa, who, to his credit, keeps a poker face of encouragement, but who I know is slowly dying inside. Any good trainer gets torn up when his fighter's taking a steady beating. He takes all the punches along with his boxer. De La Rosa's no different. Diggs is his boy, and it's painful to watch this happen.

"He just ain't got it tonight," Machine Gun says. "That's what the problem is."

"He is flat, isn't he?"

"You damn right he's flat! Ain't nothing working for him."

Taylor slams a heavy hook to Diggs's body, and Diggs, again in delayed reaction, staggers backward, toward the ropes, then falls to a knee. He's doubled over, frantically sucking in air, likely trying to figure out if it's even worth it to get up.

"Shit, that was a good body shot," Machine Gun says. He looks almost wistful. In the fight game, you've got to be able to appreciate the ones you take almost as much as the ones you give out.

"Yeah, it was. Right under the rib. Bet it hurts like hell."

"Get up, Diggs!" Machine Gun yells. His voice is louder now. And clearer. "Get the hell up!"

42

The ref begins to count. "One."

Diggs's mouthpiece is half-hanging out of his mouth, nothing but a plastic clump, filled with layers of caked and fresh blood, mixed with pools of saliva.

"Two."

"Get up now, Diggs!" I yell, even though there's no shame if the boy doesn't get up. He's taken a pounding tonight, and it's clear he can't win this fight.

"Three."

"He ain't getting up," Machine Gun says. "That body shot took the last bit of energy he had left. It's over."

"Four."

Diggs spits the mouthpiece out on the canvas. It's all over.

"Five."

"Stay down, Diggs!" I hear behind me. "You ain't got a chance nohow!"

"Six."

De La Rosa is next to Diggs again, saying things I can't hear.

"Seven."

Al and Jon are standing up again, along with the other members of media row. I wonder what they thought about my fight tonight, if they'll say anything about it on television later.

"Eight."

Diggs puts his gloves on the canvas and leans forward. He's on all fours now.

"Nine."

He begins to rise, stumbles to his feet, then stands in front of the ref.

The ref takes a long, hard look at Diggs, takes a look deep into his eyes to see how Diggs is. A fighter's eyes can tell a lot to a ref.

If they're still hazy and unfocused after a knockdown, the ref might stop it. If they're clear, there's a good chance he'll let it go on. Since it's not particularly Diggs's eyes that are messed up right now—rather, the rest of him—it looks like the ref might let it continue.

The ref nods his head, wipes Diggs's gloves with his hands, and picks up the mouthpiece. The ref then walks Diggs to his corner. De La Rosa is on the ring apron like a jackrabbit, but he takes his time in giving the mouthpiece a rinse. The more time De La Rosa buys, the better for Diggs.

"He's got to step in with the jab and tie him up," Machine Gun says, leaning into me again. "That's what the hell he's got to do. Then he needs to spin off. Just like last time."

After De La Rosa sprays a couple bursts of water over the plastic, the ref waves Taylor in for the kill. Taylor's body is soaked with sweat, and I can tell in his eyes that he wants to end it. Eight rounds may not sound like a long period of time for some people, but to Terrence "T-Bone" Taylor, a man who hasn't been past nine rounds in his past three fights, eight is practically an eternity.

Taylor leads with his head, ready to blast Diggs's body. I can tell this because Taylor has his right carried low, at the hip, and will likely try to bounce the right just off the lower part of Diggs's rib cage, trying to create even more pain there.

But Diggs must see this, because he steps forward with that power jab and fires into Taylor's unprotected head. The jab lands, and Diggs is inside immediately. Their heads clash briefly. When the ref breaks the clinch, Taylor steps back and is pawing at his left eye.

Machine Gun almost falls over. "He's bleeding! That bastard is bleeding!"

"Diggs cut him!"

Taylor touches the wound a couple times. It's a deep cut, just above his eyebrow. The blood is streaming into Taylor's eye, making it hard for him to see.

"Go after it, Diggs!" Machine Gun screams. He leans forward in his excitement and falls into the man in front of him, who turns around and gives Machine Gun a hard look. I take my glasses off. When he realizes I'm the guy who fought earlier, he gives us a nervous grin and goes back to watching the fight.

"Nail him with the jab!" I yell, jumping up and down. I can't believe Taylor is actually cut. But was it the head butt that caused the cut, or was it the jab? The rules state that if a cut is caused by a head butt and more than four rounds have been completed, the fight is decided by the judges' scorecards. Diggs would then certainly lose. He's lost every round so far.

But there's another chance: If the ref rules it was the *jab* that cut Taylor—and if Taylor can't go on—we would have ourselves a brand-new world champion.

The ref usually makes an immediate determination of how the cut occurred, by a punch or a head butt. But he don't do that here. Must be caught up in all the excitement. He may catch hell later, though. That's for damn sure.

Diggs looks bewildered by his good fortune but, lucky for him, comes to his senses quickly and decides to get to work. Though weary and pounded, he pumps his jab out at Taylor, who covers up in a shell-like defense, probably hoping to get to the end of the round so his corner can get to work on that cut, find some way to close it up.

A right hand from Diggs lands, and Taylor backs up even more. He's on the ropes now, and for the first time in seven rounds, Diggs is on the offensive, putting jabs and rights together. Taylor covers up well, but Diggs, who hasn't thrown much of anything until now, begins to unload. He throws a gorgeous seven-punch combination, starting with the jab, following with a straight right—both are blocked—then the rest connect: right uppercut, left hook to the body, left hook to the head, right hand to the head, left hook to the head. Taylor winces and blood continues to flow into his eye.

Diggs lands a couple more shots to the body as the bell rings, ending a wild round. The crowd, which had grown silent, is now on its feet, cheering.

In Taylor's corner, I can see the cutman, Al Sito, working frantically. He's got a styptic pencil deep into the cut, trying to close it up, and with his other hand begins to put large slabs of Vaseline over the injured eye, covering the entire area. You never know with cuts, but this one looks nasty. Anytime there's a cut that has blood flowing directly in the eye, it's a bad sign. Refs are much more prone to stop the fight when vision of one of the fighters is affected.

Soaked with sweat and looking like a man who's waiting in the delivery room for his first child, Machine Gun grabs my shoulder. "He needs to keep that jab in Taylor's face," he says. "He just needs to open that cut back up."

"Damn straight. If he's got anything left, he needs to let it all ride this round."

"Man's not likely to get another chance like this."

"Not in this lifetime, anyway."

Machine Gun breathes deeply, like *he's* about to go out for the ninth round. "Shit, Scrap, he could be the new champ!"

"Don't jinx it. Boy's got a lot to do, still."

"You think it was the jab or a head butt?"

"Could be either."

Machine Gun shakes his head. I can tell he's trying not to smile, but he does anyway. "Who'd have thunk it? Diggs could be new world champ?"

"Not me. That's for sure."

Round nine begins, and Diggs is doing what I hoped he would. He's laying it all on the line, using the last bit of energy he's got and trying to put Taylor away. Me, I haven't seen Taylor in this defensive a position in I don't know how long. Can't remember the last time I saw the man take more than one or two backward steps, and here Diggs is, backing him into the ropes again, throwing combinations.

Taylor punches back. He lands a couple of good left hooks inside that shake Diggs. But Diggs answers with a right of his own that hits Taylor just above the cut eye, reopening the wound. Blood pours into Taylor's eye again, and he goes back into a shell, keeping his back on the ropes. Diggs jabs three times, lands none of them, but it sets up another right. It lands and Taylor's head snaps back. His eye is painted crimson now, blood spilling everywhere, into his eye, around his eye, above his eye. Taylor has to keep it closed, there's so much blood getting in.

"Stop the fight!" Machine Gun yells. "Ref, you got to stop the fight. The man can't even see!" A vein's protruding from Machine Gun's neck, he's yelling so hard.

"Stop it, ref!" I add, even though I know he can't hear us.

Forty-five seconds into round nine, the ref gets in between the two fighters, takes a long look at the eye of Terrence "T-Bone" Taylor, undefeated world heavyweight champion, on his eleventh title defense, and waves his hands over his head.

He's stopped the fight!

Now all we have to do is wait for the ruling.

Was it a head butt that opened Taylor's cut, or was it Diggs's jab?

There's all sorts of pandemonium going on in the ring. Taylor's camp is arguing with the ref. So is Diggs's camp. A mini-riot breaks out between the two groups while Diggs and Taylor sit on their stools, exhausted.

The two groups inside the ring have simmered down, now that security has gotten involved. They separate the two camps, restoring order. The ref waves to both fighters and they go to the center of the ring. It doesn't look like either fighter knows the ruling yet.

Taylor has a butterfly bandage over his cut eye, which no doubt will need serious stitches. Diggs, on the other hand, limps over to the ref, holding his right side. He could have some broken ribs from the looks of things. That body shot Taylor knocked him down with probably snapped something inside him.

Brandon, the ring announcer, grips the mike in his hands. The entire crowd, loud as a hurricane earlier, is now completely silent.

"Ladies and gentlemen, referee Daniel Madison stops the fight forty-five seconds into the ninth round, ruling that Terrence 'T-Bone' Taylor cannot continue due to a cut over his left eye. The ruling is that . . ."

"Got to be a jab," Machine Gun says.

"Shut up, man. Listen to what they say."

"*Has* to be a jab."

". . . a *punch* from David Diggs opened the cut. As a result of this cut, the winner by a technical knockout, and *new* . . ."

Machine Gun jumps on his good foot and his crutches hit the floor hard. He falls into me. I grab him. He's hugging me and I'm hugging him back. The crutches are still on the floor and I figure I'd better pick them up before somebody steps on them and breaks 'em.

". . . heavyweight champion of the world . . ."

My stomach drops and I try to take in air.

". . . David 'Dynamite' Diggs!"

Diggs falls on the canvas to his knees and places his hands over his face. De La Rosa pumps his fist in the air several times and falls to the canvas with his fighter, hugging Diggs's pained side while Diggs lies on the canvas, sobbing.

A mixture of boisterous boos and some light cheers fill the arena. From the sound of things, it's not a popular decision. And why should it be? Diggs was getting his ass kicked for eight rounds before the cut opened up.

After taking out Patterson the second time, Liston signed to defend his title against Cassius Clay in February of 1964, at Miami Beach. Clay, an Olympic gold medalist, was almost unanimously picked by sportswriters to get hammered out of the ring by Liston. They all said Clay talked too much, didn't hit hard enough, and had a poor defense. Clay was only twenty-two years old and only had a handful of fights under his belt. Liston, on the other hand, was a seasoned veteran and was coming off those two brutal first-round knockouts of Patterson.

Only three sportswriters out of forty-six picked Clay to win the fight. Odds were seven-to-one against him.

Liston was overconfident going in, not training that much, thinking he'd knock Clay out whenever he wanted.

What happened, however, changed the course of boxing history. Clay was more of a fighter than anybody ever dreamed. He jabbed Liston to death, and after surviving a couple scary moments, began actually hurting Sonny Liston. *Hurting Liston!* It had never been done before.

After the sixth round, Liston claimed he dislocated his shoulder and couldn't continue. Clay, to the amazement of everybody, was the new champ.

Later, Liston was sitting in a hospital, battered and sore, and his manager summed up the scene. "Sonny looked like a lump of clay there. He was just swollen all over."

Liston could barely make out a complete sentence, so thorough was the beating. He hadn't said anything since leaving the arena, but finally turned to the manager. "That wasn't the guy I was supposed to fight," Liston mumbled. "That guy could hit."

Ricardo Pinango, featherweight champ from Bogotá, Colombia, is speaking into the microphone at the start of the postfight press conference. Pinango fought just before me and Rocket on the undercard. Even though Pinango's got the goods—he's undefeated in thirty-one fights and has held the featherweight belt for the better part of four years—feathers just don't bring the interest the heavyweights do. If this were a fair world, Pinango would've made more than the forty thousand dollars he likely cleared for tonight's fight, his tenth title defense, which he ended in the first round with a vicious knockout.

"*Mis puños,*" Pinango, who doesn't speak a lick of English, says proudly to the gathered reporters, and holds up his fists. He's got a translator sitting next to him, and the translator explains to everybody that Pinango has just said that he's cleared out the division, is glad Vegas has allowed him to fight here, he looks forward to his next challenge, and praise be to Allah.

Everything makes sense to me but the last part because I figured Colombia was a Catholic country.

The media yawns through all this. What they want is for Diggs and Taylor to come out here, so they can start peppering them with questions like "Was it a jab or head butt that opened the cut?" and "Will there be an immediate rematch?"

Pinango says one or two other things in Spanish that nobody really cares about, except maybe for Telemundo, the Spanish station that broadcasts down into Colombia. I hear Pinango is well liked down there, despite his possible religious difference. He's really a funny little guy, with a boyish face. But he packs a wallop in that left hook. Hits like a wrecking ball.

Dickie Rapp, a reporter from *Sports Illustrated,* stands up and hollers, "Amos, give us your take on tonight's title fight!"

I figured this would happen sooner or later. Until Diggs and Taylor get in here, the media is going to want to talk to *me* about the title fight. Who is David Diggs and how the hell did he win this fight? You're the sparring partner, so tell us, they'll say. Tell us everything.

I smile, make sure my teeth are showing through nice and clear, and say, "Well, Dickie, I should know better than anybody what David Diggs brings to the table. That's a quick jab, good movement, and great boxing skill."

"Right, Amos. But the fight. What's your take on tonight's fight?"

"David Diggs is the new champ. That's my take on the fight. He beat Taylor fair and square."

"He was getting his ass kicked, pardon my French, before he got lucky and opened that cut."

I know what Dickie's trying to do. He's a crafty old newspaperman, been at *SI* for nearly thirty years, and writes good, clean copy. More knowledgeable on the fight game than Billy Graham is on the Bible. He's trying to goad me into saying something good.

The media didn't like Liston. They didn't like that he was an ex-con. Thought he wasn't smart enough to be champ, thought he was rude to them. Which, at times, he was.

But the media often asked Liston stupid questions. And he would respond with a unapologetic bluntness that pissed 'em off.

"How long would you like to retain the title?" one reporter asked while Liston had the belt.

"Well," Liston said, "that's like God asking a man how long he wants to live."

The media lashed back and were often mean to Liston. They constantly questioned his age, saying Liston was older than he claimed. Truth was, those around him said that even Sonny didn't know how old he was. He was one of dozens of kids and was never quite sure. Being questioned about it embarrassed him.

Once, when Liston was in training for a rematch with Clay, the press got downright cruel.

"You talk about your sparring partners being better [this time]," a reporter said to Liston.

"I got Amos [Big Train] Lincoln," Liston said. "He's six feet three, and I got another one from Pittsburgh, he's six feet three."

"So they'll be something like Clay in style?"

"Much better."

"Lincoln," the reporter said. "He says that by the time he gets a chance at you, you'll be in jail."

There was a silence. Liston did not speak. Would Lincoln have said something like that? If so, why? Liston didn't know that Lincoln had anything against him.

Finally, the reporter admitted that he had been lying: "I was kidding. Amos didn't say that."

"I didn't think Amos would say that" was Liston's response.

Even though I'd like to be in the media, I tend to be wary of 'em in interviews. It's almost like they want you to say something crazy

52

or stupid, so they can put it in print or on air. Me, I'm not going to be like that when I get my break. I'm gonna be fair.

I respond to Dickie's claim that Diggs got lucky tonight. "That's where you're wrong, Dickie. David Diggs is known for his jab, and his plan was to keep sticking Taylor with it until something happened. Well, you all were there." I throw my hands up in the air for emphasis. "Something finally happened."

"But wouldn't you agree that Diggs was getting beaten soundly before the fight was stopped?" This is from Jack McCalley, from the *Boston Herald*. He's got a monotone voice but also knows the fight game well. He's a nice guy, the type that always seems to have a scoop on somebody else. A real pro.

"I haven't checked the scorecards yet, gentlemen," I say, giving them nothing. Which is exactly what I'm supposed to do. Do they think I'm gonna say something crazy, like Diggs was getting his butt whipped (which he was)? That happens, Renetti, Diggs's manager, has got reason to can my ass before I can start making some real money with the new champ.

"Well, you don't need to look at a scorecard to know that Diggs had lost every round of this fight."

"Gentlemen," I say as diplomatically as possible, then place my hand on Richards's shoulder. "There's a young man right here, Randall 'Rocket' Richards, who just fought a damn good fight tonight. Won a decision over a crafty old veteran and looks to be going places in the division. Diggs and Taylor'll be out momentarily. How about you talk to this young man some before they come out here, ask him a few questions about our fight tonight. What do you say?"

The group lets out a collective groan, knowing they aren't getting any good ones from me tonight. After a few dull responses from

Rocket, who needs to take a course in PR if he ever wants to fill an arena, I get asked a question from a local television station. "Scrap Iron, did you think Diggs was going to walk out of here with the belt tonight?"

I stand up again and lean forward, so the camera can get a better angle of me. "I'll tell you what I thought before the fight. I thought that you never, ever know what's going to happen in this game. 'Cause if you've been in it long enough, you realize that anything can happen. Anything at all."

Round Three

Taylor enters the pressroom first, walking fast, a thick butterfly bandage still plastered over his wounded eye. He's wearing black sweats that have his name inscribed on the shirt: "Terrence 'T-Bone' Taylor—World Heavyweight Champ." No longer true.

Taylor's entourage of trainer, manager, and other hangers-on flock behind him. Taylor looks pissed as he sits down to begin the press conference. Leans into the microphone and the room lights up from the camera flashes.

"First of all, let me say that the ref's decision was absolute bull-shit!" Taylor says, his voice deep and threatening. Some members of his entourage reaffirm Taylor by chorusing, "Yeah, man—bull-shit!" and "Tell 'em what the deal is, T-Bone!"

Taylor continues, "Anybody watching that fight had to see a head butt opened up my cut. The man should've been disqualified!"

"Terrence, will there be an immediate rematch?" asks David L. Sampson, from the *New York Times*. Sampson's one of those guys who looks like he'd put his middle initial in his byline. Small, wire-rimmed glasses, balding up top but his hair slicked over the bald spot to make it less noticeable. A real geek.

"I'm not finished yet!" Taylor hollers, pointing a threatening finger at the entire group of media. "Nobody speaks till I'm finished!"

The room gets quiet real, real quick. Not hard to do when you're a man of Taylor's size—an angry man at that—who has just lost the world title on a technicality.

"I want everybody to know my feelings on this. The ref's decision is bullshit. We're going to protest the decision. You all saw what happened out there. I was kicking that boy's ass for eight rounds until he head-butted me."

Jack Nylon, who works for CNN and has a reputation of acting fearless in the face of threatening figures like Taylor, stands up. "Terrence, are you going to demand an immediate rematch?"

Taylor stares in fury at Nylon, once a star linebacker in college. Nylon doesn't take mess from pampered athletes. He's still football big and has the build to get away with shit like cutting off the former heavyweight champion of the world just when he's been told not to.

"Didn't I just tell you all to be quiet?" Taylor says. His eyes are narrowed like razor wire. "Didn't I just tell you all to let me speak?"

Nylon stands his ground. "I take it you're not interested in a rematch, then. Is that what you want me to report?"

Taylor goes for the bait. "Hell, no. I'll fight that son of a bitch anywhere, anytime."

"Replays have showed that it was a jab that opened the cut up."

Taylor leaps from his seat and begins to climb over the press table. A couple of his boys grab him by the waist and try to settle him down. "Man, you want me to come down there and take care of *you*? I already done told you all it was a *head butt* that opened the cut, not no damn jab." Taylor puts his hand on the bandage. "Diggs couldn't break an eggshell with that jab of his, let alone open up a cut!"

Nylon plays it cool, even though I wouldn't mind seeing the two of them tangle. Nylon still keeps in shape and hit like a motherfucker when in college. Played for Alabama and was known for his fondness of laying people out. His nickname for the Crimson Tide was Body Count.

"You want to come down here and tangle, Terrence, go right ahead. But that footage of you trying to come down here is gonna air on tonight's show. I'd suggest you call off such behavior unless you want to do more damage to your image."

Taylor's shrugging his boys off, telling them to get the hell away from him. He seems calmer now, maybe a little more open to reason. He looks over to me—I'm right next to him—and shakes his head in disgust. "What the hell is *he* doing here?" he asks, to nobody in particular.

"He fought on the undercard," says some faceless reporter. "He's also Diggs's sparring partner."

"Oh, yeah. Sparring partner for the new champ, isn't he?" Taylor says it in a way that's supposed to be demeaning, I can tell, 'cause he throws his hands up in the air like he's real impressed. "So what's your take on the fight, Mr. Big Shot Sparring Partner?"

"Come on, now . . . ," I say.

"Nah, man. Tell me. What's your take on the fight?"

I shake my head. This isn't going anywhere good.

Diggs enters the room, walking slowly to the podium, not bothering to sit at our table. He's flashing a million-dollar smile, has sunglasses on just like me, and is wearing the usual blue-and-white sweats he runs in.

The media gets up and begins to fire questions at the new champ.

In all the commotion, I lean over toward Taylor and whisper, "I'll tell you something. It doesn't really matter what I thought about the fight tonight. 'Cause what *happened* is that you lost your belt. That's all that matters." I give him a satisfied grin, turn back in my seat, and listen as Diggs gets ready to talk.

"Glad to be champ, baby!" Diggs blares into the mike, standing up, waving his hands over his head. "World champ! Sounds good, don't it? Champ of the whole wide world!" He gives a goofy grin to the media and coughs, holding his pained side.

Diggs gets hammered with questions.

"Is there going to be an immediate rematch?"

"How bad are you hurt?"

"Did you feel like not getting up in the eighth when Taylor knocked you down?"

But Diggs is so excited that he doesn't answer any of the questions. He's in his own little world. A place called Diggs-land.

"I'm the champ, baby! Can you believe it? I'm the champ!"

"Did you think it was your jab that opened the cut, David?" Nylon asks.

"Champ of the whole wide world! Can you believe that bad mama jamma?"

"What was going through your mind before the last knockdown?" Sampson asks.

"The world's a damn big place, and I'm champ of all of it!"

"Does Taylor hit as hard as advertised?" asks Al.

"I ain't never been outside the States before, but now I'm champ of *everything*!"

"Don't you think it was just a lucky punch that won you the belt?" asks Al Grottinger, also of *USA Today*.

"How 'bout Tasmania? I want to fight soon in Tasmania. It exists, don't it? Like the Tasmanian Devil, that funky lookin' dude on Bugs Bunny? I wanna fight there!"

The media can't believe it. They can't get a decent quote out of Diggs. He's like a little kid, rambling on about how he's champ and all. He's so happy that even Taylor doesn't quite know what to make of it. Taylor just sits and stews while Diggs makes an ass out of himself.

"Gonna party like it's 1999, baby!" Diggs yells into the crowd.

"It already *is* 1999," Sampson says.

"Yeah, it is," Diggs replies, smiling and shaking his head. He's happy as a kid with a stack of fresh baseball cards. "Ain't it great?"

Renetti finally steps up to the podium and tells the media that, yes, there will be an immediate rematch. The contract called for a rematch within six months in the event that Diggs won the belt. Renetti says he intends to honor the contract. A rematch will be signed as soon as possible.

This doesn't surprise me. A rematch with Taylor will draw Diggs the purse of a lifetime, something in the tens of millions, certainly more than the seven hundred thousand dollars he got tonight.

Seven hundred thousand dollars! Shit. Even that's a lot of money.

But I can't complain. I've got my twenty thousand dollars coming to me, since I went the distance. Davis is standing over in the corner, ready to cut the checks.

I sure can use twenty thousand dollars.

Just as Renetti is doing all the diplomatic stuff—like telling the media how honored they are to win the title, how great a champ Taylor is, and how Diggs is going to do everything in his power to be a great role model for kids—Diggs hovers back into the mike and shouts, "And one more thing: party at my place tonight, baby! We're partying all night long! The Riviera is where it's at! Bring the ladies, bring the wine, bring yourself, and we'll have a time!"

The reporters, who no doubt now think Diggs is out of his gourd, give a rowdy laugh to this. Guess they're in good spirits. Hell, it's not every day the *media* gets invited to a postfight party.

I've got my check in my wallet—twenty thousand dollars sure is a pretty sight on paper—and me and Pinango, the Colombian featherweight champ, are kicking back on a couch in a huge suite of connected rooms that Renetti rented for the postfight party. A girl who's got to be a stripper is sitting on the couch with us and we're all doing vodka shots. It'll help to dull the pain my body's feeling.

Pinango's small, but the kid can drink. We don't understand a lick of what each other's saying, but it don't bother us. The goal isn't to understand, necessarily. It's to get slap-ass drunk.

The stripper's doing shots with us, giggling with a helium-rich voice, telling us that Vegas is a great place to be in her line of work.

"People tip real well," she says. "But the only problem is they all expect sex." She sighs, tosses her hair back. "If you're a *true* stripper, like me, you don't do sex. Not for money, anyway."

"Really?"

"No," she says firmly, giving me a look. "That would make me a *prostitute*! My mother raised me better than that."

Pinango's got a glazed look in his eyes, and I can't tell if it's from the drink or because he's staring at the stripper's large, bouncy breasts. She's wearing a tight crushed-red-velvet dress that shows 'em off nicely.

"*Son falsas esas?*" Pinango yells at her. His little eyes are almost half-shut from the drink.

"What'd he say?" I ask.

The stripper smiles. "He said, 'Are those fake?'"

"You speak Spanish?"

"Yeah," she says. "And French, too. Bet you didn't know a stripper could be multilingual."

"Guess I just never thought about it."

"*Sí,*" she tells Pinango.

"Well, I'll be damned." Man like me doesn't get to see a fake pair every day. They sure do look nice. Big and round. Bet they feel nice, too.

Pinango stands up, wobbles a bit, then gets down on a knee, right next to the stripper. Looks as if he's about to propose marriage. *"Te daria un montón de hijos!"* he yells. *"Soy tan fértil como la tierra de mi pais!"*

She begins to giggle.

"What'd he say?"

She giggles some more.

"What? Tell me!" Of all the times not to know Spanish.

"He said, 'I would give you dozens of children. I am as fertile as my country's soil.'"

"Well, I'll be damned." I nod my head a couple times, put my arm around Pinango. The little guy has the balls of a heavyweight. I got to respect that. "I think he likes you."

"Looks that way."

"I'm gonna go get me another drink. Hope you'll excuse me."

"Sure."

"You'll be okay here with Pinango?"

"Sure. He's kind of cute."

Damn. It'd be nice, for once, to have a stripper call *me* cute.

I finally track down Diggs, who's being mobbed by media guys trying to get the inside dope on the new champ. But Diggs, I can tell, isn't exactly in a media mood, because he breaks free of the crowd and runs around the room, chanting, "Who's afraid of the big bad Diggs, the big bad Diggs, the big bad Diggs?" He's prancing on the tips of his toes like a ballerina, half-drunk already, apparently having the time of his life. Thank God Renetti wouldn't allow any cameras in here.

"Scrap! What up, baby?" His voice is hoarse from all the yelling he's done in the last hour or so.

"Hey, Diggs. Congrats, man. Great job tonight."

He gives me a big, sloppy kiss on the cheek. "Man, I can't believe it, man, and you helped me, man . . ."

Diggs continues to mumble things—half of 'em don't make sense—and keeps me in a fierce hug.

I give him a couple hard slaps on the back and move away a step. "You're the champ now, Diggs. Got yourself the belt and everything." I take a good look at him, size him up. "Damn."

His face is a swollen mess. Diggs's lower lip is twice its normal size. Then I remember mine probably looks almost as bad from all those right hands I took from Rocket.

"It was a helluva fight, wasn't it?" Diggs says, his eyes glazed from the drinks.

"Sure was. You really sucked it up in there. I'm proud of you."

"Thanks, man. Taylor sure can punch."

"Yep. But you took it well. You took it like a man."

Diggs begins to bounce on his toes again and, despite the pain he must be feeling in his side, starts to shadowbox, sticking out his jab several times in the air. "We got a rematch to train for soon, Scrappy."

"You're gonna make yourself a lot of money."

Diggs smiles at this. "Yes, I am. *Lots* of money." He looks around the room quickly, like he's searching for something. "Which reminds me, I got to go talk to Regina. She works in town—gonna hook me up with some ladies, you know what I mean?"

I figured as much. Man like Diggs, who's gone without it for a couple months now, has probably been thinking of nothing but getting a little ever since training camp. Can't blame him. After a while a man starts seeing visions in his head—little fantasies, really—about how good it is and how much he's missed it.

"What kind of ladies you talking about, Diggs?"

"Aw, man. You know. The best money can buy."

"Hookers?"

"Sure, man. This is Vegas after all, ain't it?"

"I'd be careful, Diggs. You never know . . ." And you never do. Some of these Vegas hookers don't make guys wear rubbers. Got to be careful about that. Might wake up one morning and see something yellow down there. Yellow ain't no good. Neither is HIV.

"Man, c'mon. I just won the belt. Can't a man do some celebratin'?" He stares at me a second, his eyes unfocused, and smiles. "Hey, you know, I just realized that *celebratin'* and *celibate* kind of sound alike. They sound *exactly* alike! Ain't that true, Scrappy?"

"Never thought of it before," I say.

"You know, I won a spelling bee once, a long time ago. Think it was the third grade or something. I beat some kid out by spelling some word right—I can't remember which one it was now." Diggs's face looks serious. "What damn word was it? Ah, hell. I can't remember."

"Well, that's great, Diggs. That you were spelling bee champ and all."

"Yeah. I was real proud of it. So was my momma. She was real proud."

Diggs's mother died of cancer last year. He used to call her after every fight, and when he heard her voice, he'd cry these hot, happy tears in the locker room after the fighting was over.

"Well, she'd be real proud of you now. I know that much. She's probably looking down and smiling at you right this instant."

"You really think so? 'Cause that would be great if she was. That would really be great."

"I think she is, Diggs. I really think she is." He pinches his nose and a couple of big tears drop out of his eyes and spill off his cheeks, onto the floor.

"All right, then," Diggs says, slapping me on the shoulder and giving me another hug. This one he doesn't hold as long, though. Gives me a hard pat at the end and we move apart. Diggs turns around, then gives me a final wink. "Gonna go get me some ass now," he says, and disappears into the crowd.

I'll give Diggs this much: The man certainly knows how to ruin a sentimental moment.

I'm pouring some vodka into my glass and splashing it all with a little tonic water—which'll kick the edge down a bit. It's getting late and I'm trying to taper off. The glass is just about filled when I notice a familiar face walking up to me.

It's Nylon. He's got a tweed sport coat on and saunters up to me, carrying a fresh bottle of Jack Daniel's.

"Don't you have to go on air soon?" I ask him, staring at the bottle.

"Nah, Scrap. Already did my report for the evening. Told millions of viewers all about the big upset—and about the former champ's inability to control himself after the fight. We showed that nice shot of Taylor climbing over the podium, trying to get at me."

We both give a good laugh over this, but my ribs hurt like hell so I try not to laugh too much.

"Tough fight tonight, though," Nylon says, filling a clean glass with some Jack and a bit of Coke, just enough to keep him out of trouble.

"Yeah, it was. That kid's not bad."

"Really? You think he can go places?"

"He's *white*. Course he can *go places*. Any white heavyweight can, given the right management."

Nylon takes a long sip. "Right. But you know what I mean. Can the boy actually fight?"

"I think so."

"What makes you think he's different than any other white boy who puts on gloves?"

"Jack, you've known me how long now? Six, maybe seven years?"

"Something like that."

"And I've fought my share of white hopes."

"True."

"Well, this kid Rocket *can* fight. He takes a good shot, goes to the body like a jackhammer, and he doesn't get tired. Believe me, he's got himself some tools. They find the right opponents for this kid, he could really do something."

Nylon holds the glass in front of him and stares at me. He's a good-looking guy in his mid-thirties. Small mustache, always neatly trimmed. Rugged features, like his face could be carved into a mountain.

"The question is, Scrap, could he beat Diggs right now?"

"C'mon, Jack. You know I can't talk about the man I spar for."

"No, no. It's off-the-record. I'm just curious. What would happen if he and Diggs got in the ring?"

I don't say anything for a moment because to answer too soon wouldn't be proper, like the answer is automatic. Which, to be truthful, it kind of is. "You'd have a new champ if Diggs and Rocket ever got in the ring together. That's what would happen."

"Damn. Really?"

"Yeah. Not a doubt in my mind. Rocket goes to the body well, and he holds his hands up pretty high. As good a jab that Diggs has, it wouldn't work against Rocket. He'd just pick the jab off, work Diggs's body, probably wear him down late and stop him." I look at my glass. "That's the kind of fight it would be."

My glass is getting empty. Nylon pours some more vodka in there. "Take the pain away from those body shots," he says, smiling. "You know, I remember after home games in Tuscaloosa, the team used to go out and tie one on, especially after we won a big game." He smiles big, just thinking about it. "Especially against a team like Georgia or Florida. Man." He sighs. "I remember the best part of it was that you forgot how damn sore you used to get a few hours after the game was over."

I step away from the bar and try to straighten my back out a bit. It's starting to stiffen up, and the lumps on my face are beginning to get sore. Tomorrow's gonna be a painful day, especially when I first get out of bed. If I'd of won, it'd be a good sore. But when a man loses, there's no such thing as a good sore.

Nylon looks at me kind of reflectively, like he's sizing me up. "Say, Scrap, what are you doing tomorrow morning?"

I stir some of my drink with my index finger. Seems like all the alcohol is near the bottom of the glass. "Sleepin' in, most likely. Gonna be hard to get up tomorrow, if you know what I mean. Why?"

"I was just thinking."

"Just thinking what?"

"Well, I know how you've been wanting to get on television and all. And Diggs is the new champ now."

"And?" I'm getting kind of excited, but don't want to think anything too much. Not after what happened with Al and Jon.

"And I've got to run a quick report tomorrow morning. Live from Vegas. Kind of a summary of what happened this weekend. It might be kind of cool to have the top sparring partner of the new heavyweight champ show us how Diggs won the belt."

"Ha! You mean explain how Diggs landed a lucky punch?"

"No. I mean, you could show us what Diggs's game plan was going into the fight. Maybe explain to the viewers what T-Bone was doing well, then what Diggs was trying to do, maybe how Diggs's jab eventually opened up that cut. Kind of break it down for our viewers, but in layman's terms."

"Why not get Diggs on there?"

"You were at the press conference. There's no telling what that nut's gonna say. I want an interview, not a circus."

"You got a point."

"So tomorrow morning it is. You're staying here, right? Meet me in the lobby at nine. We'll go over what we need to talk about, stuff like that."

I put my drink down. This is gonna be good. A spot on television! At last. "One more thing, Jack. Uh, I don't really got anything nice to wear. You know, just sparring out here and all. Didn't have to really wear any nice clothes to Vegas."

Nylon waves his hand. "Don't worry about it. We've got people for that." He shakes his head. "Hell, tell you what. Meet me here at eight, we'll run by Caesars. Pick out a pair of pants and a sports coat for you. Make you look real sharp."

"Hey, man. That sounds great."

"Sure it does, my man. And you know what?"

"What?"

"That's what company credit cards are for." He gives me a smile and a wink. Then he's out the door.

Pinango's gone and passed out. The stripper, whose name is Carli, is waving her hands quickly over Pinango's face. She doesn't get a response from Pinango, who's so out of it that he's snoring.

"Too many shots, I guess," I tell her. Pinango's little head is in her lap, her toned and tanned legs supporting him. Her skirt is tight and riding high and I can see all the way to her upper thighs.

"He must have a low tolerance level," she says. She pats the open area on the couch next to her. "Sit down." She gives me a smile. Her lips are red and moist.

"Well, he probably hasn't drank anything in a couple months, seeing how he's been in training and all," I say. "Throw all that hard liquor in a man's system after months of not drinking and it'll mess a person up."

She's sipping some tall, fruity drink. Slivers of pineapple and thin orange slices are floating at the top like survivors of a sunken ship. "I don't know how you men *do* it," she says. "I couldn't give up my drinks for a week, let alone *months* at a time."

"Not all men quit drinking during training," I tell her. "Hell, Julio Cesar Chavez, the great Mexican champion, he used to drink beer like it was tap water when he was training. Tecate, I think it was."

"Oh," she says lazily. She places her hand on my arm. "So, how does it feel to be working for the new champ?" Her hand is smooth and warm and soft. She runs her index finger up and down my arm a couple times, causing the hairs to stand on end. "Are you excited?"

Talk about a loaded question.

"You must be excited," she says. "I would be if I was working for the heavyweight champion of the world."

She has a good point. I haven't really thought about it much, mainly because I have mixed emotions about what all happened tonight. I got my shot in Vegas after all this time but got beat pretty good. Then Diggs went out and pulled a miracle out of his ass. "Guess it hasn't sunk in yet," I tell her. "Things have just been moving so fast."

She pats poor little Pinango's head. He looks like a Colombian angel lying in her lap, snoring away, arms crossed, this big smile stretching wide across his face. Hell, I'd be smiling, too, if I was passed out in a stripper's lap.

"Speaking of things—or people—moving fast, it seems Mr. Pinango here has finally slowed down. You know, he was pulling some pretty quick moves on me."

"Was he now?"

"Yes, he was. He kept trying to get me to go see his room with him."

I don't quite know what to say to this so I keep quiet.

She bites her lower lip. "It'd just be a real big shame if I didn't get to see *somebody's* room tonight, though."

"Would it now?"

"Yeah," she says, stroking my arm again lightly, lightly, knowing exactly what kind of response she's getting out of me.

I got to be on set with Nylon early tomorrow, so what I *should* do is go on home by myself and get some sleep. She's just one of dozens—women who see a man's elevated status and want to be in it with you for a little while. These kinds of women are always available after fights, always lurking, waiting, it seems, for the right opportunity.

I should go home, sleep, be fresh for tomorrow.

But she's still stroking my arm, Carli, the stripper-who's-too-good-to-be-a-prostitute but for the right amount of money will dance around a man's (or woman's) hotel room in nothing but a G-string.

Only problem is I haven't had any in a while—not for the months I've been in camp with Diggs. Hell, a man can always catch up on sleep later. Nothing a couple cups of coffee can't help me out of in the morning.

I grab Carli's hand and she stands up. As she grabs my arm and I turn around to walk out of the party, I notice that she's let Pinango's head flop into the cushion, facedown. I take a quick step back and put his head on a soft pillow. He continues to snore. "Sleep well, little champion," I say, and take Carli's arm once again.

Liston liked women, too. Once, when asked how he got fired up for a fight, Sonny said he imagined his opponent was the only person standing in the way of him and a night with Lena Horne.

Fondea Cox, his former sparring partner, said when Sonny wasn't training, his big sport was women. "He used to get the hotel rooms and pick up women left and right," Cox said. ". . . We would go into a new town, and we would have girls in there . . . and it's amazing the things that they would do."

Sonny knew there was a balance between working hard before the fight and playing hard after the fight, and he did both. When a man works his body into tip-top shape over a period of time, when he sacrifices so much of himself in battle, he needs to know there's something waiting for him afterward.

A man can get beat on in the ring only for so long. After a while, he needs somebody to be next to who won't hurt him.

"Carli; hey, girl, wake up." I shake her shoulders a couple times but she doesn't respond. "Come on now, you got to get out of here."

I've shaved, showered, and I'm ready to head out the door and meet Nylon. I don't know what time I finally fell asleep last night but it was definitely after three.

I gently grab her by the back of the head and shake.

"Ummh. Yeah?" Her eyes open slowly.

"You got to get up, girl. I have to leave."

She reaches for me, trying to pull me close to her.

"Can't we play a little more this morning?"

"Naw. Look, I really got to go. Got an appointment I can't be late for." I pick up her shoes and dress and toss them onto the bed.

"Can't I just stay here?" she says in a pouty voice.

"No can do. I leave, you leave. That's how it works." I stare at her extra long to make sure she gets the message.

"Fine," she says, suddenly in a bad mood. She throws on her dress faster than she took it off last night and steps into the heels so quick she loses her balance and stumbles to the door. I don't feel bad that she's angry; she knows I'm a fighter and I don't live in Vegas, so nothing else but an occasional visit to my hotel room is gonna happen.

"Been a pleasure, Carli," I say as she opens the door to leave.

Carli turns around, eyes puffy and face lighter without the makeup. "A real pleasure," she says, giving me a sarcastic smile.

Just before she walks out the door, I throw it to her. "Catch!" I yell as it sails over her head. Carli makes a nice catch and pulls it in, stuffing it into her purse with a huff.

Her black G-string. What a woman.

I've got to say, the new threads are nice. I've got me a light green sports coat smoother than a baby's skin and a pair of hundred-dollar black slacks that give my legs plenty of room to breathe. To top it all off, Nylon picked out a ninety-dollar black turtleneck to wear under the coat. Ninety dollars for a turtleneck!

We've gone over what I'm gonna say about a dozen times, but I still feel a little nervous. Maybe it's because I know that the chances of this getting cut are pretty slim. Nylon says he absolutely has to fill up some airtime, and he doesn't have anything new to report. He's gonna ask me about Diggs's training camp, how Diggs trained for the big bout, maybe what our plan with Taylor was, stuff like that. I cleared it all with Renetti. Any exposure for Diggs at this point is good: It'll help start the demand for the rematch.

Diggs got on a plane earlier this morning for New York City with Renetti. They're hitting the talk show circuit come Monday morning. "Just don't say anything crazy," Renetti told me before he left, along with the news that I had the next month off, to give Diggs's eye enough time to heal. He did, however, hand me a check for five thousand dollars—a bonus that I didn't expect. Did it for Machine Gun, too. Don't know if Renetti sent TNT a check or not, or if he even knows where TNT is.

So I got twenty-five big ones, a spot on national television, and I'm the lead sparring partner for the new world heavyweight champ.

Right before we're about to air, I take a big sip of bottled water. Wet my lips because I want to be able to lift my upper lip when we get on air, 'cause then my teeth'll show through a lot better.

Filming begins. We're outside the Thomas & Mack Center, same spot Al, Jon, and I were, and Nylon's rehashing everything that happened last night. Then he says, "And with me this morning is the top sparring partner for the new champ, Amos 'Scrap Iron' Fletcher. Amos fought on the undercard last night and lost a tough one to Randall 'Rocket' Richards, but has been nice enough to come out here today and give us the inside scoop on the new champ."

I smile, liking the way that Nylon said I've been nice. It makes me smile, which makes me show my teeth, and all these things, I figure, are positive. Everything's a chain reaction of good this morning and I'm happy as hell to be here.

"Tell us, Amos, what was the game plan for Diggs going into the fight?"

I make sure to grin real wide into the camera, then look to Nylon. Important to keep eye contact with the guy you're talking to, Nylon told me earlier. "Well, Jack, Diggs's game plan was to utilize the ring space and work his jab on Taylor, see if he could get the fight into the later rounds. David Diggs has always had a good jab and good movement, and we decided early on in training that the best chance for him to beat Taylor was to combine those two strengths into his fight plan."

Nylon gives me a knowing, interested look, and I quickly realize this is what good television people do: They look interested, real, real interested, to the people they're talking to. It's a good lesson to learn. I might be reciting the vaccine to cancer, for all the viewers know, Nylon's so into what I'm saying.

"Diggs kept fighting on," Nylon says. "Even though he was way behind on all scorecards. In fact, he'd been dropped twice in the bout and was marked up pretty bad. Did you think at any point that Diggs might quit?"

"No. One thing about David Diggs is that he's a disciplined fighter. He's serious about his roadwork and about getting himself in shape. And I tell you what, Jack, he stuck to the fight plan well, even though things weren't going his way. He hung in there and made something happen. That's what champions do. They take care of all that good shit."

Nylon gives me a look. We're live and I've just said "shit"! I take a deep breath and try to focus. No more bad words. No more bad words. Got to keep it clean. Got to keep it clean.

"Indeed, great fighters do take care of business," Nylon says, recovering quickly. "Amos, your thoughts on the rematch, which, apparently, based on information I've received from Diggs's manager, Mike Renetti, will occur in exactly six months, possibly again here in Vegas."

"Well, it's gonna be a tough assignment for Diggs. That's for sure. We gonna take a month off, then go back to training camp and figure out what he can do better next time. But Taylor's going to have to do some figuring, too, because he's always going to have that cut now. That's something he's going to have to deal with the rest of his career."

"True. Will the cut be a target for David Diggs in the next fight?"

The question is a silly one, which is exactly why Nylon asks it. It serves an obvious but important purpose: to accentuate that Taylor does have a weakness now, so even though he was beating Diggs's ass in the first fight, the second one isn't automatically a gimme. "Absolutely. Anytime a fighter is cut, it becomes a target for every future opponent. And a fighter like Diggs, who has a sharp jab that can cut you up, will certainly take note of that cut and aim for it."

"Amos, thank you so much for joining us. Good luck to you in your future fights, and good luck in Diggs's training camp."

"Thanks, Jack. It's been my pleasure."

When I'm done, I make the trek down to the jail. I checked *USA Today* earlier and saw that it's eighty-one degrees and sunny in Rio de Janeiro. Warmer than here. I don't know of anybody who ever fought in Rio. But I wonder what it would be like to fight there. I hear the women are hot-blooded down there. If I went to Rio to fight, I might never leave.

Must be that Latin blood. Latin women. Just like Latin fighters. They got that fire to 'em. That spark. Latin fighters all got that *machismo*. That pride that says I'm the best and I'm gonna do whatever it takes to whip your ass. I like that in a fighter. In a woman, too.

I see him after a brief wait.

"Scrap, what you doin' here?"

"Came to see you, man. How you holdin' up?"

"Man, shit." TNT looks to the ground, like he's embarrassed. Then he looks up and sees my chopped-up face. We're separated by this glass wall, TNT on one side, me on the other. Everything smells like disinfectant.

"I fought Rocket Richards," I tell him. "Hell, they needed somebody to replace *your* crazy ass. Machine Gun broke his ankle so I was the only guy left."

TNT doesn't ask me how I did. "Hope you at least got paid good," he mutters. "I guess the good news is that Diggs won."

"Yeah. He did real well. He's banged up, but he's champ. And I know you can't believe that shit. Just like I can't."

TNT smiles.

"Now tell me, man," I say. "How you holdin' up in here?"

TNT looks tired. I'd have a hard time sleeping in jail, too.

"The other fellas don't bother me much, I guess," he says, eyes sullen. "They tell you anything when you come in?"

"They said you solicited an undercover cop posing as a hooker."

TNT lets out a big sigh. "Yeah, well, she sure didn't look like no cop, Scrap."

We could go on here all day so I get to it. "Did you call anybody? Everybody gets a phone call."

75

"Who was I gonna call, man? Renetti don't want to talk to me no more and I ain't got no family that could have come bailed me out."

"You don't have *any* family, TNT?"

TNT looks down. "None that'll talk to me, at least."

I decide not to press it.

He doesn't say anything for a while and neither do I, and I start getting agitated with myself, because I know what I'm about to do. I've got twenty-five big ones on me and here's this guy I've trained with who's in a jam. Even though I know it's a bad move to lend another fighter money, I can't let the man just sit in here by himself. TNT's a *fighter,* after all.

"Look, TNT, Renetti gave me a five-grand bonus for being in training camp. Your bail is five grand. I got paid good money to fight Rocket. So this bonus, well, it's just icing on the cake."

"What are you talkin' about, Scrap?"

"It means I can get you out of here today."

TNT looks at me like he can't believe it. He presses his face closer to the glass and puts his huge hands up against the glass that separates us. "Thanks, Scrap. Man, I really do 'preciate all this. I'm not gonna forget this."

"You just stay out of trouble. You hear me?"

"Yeah, man. I hear you."

Later on, I come on out to where I always come when I need to reflect—to Liston's grave. I've bought a fresh bouquet of flowers. They gave me a mix that cost thirty bucks but has different colors of purple, yellow, and white. Easter-type colors, it seems, even though it isn't Easter right now.

Used to be that people came by every once in a while to Liston's grave. Talked about the man and what he did in the ring, then maybe paid a small tribute by saying something like "He was world champ for a while. Till he lost to Ali." Then they'd leave Sonny, buried here in the green grass and peat moss, under this headstone, doing whatever it is dead fighters do when their bodies are deep in the ground and their gloves are forever off.

But I don't think many people come out here anymore. Not often.

I place the flowers in the metal urn atop his headstone and pour a little water from the glass vase they came in. Then I stand back, staring at the headstone, and wonder what Liston's thinking right now, wherever he is.

"Man, Sonny, you ain't gonna believe what's going on around here." I say all this real lowlike, so if a cemetery worker was to come by, he wouldn't think I've lost my mind. "Diggs won the belt, I'm on television, and money's holding up okay. Can you believe it?" I shake my head. "You know, Diggs has the same lineage as you now, Sonny. You both heavyweight champs. You to Ali to Frazier, on down the line to Diggs. Life's crazy, ain't it, Sonny?"

I feel a calm come over me every time I talk to Liston, like he's here, atop the headstone, in spirit, listening to me. Maybe nodding his head and saying, "Hey, kid, I know it's tough for you and it might even get tougher. But don't give up on the world. Good things can happen if you let them."

Good things happened to Sonny, too, but only in spurts. Long-term good stuff just wasn't meant to be for him. Some of us, we're just not meant to be happy for long spells.

And Sonny, no matter what good things happened to the man, it always seemed to go right next to something bad.

Take Denver, for example.

Sonny started out in St. Louis—won a Golden Gloves title there. He was beginning his pro career there, too, but found himself getting into trouble with the law. Once, Sonny beat up a St. Louis policeman, took his gun, and left him lying in an alley with a broken knee. Liston went to jail for the incident, even though he said the policeman attacked him first.

When a local cop finally told Sonny that if he didn't leave St. Louis, he'd "end up in an alley somewhere," Liston left. He didn't need that kind of mess. Moved to Philadelphia, which wasn't much kinder to him. Sonny was still picked up by the police for charges like loitering on a street corner (which was later dropped) and impersonating a police officer (which was also dropped).

And then there was the cold reception Philadelphia gave him when he won the belt. It was almost as if the city was saying to him, "Hey, kid, can't you find somewhere else to live?" He was once stopped in Philly for "driving too slow" through Fairmount Park.

In 1963, Liston, fed up with the harassment, moved to Denver. "I'd rather be a lamppost in Denver than the mayor of Philadelphia," he said at the time.

The Rocky Mountains weren't much kinder to Liston, who at this point had built a reputation from the police departments of St. Louis and Philly. A clean slate in Denver just wasn't going to be possible. One of Liston's former sparring partners, Roy Schoeninger, said, "For a while the Denver police pulled him over every day. They must have stopped him a hundred times outside City Park. He'd run on the golf course, and as he left in his car, they'd stop him. Twenty-five days in a row. Same two cops. They thought it was a big joke. It made me ashamed of being a Denver native. Sad they never let him live in peace."

Peace was something that Liston didn't find in any city. Maybe it was only in the ring that Liston truly found happiness. Who the hell knows? There were times—I've seen on videotape—when Liston was holding a little kid in his arms, or getting his hand raised after a fight, times when I could see a wide smile break across his usually sullen face, and the whole thing lit up like a firecracker in the night. Sonny had a helluva smile, and it's a shame—a damn shame—people didn't get to see it more often than they did.

Round Four

We're back in training camp. A month has gone by and Diggs is back from his talk-show tour, fresh from appearances on *Letterman, Conan O'Brien,* and *Leno.* Everybody wants to know who the new champ is, wants to put a mike in front of Diggs, 'cause he'll say anything.

I've been keeping busy by doing some work with Nylon. He asked me to cover a middleweight title fight last week with him. I did quite well. Said all the right things, smiled a lot into the camera, and flashed my teeth plenty. I even kept clean on the bad words.

My analysis of the fight was right on: I told the viewers to look out for the challenger's left hook to the body, because it was the best I'd seen in a while. He really knew how to punch hard to the liver, and also right in the solar plexus area, a place most fighters ignore— but if you land there, watch out. A man can deflate instantly. Bob Fitzsimmons won the heavyweight title that way, back in the late 1890s—landed a perfect punch to the solar plexus that knocked out Jim Corbett. So I knew this kid had a chance at the belt when I saw his bodywork. He had that solar plexus punch down to a science.

Knew exactly where and when to throw it. I figured he'd try it in the title fight and maybe see some results from it.

Then wouldn't you know it, the challenger knocked out the champ in the seventh round with a left hook to the body! Nylon and the other CNN boys gave me credit on that one. Told me that it showed great insight on my part. They've asked me to come back for more work in the near future.

Been using Vegas as my base of operations, too. Since I've technically been off Diggs's training camp payroll for the past month, I had to find my own place to stay. But I liked the Riviera. It's nice enough, clean, and convenient for what I need to do. So I struck a deal with one of the hotel managers. Told him I'd make sure to convince Diggs to stay here again for the rematch.

Diggs really likes the Riviera, so odds were he was gonna ask to stay here again anyway. Most fighters are superstitious to some degree, and with all the luck Diggs had on his side last fight, there's no way he'd risk changing hotels for the rematch. Might throw things out of whack.

But the manager didn't know this. From what I told him, Caesars was looking like a top contender as a place for us to stay. Change of scenery might not be a bad idea this time out, I explained.

He asked me what it would take to convince Diggs to stay here again. Because having the heavyweight champ in your hotel's a big deal in Vegas. Anything that gives one hotel an edge over the others is a big deal.

I told the hotel manager that I couldn't guarantee anything— that Diggs was a big boy and he made up his own mind about where he stayed. I could only steer him in a direction.

The hotel manager said fine. No guarantees. But to steer Diggs in a particular direction—what would that take?

I paused. A good negotiator always pauses. Partly for effect, partly to think about terms and conditions. Plus, it gives a man confidence to know he can create silence when he wants. Leave no sound in the air for a good while, make the other man think about the silence and what's gonna come next.

"How about a room for a month? Free of charge?" I asked him.

The manager nodded quickly and I knew I could get more. Man like him nods quickly, it's for a reason. There's more to be gotten.

"Plus free meals—buffet, room service, the works. After all, a man's gotta eat."

He nodded slower this time, but nodded just the same. Now I'm thinking, I've got a free place to stay till camp starts up again, and food to boot. Anything else is gravy, so go for the good stuff.

"Plus free gambling money every day. Five hundred bucks credit on the house."

"No can do," the manager said. "That's out of the question. I couldn't get approval."

I nodded real slow, like it might be a deal killer. Always pays to nod slow, like you're in deep thought. Makes the other party nervous. "I don't know what to say then," I told him, then created some more silence, which I knew was spooking him. "Caesars just might be willing to offer me credit."

He looked around the room a bit, wondering what the hell he could throw at me to keep a buzz in Diggs's ear. We finally agreed that he'd give me shuttle service whenever I needed it. Not exactly casino credit, but it worked for me. And he was happy enough, because Diggs is getting to be a hot commodity.

Just two nights ago Diggs was on CNN on *Larry King Live* and was telling Larry that the words *champ* and *chump* are almost spelled *exactly* alike, save for a vowel in the middle. Then Diggs threw the word *chimp* into the mix and said that sometimes he wishes he was a chimp, because they got an easy life hanging on trees and eating bananas all day long. Diggs went on to say he eats two bananas every day and always before fights because the potassium bananas have helps retain water under the harsh lights in a boxing ring. Which is true enough. Bananas *do* have potassium, potassium does help a man retain water, and Vegas lights can be real hot, so anything that gives a man an edge in such an environment is important.

Larry laughed long and hard over this, but Diggs wasn't laughing. He was just being Diggs. Seems like the former spelling bee champ and part-time philosopher is getting to be a big hit.

Back in the ring, and me and Diggs are getting it on. Four rounds today, and this is our third serious sparring session since camp opened up two weeks ago. Diggs's timing has been off but it's coming back now. His jab's getting quicker each time I spar him, and he's starting to move around the ring better. The man has swift legs and it's just a matter of him getting the spring back in them by doing his morning runs.

We're in round two. Got the eighteen-ounce gloves and leather protective headgear on, black headgear that Diggs said he wanted us sparring partners to wear because black is a color he associates with death and destruction, and he wants this to bring out his hate for Taylor, which before now I didn't know he had.

"Of course I hate Taylor," Diggs told me earlier. "The man beat me up good last time out."

The man wants black, give him black.

And I'll give Diggs this: He's taking training more seriously this time. He knows what Taylor's got to offer after being in there with him. He wants to be in the best shape possible. Plus, he knows that Taylor's gunning for revenge and wants a piece of his ass in a big, bad way.

I throw a lead right to Diggs's head. His rib's still a bit sore, and De La Rosa wants me to go easy on the body for at least a couple more weeks. Diggs slips my right and counters with a right of his own. It's quick and snaps my head back. Diggs steps in close and lands a quick left hook to my body, pivots, and fires a three-punch combination: jab, right hand, left hook. All three land. I'm against the ropes and Diggs throws a hard jab. Before I know it, I'm tangled in the ropes, my head dizzy like I've been on an upside-down Ferris wheel, the top half of my body leaning like Silly Putty on the top rope, my knees suspended by the lower rope.

"Time! Time!" yells De La Rosa. I hear the voice echo a couple times and see a blurred vision of a man enter the ring.

What you doin' on the ropes and what is he doin' in the ring and what the hell is that ringing?

I think I see a man's hands flailing over his head and I think I see Diggs standing back, his gloves resting on the ropes, and I feel somebody grabbing me, helping me to my feet. My head is still spinning and I try to shake it off, wonder what the hell just happened.

"Okay, enough for today. We take a break now, okay?" De La Rosa's voice is pounding in my head and I realize what is going on: Diggs just nailed me and I was on the ropes, defenseless. If it wasn't for De La Rosa stepping in, I would have gone down.

As it was, the ropes were the only things holding me up.

My mouthpiece hangs out of my mouth halfway and I spit it into De La Rosa's hands. I take in some air and try to let my head clear. "Okay, no problem—don't worry," De La Rosa says. "You'll come back tomorrow good as new. Get some rest now."

Diggs is standing over in one of the corners of the ring, his gloves down at his side, and through his mouthpiece his voice is a muffled roar. "Sorry 'bout that, Scrap," he says. He punches his gloves together and they make a slapping sound. They've got a new guy in camp—Jarred Dougal—who's going to be sparring with Diggs in my place. Just because I can't finish the round doesn't mean that Diggs is finished for the day. There's still work to be done. Dougal's geared up and in the ring—where I should be right now but I'm not because I just got my bell rung like a motherfucker.

I'm watching television in my room when I hear the door knock. My head is still pounding even though I took some aspirin to cure the throbbing. The right side of my temple feels like glass has crashed inside it, screaming, pounding, ready to slice into my brain. The aspirin should've killed the pain by now but it hasn't.

I open the door and see De La Rosa, a small cigar in his shirt pocket. Sometimes he smokes them at night when the training's done and there's nothing left to do but think about the next fight.

"How you feelin'?"

I lean against the door, do my best to look alert, even though I'm tired. "Better. Feeling better. Guess he got me good today, didn't he?"

"Happens. Sooner or later, everybody gets their bell rung. You know how it goes."

"Don't I, though."

"You looked dull in there today, Scrap. Not as sharp as usual. In fact, I was gonna talk to you about this, but ever since the fight with Rocket, you been off. I think that fight took something outta you."

Now I may have some things against De La Rosa, because he's the man who went looking to get TNT in trouble and all, but I've got respect for what he says about boxing. He's been in the game longer than I have and really gives a damn about his fighters.

"You think I've lost something?"

De La Rosa's arms are crossed like swords and he shakes his head. "Yeah. Maybe. But you got to realize it happens that way sometimes. One good, hard fight is all it takes to wear a man down. Still too early to tell, but your reflexes seem slower. Could just be you're workin' yourself back into shape, could just be that your timing's off. Hell, none of us been trainin' the past month."

"Yeah. That might be it."

There's this pregnant silence in the air and I don't know whether to ask De La Rosa into the room. My room is still free, compliments of hotel management, so I don't have to share it with a sparring partner like last time.

"Anyway, just thought I'd come by to talk to you. I think you'll be okay. Just get some rest tonight and we'll see how it goes tomorrow. Okay?"

"All right."

De La Rosa nods and turns to leave.

I follow him into the hallway. "Hey, man. I'm gonna be okay. But thanks for coming down here anyway."

De La Rosa gives me a look. "I hope so," he says, and goes back to his room.

I know Diggs like a book by now. We've sparred more than a hundred rounds together, so fighting on even terms with him in sparring shouldn't be that big a deal. But ever since we've started training for the rematch, I've *known* something in me was off. My timing's not there, I'm slower than usual, and I can see punches before they land, but can't seem to get out of the way.

It's damn frustrating.

De La Rosa's right. Sometimes it just takes one fight for a man's skills to go. Rocket *did* pound on me pretty good, and maybe part of me stayed in the ring that night.

Getting beat on makes a man do funny things. Like when Patterson lost to Liston the first time. Floyd reacted in a weird way— he left the country. That was the effect that Sonny's fists had on him.

Not long after the fight, Patterson, wearing a fake beard as disguise, flew from New York to Madrid. There was no particular reason that Patterson went to Madrid. He simply looked at the flight board and saw that a plane to Spain was leaving soon.

In Madrid, Patterson faked a limp and walked around some of the worst areas of town. He stayed much of the time in his hotel room.

"You must wonder what makes a man do things like this," Patterson said. "Well, I wonder, too . . . And the answer is, I don't know . . . But I think that within me, within every human being, there is a certain weakness. It is a weakness that exposes itself more when you're alone."

In the ring, a fighter is *always* alone. Facing his fears, his weaknesses. In the ring, the only person who can help you is yourself. Now it's time for me to help myself—so I don't lose my job as a sparring partner with the heavyweight champ. All I've worked for could go down the drain if I don't do well today.

I got to hang with Diggs for the rounds we work. I know this like I know the game of boxing. There's no room for mistakes.

Diggs and I are back in the ring, mouthpieces in, bell about to ring. The moments before the bell rings for a sparring session—no matter how many times a man does it—there's still this gut level of fear mixed with adrenaline that gives a rush, a rush no drug can achieve. My stomach rages and howls quietly as the bell clangs and Diggs and I meet in ring center, hitting our gloves together like we always do to start the first round.

He's moving around in small circles, pivoting left to right, out of my punching range, something new he's trying for this fight. De La Rosa figures if Diggs stays outside of Taylor's reach, Diggs can utilize his superior hand and foot speed to jump in at odd angles and throw quick flurries. It's a good strategy and Diggs is working it well so far.

Diggs has always been quicker than me, but I've still managed to do well against him by making him do things he doesn't want to. As a more experienced fighter, one of my strengths has always been to make the other fighter fight *my* fight. There're many ways to do this. For Diggs, he likes to stick and move—flurry and run. But me, I like to get inside and work, go to the body, take a man's legs away. So I power jab (which Diggs does now, too), lean on the ropes and let the other man come to me, stand still, wait for the other man to throw something, then counterpunch.

I go back into the ropes and wave Diggs in, a temptation he can't refuse. He moves quickly to his left, on his toes all the while, then shifts hard to the right like a sports car in traffic, still bouncing, throwing a right-left. He pivots. I block both punches, throw a left to the head that grazes his temple. I'd really like to go to the body now, because even if a man's timing is off, he can still land effectively to the body. A man can always move his head side to side to avoid punches, but the body is harder to move. It's a still target usually, and that's what I need right now.

But De La Rosa says no body, so I don't go there.

Diggs jumps back outside and pumps his jab at me. I parry the first with my gloves, but his second one lands. I'm thinking now more than usual, thinking of what I can do to slow Diggs down, to give him good work. I jab and he blocks it, then jab again. The second one lands and I advance inside. Diggs ties me up. I spin off and throw a quick flurry. Most of the punches miss, but it keeps Diggs off-balance, causing him to think defensively. I'm a little winded, but manage a couple more combinations, moving in behind my jab, not letting Diggs get his feet set. Just as Diggs is back and bouncing, ready to fire some hard jabs, the bell rings. I've made it through.

The pay-per-view sales have been slow so far, and I can't say that I'm surprised. Who wants to pay good money to see a rematch for a fight that wasn't competitive the first time around? Taylor's favored to beat Diggs's ass, and the only hope for a Diggs win is another lucky cut.

Rematches usually happen either because the first fight was great or because there was a big upset. Diggs-Taylor II falls into the latter of those categories.

Me, I've never been high on rematches. Rarely does a second fight between two men live up to the promise of the first one. There's an exception every now and then—like Sugar Ray Leonard–Tommy Hearns II—but for the most part, people go away from a return bout disappointed.

Ali-Liston II was ugly. Liston got himself into fantastic shape, training with Spartan effort. He wanted to prove the first fight was a fluke, so he trained hard. Then, three days before the fight, Ali went to the hospital for a hernia. The rematch was rescheduled, and Sonny was never the same.

The fight was held in Lewiston, Maine, at St. Dominick's Arena. Why the hell the fight was in Maine spoke volumes about the Black Muslims during this time. Nobody else wanted to hold the fight, with the Muslims following Ali around and all.

So Maine it was. And while Liston waited for Ali to recover from his injury, he did nothing, really, except grow older. Ali was still young, maturing, growing into his body, learning more and more how to use it as a weapon.

But Liston had trained so hard earlier—just to see that training go to waste—that it was hard for him to train that hard again. Training is tough and it can prey on a man's mind after a while.

Those close to Sonny said he couldn't put himself through the grueling routines of training again. Some said he was losing his mind.

The night before the fight, Robert Lipsyte, a boxing writer, came into Liston's room to talk. The room was dark. Shades down, nothing but a television set giving the place any light. Sonny sat next to the set, transfixed. Didn't even notice Lipsyte. On the television, a movie was playing. Zulu warriors were getting mowed down by white men with machine guns. Blood was spilling everywhere. Liston said nothing. Just sat there and watched the Zulus get killed.

"His mind is blown," Dick Gregory, Liston's friend, also in the room, said. "He's gonna lose fast."

Sonny did lose fast. Ali knocked him out with one punch in the very first round.

When I'm in a training camp, grinding away, sparring the rounds, my body getting sore in places I didn't know I had, I call it The Routine. Every day when I go in, I know what I'm getting. Only thing that might change is the number of rounds I work. Some days may be four, some days as many as six. Rarely do I go more than that. That's what other sparring partners are for.

If it's a ten-round day for Diggs, I might go five, then another guy might come in for another five. A fresh body so Diggs gets good work. Fresh bodies make him work harder, make him stay sharp. Not exactly fair to Diggs, but camp isn't about being *fair*. Life in the ring's not fair. It just *is*.

Despite the lack of pay-per-view sales, some reporters are staying close to Diggs's training camp, hungry for any news about the rematch, or perhaps a quote from the champ, which, most nights, gets a clip on the evening news.

I see Al across the room, standing still, cameraman at his side. I step out of the ring, having just finished four tough rounds with Diggs.

"Hey, Scrap," Al yells. "You got a minute?"

I eye the floor a moment as De La Rosa unties my gloves. My shirt is soaked and I feel trickles of sweat pooling past my eyes and down my cheeks, over the areas of my face that haven't been lubricated. "Kinda busy. Got to hit the showers, you know." Al's got some nerve. He still hasn't called to tell me why they cut my segment. No matter. Nylon and I are working good together on CNN and there's a fight in a couple weeks I'm supposed to help on.

"I just need a minute, Scrap," Al says. "In response to something Terrence Taylor said earlier today."

Taylor? Now what the hell would Taylor say about *me*? Last time I talked to Taylor was the title fight.

I walk over to Al, hands still wrapped, protective cup sitting on my hips. I notice the camera is on.

"You wanna turn that off?" I point to the cameraman, a short, stumpy guy wearing a baseball cap touting the MGM Grand Casino.

The cameraman looks to Al and Al nods. One thing I've learned is to have all cameras off when talking to the media. Never know what they're going to ask. Always helps to be prepared.

"So what's Taylor saying about me?"

Al clears his throat and runs his hands over his shirt, which could use a good ironing. He needs to pay some attention to his wardrobe, plus his mustache could use a good combing. He has some wild hairs sprouting up out of the natural order above his lips.

"He mentioned something about the Diggs fight and you and he talking in the casino before it. He mentioned money being offered."

"He mentioned that?" What, Taylor turn crazy all of a sudden? I shrug. "Yeah. All that happened."

Al puts his hands in his pockets and the cameraman keeps staring at him, like there's more to come. There's this moment of quiet and Al finally breaks it. "Scrap, he's saying *you* asked him for money in exchange for information on Diggs. He's saying he said no way, but you kept pressing anyway."

"He said *what*?"

"That's what he said. I just wanted to get your response."

My response? How about my foot up Taylor's lying ass? "It ain't true, Al. None of it."

"So you deny everything?"

"Man, of course I deny everything! Fact is, Taylor's the one who offered *me* money. I did see him in the casino one night, when I was looking for TNT. Taylor sat me down and started asking about Diggs. I told him I didn't work that way and then he offered me some cash for specifics. I told him no. End of story."

Al's got this dull look on his face, like he's just swallowed a pill and can't yet decide how it tastes. "Why didn't you let anybody know about this?"

I shake my head. The man's got some kind of nerve, coming in here and asking me questions like this. I start to undo my wraps. "Look, man, what I told you, it's the truth. You known me how long now? Four, five years? And I've never given you a bad tip. Now you come in here asking me if I wanted money from that scumbag in exchange for secrets? I ain't believing this, Al. I really ain't believing this . . ."

"I've got to report what I hear, Scrap."

I let the rest of my wrap unravel and it hits the floor in a pile. "The hell with what *you hear,* man. What do you play me for? Man, I'm on the up-and-up. Always have been, always will be. You got Taylor over there," I say, pointing to a window. "Crying like a baby because he lost his title. Just looking for an excuse. And you're *buying* it, man. You buying his bullshit, and that's all there is to it." I wipe some sweat from my forehead with the palm of my hand.

"Scrap, you've got your job to do. I've got mine."

"Which means?"

"Which means this: I've got an ex-champ who says one thing. I've got a sparring partner for the new champ who says another. But they both agree that they talked in a Vegas casino before a title fight and the subject of money came up. They have differing opinions about who offered who money. So there's a controversy. Differing opinions. Now, I'm not a private investigator. It's not my job to find out who's telling the truth here, though I'd die to know. But just like you've never given me reason to doubt your word before, neither has Taylor. He's always been straight with me."

"So you're gonna run with it?"

"Scrap, it's my job. If I don't, every other television network and newspaper will."

I look to the floor, to the hand wraps, lying there, layers of bunched cloth. I'm not going to look into Al's eyes and give him the satisfaction. Sonny wouldn't have. I know that. "Get on out of here now."

"Scrap . . ."

I wave my hand at him, eyes still fixed on the floor. "Out, man! You hear me? I said *out!*"

Only thing to do now is see how this plays out. I got a feeling it's not going to be pretty. The sparring partner for Diggs, accused of wanting to exchange camp secrets for money? Damn. They say shit rolls downhill. Well, at the bottom of all the hills in the world, there's one just for fighters. And at the bottom of *that* hill is a place specially reserved for sparring partners, where the shit can't run down no further.

A little past eleven and I'm watching to see if Al reports what I think he's going to. Sure enough, there he is, wearing a navy blazer and white shirt—tuxes being just for fights—with Jon standing next to him, his beard badly in need of a trim. The two have these furrowed brows, which, I've learned from watching newscasts, is necessary when presenting the public some sort of negative news. In this type of situation, it's key to show some wrinkles in the fore-head, to let the viewers know you're concerned.

And that's what Al and Jon are doing now, showing concern, great concern, like a world war might just have broken out, and wouldn't you know it, they're the ones who got to tell the rest of us. Al goes first.

"Well, the big news today stems from conversations I had earlier with both former world champ Terrence 'T-Bone' Taylor and the lead sparring partner for current champ, David Diggs, Amos 'Scrap

Iron' Fletcher. Taylor said today that the week before his title fight with Diggs, he had a conversation with Fletcher in a Las Vegas casino. Taylor maintains that Fletcher asked him for an undisclosed amount of money in exchange for secrets from Diggs's training camp, where Fletcher has been employed for the better part of a year. Fletcher confirms that the casino meeting *did* take place, but that events occurred the other way around, that Taylor offered him money in exchange for camp secrets."

Al cuts to a video of what I take to be a filmed interview earlier in the day with Taylor, who's sitting outside a boxing ring, sweat on his forehead, a white towel draped lazily across his shoulders. "He came into the casino and asked me how much would I pay him for access to some camp secrets. I told him that I wasn't interested in that kind of transaction." Taylor's nodding all the while, as if by doing this he's going to convince people that *his* story actually took place. "Surprised me, too. 'Cause I always thought Scrap was a stand-up guy. At least until recently. Money will make a man do some crazy things I guess."

The son of a bitch.

The camera cuts back to Al, who gives the audience a sober stare, turns to Jon, and says, "I was able to track down Amos Fletcher earlier today at Diggs's training camp. Fletcher had just finished a brisk workout with the world champ when I caught up with him. Needless to say, Fletcher was in anything but a happy mood when he heard of the allegations."

Then, before my disbelieving eyes, Al begins to show clips of our conversation! He told me—the man told me as plain as can be—that the camera was off. Off! But here he is, and here I am, in a montage of video clips, short, angry sound bites from our talk.

Me saying, "Man, of course I deny everything!"

Me saying, "I did see him in the casino one night."

Me saying, "You buying his bullshit, and that's all there is to it."

Me saying, "Out, man. You hear me? I said *out!*"

Al gives the audience the same look and turns to Jon again, who's a little wide-eyed, likely for show, since I'll bet he's already seen my interview a dozen times. By being bug-eyed, Jon lets the audience know he's *shocked,* absolutely shocked, by what he's just seen. He's letting the audience know that it's okay if they're shocked, too.

"Jon, I've spoken with both men, and to be fair, they've always seemed like straight-up, decent guys to me. Very candid and honest. But the situation we have here is that one of them is lying."

It's Jon's turn. He looks deep into the camera, his eyes narrowed a bit, almost trancelike. "Al, it certainly is baffling to both of us, veterans of the fight scene, why one of these men would be lying. It's interesting to see Fletcher's reaction to your news because he's usually a very agreeable man, and to see him fly into a rage like this is quite shocking."

Al: "Well, it was, Jon. He did deny everything and even said he believes Taylor is just upset that he lost the title and is looking for a scapegoat. That is possible. Certainly, it at least brings a bit more intrigue to the upcoming Diggs-Taylor rematch, which has been receiving only lukewarm interest so far, as most boxing experts believe that Diggs was very fortunate to have won the first fight."

Jon: "We'll continue to keep on top of this story, and as events transpire, ESPN will be the first to bring them to you. Now, back to the studio."

Those bastards. Filming me when they said they wouldn't. Dubbing my clips to make me look like a fool. Questioning my integrity.

This isn't the last they've heard from me. I guarantee that. First,

I've got to go talk to Renetti and Diggs, smooth things over with them. I'm sure they saw this tonight, and I don't want to sit on it until morning. Best to get it all out in the open.

Next, I've got a score to settle with Al and Jon. Time for them to rectify some pretty bad mistakes they've made.

Renetti beats me to it.

Just as I'm getting ready to leave the room, there's a knock on the door. It's Renetti, standing in a white T-shirt and faded blue jeans, hair every which way. Was probably dozing in bed when Al and Jon came on, then his ass woke up *real quick* when he heard what they had to say.

He doesn't ask me if he can come in. He just walks past me, shuffling on the carpet in his slippered feet, going toward my window, where the shades are closed.

"Why didn't you tell me?" His back is still turned, peering through the shades and out into the neon Vegas night. Guess I should have expected as much.

"Don't know." And it's the truth. What with Diggs getting ready for his shot at the belt and all, I didn't want to cause any distractions. I tell Renetti and next thing I know, Diggs is catching wind of it and his mind is on that rather than the fight. Instead of moving away from Taylor's right hand—shit he should be concerned with— Diggs is focused on why Taylor's throwing money around, trying to get secrets. These kind of things can mess with a man's mind before a fight, and I suppose I figured it was my job to keep distractions to a minimum.

"Don't know, eh?" Renetti says in a light voice, back still turned. Then he does a slight spin, shoulders facing me at an odd angle.

"Naw, I guess not."

"This isn't just a small thing here. The way I see it, Scrap, you're fucked either way. By not telling me when it happened, you caused *this* to escalate." He throws his hands wide, like there's a big world globe in between them. "You've got the media involved and now there's no way of telling where this is gonna go."

"Didn't want to screw things up, I guess. Thought it might break Diggs's concentration. You know, it being a title fight and all."

Now Renetti looks at me, his eyes dull and narrow and cold. "Yeah, well, I'll tell you what, Scrap. I don't pay you to *think*. I pay you to *do*. I pay you"—he's pointing at me now, even though he and I both know damn well I'm the only man in the room he could possibly be talking to—"to go in the ring, get hit by my fighter so he can hit other fighters better when there's serious money on the line. So let's just drop *think,* okay? Because that never was, and certainly never will be, in the job requirement."

There's a bunch of things I could say here. Tell Renetti what I really think of him, that he's a bloodsucking leech, making money off the spilled blood of other men. Or I could throw a right hand at his nose, feeling the bone and tissue of it softly crunch when my knuckle hits it, turning the fist sharply at impact, feeling it ruin into a misshapen mass all the way from my elbow to my fingertip.

But none of these, I decide, would work. They'd only lead to other problems. And the way things are going right now, the last thing I need are more problems.

"Jake Douglas from the Vegas Boxing Commission called me just before I came up here," Renetti says. "He wants to talk to you first thing in the morning. Eight o'clock. He said he'd meet you in the coffee shop downstairs. I told him you'd be down there with your bags packed, because you were leaving camp tomorrow morning."

So this is how it's gonna play out. Me losing the job over Taylor's lie. Me having to face the Vegas Commission. Me getting talked to like a nitwit by Renetti.

"Just tell me one more thing, Scrap." His arms are folded across his chest and there's this smug look plastered on his face.

I look at the ground and focus on not swallowing.

"Why'd you do it?"

I look Renetti square in the eye and hold the gaze a long minute. "I didn't do nothing wrong, man. This here, it's a setup."

Renetti stands there real quiet for a while, and I begin to think that maybe he believes me. But he doesn't. He shakes his head. "Remember," he says, walking to the door. "Eight in the coffee shop. And have your bags packed."

Douglas shows up right on time. I'm in the coffee shop, packed bags at my side. I'm ready for the worst. Never hurts to always be prepared for the worst. Saves a lot of trouble down the road that way.

Douglas has a big belly. It sticks out over his pants, so he always wears a sport coat to cover it up. No matter how hot it is here in Vegas, Douglas can always be seen with a coat on, protecting that belly from public view. He's got a walrus mustache, too, thick and bushy, and from the looks of him he'd be better suited to being a carnival pitchman than the commissioner of boxing's most important city.

His hand collapses around mine and we shake firmly. "Amos, thanks for meeting me on such short notice," he says, like I had any other choice. Douglas has this rule. He never calls fighters by their nicknames. Always formal, always right down the line. The man has a reputation for being hard but fair.

"No problem." We take a seat at my table and I sip some coffee. "No need to beat around the bush . . ."

"No, there isn't. Amos, as of this morning I'm doing two things. One, I'm organizing a formal investigative committee to get to the bottom of this 'who did what' routine between you and Terrence Taylor. We're going to find out who's telling the truth and then we're going to take the appropriate action."

"And the second thing?"

Douglas takes a deep breath and I can see his stomach protrude through the jacket. I don't want to stare too long, though, or he's liable to notice and that'll get him pissy. "I'm putting you on immediate suspension. Until we get this sorted out."

"Suspension?" I start to stand up, then decide not to. No sense in causing a scene, at least not until I get some answers. "What about Taylor?"

Douglas gives another tired sigh and pushes the table away from him a little, since his stomach's almost touching it. "I've got to put you on immediate suspension, Amos. I don't want to do it, but I have to. Until we get this figured out I can't have you fighting here. You don't have a bout scheduled in the next few months anyway."

"But that's gonna affect my income. I just got released from Diggs's camp this morning, and a suspension means nobody in Vegas is gonna want to hire me to work in their camps. Come on, Mr. Douglas. There's got to be another way here."

Douglas's palms turn toward me and he gives me a shrug. "Amos, I wish there was some other way, but there's not. I'll get in touch with you the moment we reach a decision on the investigation."

I shake my head several times. "Naw, Mr. Douglas. This ain't right. It ain't *right*! You're telling me a man can make something up about another man and begin to destroy that man's life?"

"I've got to do my job, Amos. And that job is finding out the truth."

"Mr. Douglas, I *always* been clean. Always played it straight. You *know* that." I put my hand over my face, rub caked sleep from my eyes. "Tell me, what are you gonna do with Taylor in all this?"

"He has a fight scheduled in a few months with David Diggs. If we find that he's lying before that fight occurs, he'll be placed on immediate suspension."

Now I get up, stand for a second, and pace around the room, muttering to myself. "Bullshit, man. This here *all's* bullshit." I give myself a good two or three trips around the restaurant, then come back to my seat. Douglas is still there, looking exhausted, probably wondering who he pissed off so bad to make his morning start off like this.

"There's no other option, Amos. As of right now, you're on suspension. But I give you my word on this: The moment we find something out, I'm going to let you know first."

He offers his hand to me. I stare at it and realize there's not much else to do here, so I put mine out there, and in the middle of this Vegas hash joint, me and Jake Douglas shake. And as I look around me, people sipping steaming coffee, runny omelets and fatty bacon piled high on plates, I think to myself, *Scrap, what the hell you gonna do* now?

A call from the coffee shop's pay phone to Nylon cements the rest. "Don't know what else to tell you, Scrap. You know I believe you. I think Taylor's a lying sack of shit and I told Dale Greenburg, our vice president of operations, as much, but policy is policy. He told me no matter how unfair the situation seems, it would just kill our credibility to have a suspended fighter working broadcasts."

I expected as much. The whole shit-running-downhill thing. Right now, there's an *avalanche* of manure all over me.

"So what do I do in the meantime?"

"Just hang in there. They've got a commission investigating this thing, right?"

"Yeah."

"Good. I'm gonna start some investigating of my own, expose Taylor for the lying coward that we know he is. I'm gonna start by tracking down that blackjack dealer you told me about, the one who might have overheard your conversation with Taylor that night."

"Yeah, I hear that."

"And, Scrap, once this suspension is lifted, you'll be back with us. You've done a great job, and Greenburg even told me, 'It's too bad we can't continue to use him because he really does nice work.' Scrap, he doesn't say that about *anybody*."

"Well, right now I'd take just being able to have this suspension lifted."

"I know, brother. I know. You just hang in there, you hear me?"

Paradise Memorial is quiet this morning. Not many visitors. There's a bit of breeze in the air, a wind that isn't strong enough to be called stiff, but it's more than nothing. There's green all over. Maintenance men been keeping the sprinkler system on strong, I suppose, giving the place a healthy look. Healthy for the dead. Ha.

"Things don't make no sense sometimes, do they, Sonny?" I stare at the bottom of the headstone. *A MAN*. "People, Sonny. They push and push, don't they?" I feel it move, just a little, and try to stop it. Then I remember who's company I'm in. "It's gone, Sonny. Just about everything. Job in the camp, my boxing license, television gig. All of it's gone, man. And for what?"

It moves again. I bow my head. Decide to close my eyes, 'cause I'm closer to him with my eyes closed, like maybe he can be on his toes, in full gear, dancing up and down, no longer mythical, but real. We might even sit and share a meal together. Me and Sonny. Sonny and me. The two of us, him maybe saying, "I know, kid. I know how it can all go."

Eyes still closed, I continue, "We both men, Sonny." Maybe it doesn't really matter if it moves a little. Maybe, just maybe, it's what I need. To swallow. "You and I, we men, and in the end, that's all folks need to remember about us." I swallow again and, under my breath, almost whisper, "Men, Sonny. You and me. That's who we are. What we are."

And as I stand there, at the grave with my two suitcases, I let it go. Break down like a damn baby, right in front of all those head-stones, with Sonny watching over.

Round Five

Unc is what I call my Uncle Dwight, the brother of my dead father. I called him Unc as a baby since I couldn't say his entire name, and it stuck.

I've just gotten over to his house in Trenton, New Jersey, where I'm going to stay until I can get my life figured out. When I called Unc yesterday, he said sure, come on out. He'd heard about what had gone down with me, no doubt, but didn't mention it. He runs a boxing gym in town and makes enough to get by. It'll be a good place for me to stay for a while.

"So how's it been out in Vegas lately? Things changing much out that way?" Unc asks.

As close to the game as he's been over the years, Unc hasn't visited Vegas since the early seventies, right after Liston died. He had a fighter—a light heavyweight with some skills but not the desire—who fought a main event there once. Unc and the fighter stayed for three days in the Thunderbird, a hotel Liston used to frequent.

The light heavy didn't do so well. Got stretched in three and Unc came back to Trenton just like he always had, ready to get back to the gym and work with the fighters. It's something about Unc I've always admired: One of his boys gets beat and Unc doesn't blame anybody. Things happen, life moves on. Unc just goes about his business, keeps doing what he does best.

He has a boy fight in Atlantic City every now and then, and I remember a couple years ago he had a featherweight win a decision in Reno. But no Vegas.

"Nah, Unc. Same old, same old. You know how it is. Vegas may be glitzy and all, but it pretty much stays the same."

"You look good, son. Like you're keepin' yourself in shape."

"I feel all right. Keepin' myself in order."

"I feel good, too, son. Strong."

"That's good to hear," I say.

"Were you getting some good sparring out there? Those boys kept you busy, didn't they?"

"Sure, Unc. You know how it is. Work for one camp, do a good job. Word gets around."

"Well, you know I'm proud of you for that."

"Thanks." I change the subject. "How things at the gym?"

"Could be better, but that's always the case, isn't it?" He chuckles. "Nah, things are good. Can't complain too much. I get letters from developers every now and then. Business owners down my way say we should tear the gym down or remodel it, to make it look nicer. Remodel it! Ha! But I take it all in stride. Gotta expect people to act simple from time to time. You know the white man."

I look around the room. There's a battered green couch with yellow stuffing coming out in spots. This will be my bed until I figure out what I'm gonna do next. Hope my back can take it.

"You gonna come down tomorrow, maybe work out a bit?" he asks.

"Yeah, I think I might just come on down there. Loosen myself up. Work the bags a bit."

"Maybe show some of my boys a thing or two?" he says, laughing.

"Yeah, Unc. I'll show 'em lots of things."

Unc's gym is pure old school. It's in downtown Trenton and it's been Unc's for nearly twenty years now. Because of the location, he's had offers to sell—lots of business parks have been sprouting up here lately.

Unc's never taken those offers up, though. The gym itself isn't much to look at. Outside is some old red brick, cracking in places that could use a mason's touch. Inside it's not much prettier. A regulation boxing ring takes up most of the room, two heavy bags hang to either side of the ring, there's a couple speed bags and a large crate for the gear: gloves (some for sparring, some for bag work), protective leather headgear, protective cups, skip ropes. Kind of like a smorgasbord, pugilist style. Order your headache of the day. Cross to the jaw, or a hook to the solar plexus? Which will it be?

Unc paid the place off years ago, when a fighter of his won a couple bouts he probably shouldn't have. The guy didn't train real hard but he had a helluva punch, always an equalizer. Unc's cut of those purses took care of the place.

"It's not much," I remember Unc telling me a while back. "But it's mine."

As I stand here now, a very recent arrival to Trenton, I've got to hand it to Unc. No matter what people say or do, this place is all Unc's. All his. There's a dignity to that I admire.

"Amos, can you show this boy what I mean by 'making him pay'?" Unc's inside the ring with some kid in headgear and gloves. He can't be no more than seventeen. Black, thin. Tall, too. Unc's got gloves on and is throwing punches half-speed, giving the kid a chance to slip and counter. I step into the ring.

"I got it," I tell Unc. He nods and steps out of the ring to go help some other guy. I give the kid a look. His eyes are big and I consider this to be good news, because it means he's either scared or ready to learn something. Hopefully both. Fear's a good thing for a young man to have. Makes him sharp. "What's your name?"

"Ben."

"Ben, eh?" I roll my arms over my head a few times, loosening up some kinks. "Ben, I see what you're doing when he punches. You're slipping all right, but you're not countering when you make him miss. Let me guess, you're amateur, been boxing about a year, had about eight fights."

Ben's eyes are still big. His plastic mouthpiece half hangs out of his jaw, but he spits it into his gloves to talk. "About eighteen months and ten fights. But how do you know that?"

I get in a proper stance: my side to him, chin tucked in tight to my chest, right hand on right side of chin, left hand on other side of my face, ready to strike. "I know because I been around this game awhile. Seen a few things here and there."

I stick my left out at him, gloveless, and he parries with his right. Quick reflexes. This kid may have a chance. I do it again, and again he parries, blocking the jab with his right and opening up his palm, using it as a kind of shield. Effective. He looks at me, me at him.

"What you gonna do next?" I ask.

"Gonna move out the way."

I shake my head. Can smell the kid's body odor. It's rising up off him strong and gives the air a dirty, sweat-earned scent. "Naw. That's what maybe you *used* to do."

"What you mean 'used to do'?"

He's still looking at me hard in the eyes, another good sign, because it's hard to fake a man's eyes out. It can be done, but it's difficult. Takes guile. "'Cause you're workin' with *me* now, Ben.' And if you're gonna work with me, you're gonna do things the right way. Now, when you block my jab, jab back yourself. By blocking mine, you're stopping me from doing what I want to, but you're not making me pay."

He nods. I can tell this kid's getting it, can tell he's staying with me. Feels good to have someone get what I'm trying to show 'em.

"Got to always make 'em pay, Ben." I stick my left out again. He blocks, jabs at me real quick, and if I was an amateur like him instead of a seasoned pro, I believe he'd have knocked me right on my raggedy old ass.

But only working with the Bens of the world just won't do. I'm not some charity worker who helps kids for a living, not some guy people might one day decide to make a television movie about because I'm all "Aw, shucks" and kids sayin' "He like the daddy I never had." Ain't me. I'm about *business* in this stage of my life, and right now, business isn't too good. I still have most of the money I collected in Vegas—except for the five grand I loaned TNT—but outside of the Dow jumping up and making my mutual funds soar, I got no other income coming in.

No news from Douglas yet on any findings of the committee. Figured as much. Nobody can find the blackjack dealer who was at the table the night Taylor and I talked. Nylon went out there first thing once the story broke, but no luck. Kid was nowhere to be found. He'd quit a couple days before, apparently, and has left Vegas. Makes me wonder: Did Taylor's people pay the kid off to leave town, afraid that he'd tell the truth? Or did they tell the kid to find another place to live, otherwise his health might be threatened?

Neither would surprise me. Truth is, *nothing* in this game surprises me anymore.

Meanwhile, the buy rate for the rematch has been skyrocketing the last few weeks. Seems that all the controversy about me and Taylor's rekindled interest in the fight. Maybe what Taylor envisioned all along, the crafty bastard.

Me and Unc eat breakfasts at this greasy spoon in town called the Capital Diner. Regulars call it the Crapital but keep coming back anyway. The food actually isn't that bad. And they serve a mean cup of coffee. Unc orders a stack of cakes with hot maple syrup and a slice of thick pork roll on the side, me a three-egg omelet with cheese and onions. We both get cups of their scald-your-stomach coffee. Hell of a way to start a morning. We're sitting and talking about what we always talk about: the gym and the fighters in it, television, and the fate of New York Knicks basketball (Unc's a long-time fan). I'm stabbing some omelet on my fork. A little piece of onion hangs out and I'm ready to devour it.

"Ted Jenks lost last night," Unc says, stirring some sweetener in his coffee, the white dust disappearing into the mini-brown-liquid-cyclone of the cup. Jenks is a guy I used to spar with a while back. He was nice enough. Had a good right hand but not much else. He always went hard the last twenty seconds of every round, to try and steal it from you. He was smart that way.

"Did he now?"

"Yep." He shows me the Trenton newspaper's sports section. In small type, buried in the sports page, it indeed reports that Jenks lost a ten-round decision last night in Atlantic City. Jenks used to be in the top ten but has fallen on hard times as of late. Now in his late thirties, he's been losing more than he's been winning. "A man shouldn't keep going on in the ring when it gets to that point."

That point. Unc, I know, is trying to say something to me.

When should a fighter retire? Hell, if I could answer that question, I'd be the smartest man in the world. Truth is, nobody really knows when a fighter should hang the gloves up for good. But rarely does a man get out of the fight game too early—just about every time somebody leaves the ring, it's one fight, or several fights, too late.

Take Ali. People say he should've retired for good as early as 1974, when he beat Foreman in Zaire to regain the title. Ali had all his faculties then. But he hung around another seven years, took some frightful beatings, and was permanently damaged. Anybody who takes a good look at Ali can see that. The faculties that were once there ain't no more. He can't talk like he used to, can't make the same facial expressions he used to.

Or what about Joe Louis? He hung around too long also. Met up with a young tiger by the name of Rocky Marciano who beat the shit out of him when Joe was thirty-seven. Got knocked out of the ring in that fight.

Sonny quit fighting after beating Chuck Wepner, a white heavyweight who bled so much in his fights that he was called the Bayonne Bleeder. Liston was coming off that knockout loss to Martin, his old sparring partner. He made only thirteen grand for the Wepner fight.

Sonny fought like he was pissed at Wepner for getting so little money and gave him a beating. Cut Wepner to pieces. Wepner ended up getting seventy-two stitches in his face.

After the fight, Sonny had to give all the money back. He'd apparently bet ten grand on another fight and lost. Also owed his corner three grand.

"He handed over the cash in brown paper bags and went back to Vegas with zip," said his friend Lem Banker. "Zip exactly."

And that was it for Sonny. He retired after the Wepner fight. Went back home to Vegas for good. Vegas was a nice place for Sonny. Cops didn't bother him there. People didn't seem to care about his background. He probably figured there must have been a better way to make—and lose—thirteen grand. Probably figured that after years of getting hit in the face, it just wasn't worth it no more.

What was going through Sonny's mind in that last fight? Was he thinking, *This is the end of a damn good career. I'm sure gonna miss the smells and sounds of the gym, the training, of the crowds cheering.* Or was he thinking, *I'm glad this shit's finally over?*

Me, I'm tired. Tired of getting hit in the face and crunched in the body. Tired of feeling sore all the damn time, of feeling a muscle I didn't know even existed flare up because I got punched there earlier and now the only thing I can do about it is try to sleep a certain way so the muscle don't get more aggravated than it already is.

I'm tired of the daily grind of sparring and of workouts—tired of getting in the ring and not knowing how much damage is being done to my body each time I step out of the ring, holding an icepack over a swollen eye or smearing medicine over a nasty cut and waiting for the cut to close. Tired of looking in the mirror every time after I fight and seeing my features change just a little bit more, till maybe one day I won't recognize whose face is staring back at me.

I'm tired. Boxing is a young man's game and I ain't young no more. I'm thirty-six years old. Near Liston's age when he quit. Almost Joe Louis's age when he got knocked out of the ring by Marciano. I don't want to go out like that—getting knocked out of a ring while people sadly shake their heads and say, "Scrap used to be somethin', now he's goin' and gettin' knocked out of rings."

The head shaking would be the worst, like the people who'd be doing it would know better than me. Like I'd be making people wince because I hung around the game too long.

I never been knocked down. Not in all the time I've been a professional fighter. I'm damn proud of that. It's something I'd like to be able to still say when I'm out of the game for good.

"I'm retiring, Unc. I'm done." I eat some more egg and wash it down with the rest of my coffee. "Just thought you should know."

"You're retiring?"

"Yeah. I've given it a lot of thought and I've decided that it's time for me to move on, time for me to look at new things to do with my life. I'm getting too old to keep fighting. The Rocket fight proved to me that I can't fight at a top level no more. If I can't do that, if I can't win big fights, then hell, Unc, all I'm doing is going in there to get beat. And I don't want that."

He looks at me and nods his head.

"This suspension, it could end up being a good thing for me," I say.

Neither of us says anything for a good while.

"How about sparring?" Unc finally asks. "You gonna still look for work doing that when the suspension gets lifted?"

"Naw. Done with that, too, I guess. This here's a young man's game and it's time, I think, for me to do something else."

Unc sits quiet, takes it all in.

"Well, I can still use help around the gym," he finally says. "And you're welcome to stay with me as long as you'd like. You know that, don't you?"

"Sure do. And I thank you for it."

"That's what old men like me are for." He puts his hand on my arm and gives it a light squeeze. I can see the film of some tears in his eyes. "I know it's not easy coming to the end, son."

I don't say anything.

"You had a great career, Amos. You sparred with world champions and held your own. You fought some of the top fighters in the world. You fought in *Vegas*."

I smile just a little. "I did fight in Vegas, didn't I?" It hurts to give the game up like this, to retire in a coffee shop, without any kind of press announcement, without any media at all in front of me, asking me my thoughts on leaving boxing and maybe where the game is going now that I'm no longer going to be a part of it. But I have had a nice career. Maybe I never won a title, maybe I was never even ranked in the top ten, but I still had myself a career.

"Yes, you did," Unc says.

We move on to other topics.

"You meetin' any women out this way so far?" Unc asks.

I'd rather go back to talk of retirement.

I blow on the egg. The Capital's omelets are always hot and require a considerable amount of blowing on them to avoid burning your mouth.

"Aw, Unc, you know how it goes. Things been busy with the gym and all. Haven't really had the time." Which, of course, is a lie.

"There's always time for *that,* son." He sips more coffee.

"Yeah, well, being on the road lately and all has thrown a crimp in my style."

"Has it now?"

"I won't say that it's *totally* cramped my style."

Unc gives me this wide grin, one usually reserved for when he either hears real good news about the fight game or about some woman you've been messing with.

"Vegas woman?"

"Yeah." I sip some coffee. Unc feels like a father/brother to me. Father in that I know I can always come back here when I need to and he'll make me feel like I'm not just visiting, but that I'm at *home*. Brother in that he likes to hear all the good shit going on in your life that you'd never tell your father.

"Tell me about her."

"She's a stripper, Unc."

He keeps on smiling, looking down at his now empty plate, shaking his head. "A Vegas stripper. Damn."

"It was nothing big, Unc. Just one night. After my fight and all."

"Well, that's still okay, son. I think it's healthy for a young man to have himself some fun here and there. Keeps a man in a positive state of mind."

Unc always calls me a young man, even though at fifty-five he's only nineteen years older than me.

"How about you, Unc? Anybody interesting around here?"

He lets out this sigh and leans back in his chair. "Been on a couple of dates. But nobody who can match my Peg."

Unc's wife—my aunt Peg—died five years ago. Cancer.

"Hell, no woman's gonna do that, Unc. She was a great lady."

"She was."

"The greatest." I want Unc to know how highly I think of her still.

115

Unc gets a little tear in his eye, the result, I suppose, of having been married for twenty-seven years to a woman that he's told me many a time he loved "more than anything I've ever loved before, times twenty."

I try to break the awkward silence that follows, not knowing how the hell it got to this, two men sitting in the Capital, getting all worked up and the day hasn't even begun. Though I know the answer is simple: women.

"I guess you and I got something to occupy our time in the next few weeks, Unc."

"And what's that?"

"Got to get out of the house and meet us some ladies. Know what I'm saying? 'Cause they sure as hell ain't gonna come to *us*."

Unc does what I was hoping he would. He smiles.

I slap a ten down on the table. "I just remembered," I say, taking a last long sip of coffee. "I told Jack Nylon I'd call him this morning."

Unc nods. "Nylon, eh? You know, I always like watching that boy. He seems real fair."

"He is, Unc. I'll see you at the gym later on."

Liston met his wife, Geraldine, while out driving his car one night in St. Louis. It was raining heavily when Sonny saw this beautiful young woman standing by herself on a curb.

He got out of the car and picked Geraldine up, physically picked her up, put her in the front seat of his car, and told her, "You're a very attractive lady. You shouldn't have to stand out there and get wet."

Can't nobody ever say Sonny wasn't smooth.

They were married not too long after.

Geraldine was with Sonny to the end. She was the one who found his body in their Vegas home. "He was a great guy," she said after he died. "Great with me, great with the kids. He was a gentle man."

I find a pay phone and punch in Nylon's numbers. We've talked a couple times since I've been back. "Nylon here," he answers.

"Hey. It's Scrap."

His voice lifts. "Scrap. Hey, man. What's up?"

"Aw, you know. Just checking in."

"Right. Yeah, man. Things pretty much the same around here. No news. That's other than . . ."

"Other than what?"

"Other than I got a phone call yesterday from some guy who wanted to get in touch with you. I swear I'd heard his voice before. Real familiar."

I grip the phone tight. "Who do you think it was?"

"Well, that's it, Scrap. He wouldn't tell me who he was. Just said he was a friend and that he wanted to get in touch."

"So what'd you tell him?"

"I just said you were back in Trenton for a while."

"Jack! You don't even know who this guy was!"

"Easy, Scrap. It's no biggie. Like I said, he just wanted to know what you've been up to is all."

"He didn't give his name?"

"He hung up before I could ask again."

I take a deep breath, look around at the people buzzing to work on the sidewalk in front of me. "Look, Jack, maybe it's some goon lined up by Taylor. You know, ordered to take me out . . ."

"Scrap, take it easy, man. It's nothing like that. Probably just an old friend of yours."

I give Nylon a quick, skeptical laugh. "Yeah, a friend who don't give his name out."

"You're gonna be fine. Look, I've got to run, but you need anything, anything at all, you call me. Okay?"

"Yeah. Sure." I hang up and take a couple deep breaths, trying to compose myself. Damn, my nerves are shot to hell these days with all that's been going on.

It's not even nine and I realize I don't have a thing to do. That coffee's given me some energy, so I decide to walk the few blocks down to Unc's gym. Maybe I'll blow off some steam in there.

The gym lights are off. I flip the main switch and the overhead bulbs slowly come to life, lighting up the dusty corners and drowning out the shadows.

Unc's not here yet. Probably running a couple errands, but I'm sure he'll be in soon enough. Maybe I'll help him give the gym a good cleaning. Mop the floors and ring. I know there's some Pine-Sol in a utility closet next to the bathroom so I head down there to get it.

The bathroom lights aren't on and it's dark over this way, but I get the closet open easy enough and fish for the cleaner. This floor's gonna be spotless when I'm done with it. I grab the cleaner and unscrew the cap. Begin to pour it in a large mop bucket I find, whistling some damn song I heard earlier on the radio.

It's while I'm pouring that I feel it. A hand on my shoulder, squeezing hard, turning me around, sending my heart into something near convulsions.

I'm still in the dark, but I can see well enough to make out a silhouette, and when I do that, there ain't no doubt, not a doubt in the world, as to who called Nylon earlier. I can't believe it. My cleaner spills on the floor, soaking my shoes, and I mouth the words at first, then yell it out loud.

"TNT!"

"Hey, man. Sorry 'bout that. Didn't mean to scare you." He releases his hold on my shoulder and I step away from the mess. TNT certainly looks the same. Dreads still hanging every which way from his head, his belly a little fuller than when I last saw him. He must've gained about ten pounds since his suspension.

"Damn, man. I near had a heart attack!"

"Man, shit. Sorry." He stands there, pitiful like.

"Two questions. One, how you get in here? Two, what the hell you doin' here?"

TNT's eyes look tired. Traces of red in the pupils. Truth is, I've been wondering what the bastard has been up to. Nobody I know in the fight game's heard a word about TNT since he left Vegas, and I was beginning to get concerned.

"Uh, I got in through the bathroom window. It was loose, so I jimmied it." He gives me a shrug. "Tried knockin' on the door but nobody was here."

"And?"

"And what?"

"And what you *doin' here,* man? Why you in Trenton all of a sudden? Where you been these last couple months?"

TNT rubs his chin, a nervous tic I noticed he had when we were in camp together last. He paces around a few steps, walking in small circles. "It's a long story, Scrap. And man, am I *hungry.*"

"You broke, ain't you?"

"Yeah."

"You ain't got my money, either, do you?"

"Man, shit."

I shake my head, then give him a little laugh. TNT, after all this time. Guess I've got some stuff to tell him, too. My story, I'll bet, is just as long, if not longer, than his. "Come on. Let's grab us some food and a cup of hot coffee. There's a good place right around the corner. We can do some eating and we can do some talking."

We head on over to the Capital and TNT orders a six-egg omelet with bacon, sausage, cheese, and onion. He's wolfing it down like a man who hasn't had a square meal in weeks and talks as he's chewing.

"I was in Kentucky first, Scrap, after I left Vegas. Hung out there awhile and even managed to get a couple fights under a different name."

"TNT, you *suspended,* man! What you doin' gettin' fights under a false name? You know you could get in a lot of trouble for that."

"Yeah, well, I got in a tussle with the promoter there. He said he'd pay me five hundred bucks for this one fight, and afterwards he tried to stiff me a hundred of it. Things was gettin' ugly and I grabbed him by the throat. He gave me the money but said he'd never use me on his cards again."

"TNT, you shouldn't be fighting for no five hundred bucks! Shit!" A guy like TNT shouldn't be fighting for anything less than ten grand, and that would only be for a small fight. He's world-class.

"Next I went to this town on the west coast of Florida." TNT smiles at the memory. "You should have seen it, man. Palm trees everywhere. And beaches. There was these white-sand beaches and the Gulf of Mexico. It was beautiful." TNT looks like he's in another world thinking of the place.

"What was in Florida?"

"My ex-girlfriend. Has a place down there. Took some convincing, but she finally let me sleep on her couch. Said I just had to leave her place whenever her new boyfriend came by. One night

I was so tired I didn't wanna leave. You know how you get when you real tired, Scrap. You just want to lay in one spot and not move around none."

"Yeah, I see what you're sayin'."

"Well, the boyfriend gets there and, when he sees me, geeks out. He starts makin' noise about what he's goin' to do to my ex-girlfriend." TNT fingers his chin and his eyes grow big. "Man insults me, that's one thing. He threatens a woman, that's another."

"I hear you."

"So I threw a left hook at the guy's jaw. Had to find another place to live. Was broke at this point, still had the suspension goin' on, so I made my way to Hickory, this little town in North Carolina. Found spot work sawin' wood for a furniture company. It's hard damn work sawin', Scrap. You ever sawed for a living?"

"Naw. Can't say that I have."

"Hard damn work," TNT mumbles. "After two weeks of that, I called Jack Nylon to see where you was. And here I am."

TNT looks like he needs some help and I have a crazy idea that's so out there it doesn't bother me to run it by him.

"TNT, your suspension's gonna be lifted next month, isn't it?"

TNT wipes his mouth with a napkin and looks around the room, clearing his throat. "Yeah, but, Scrap, nobody wants nothin' to do with me, man. Even when it gets lifted, who's gonna manage and train me? People considerin' me damaged goods right now because of all the trouble I've got myself in."

I take a long sip of coffee. "What if I told you that if you did the fightin', *I'd* do the managing. And the trainin'? I mean, you can still fight. And I know the fight game, TNT. I know it well. We can get fights. I'll stay on your ass, make sure you do things the right way. Know what I'm sayin'?"

He holds his hands up before me, making fat fists out of each one, and slowly nods.

I sip some coffee and feel the cool burn settle into my stomach. What I'm proposing to TNT is probably crazy. A guy who's never trained and never managed a fighter wants to take over the career of a heavyweight who's got some issues. But TNT's got top-notch skills, the talent to make noise in the division if he ever gets motivated.

I need to make sure TNT's aware of my own problems, though, before we enter into any kind of business transaction. "You heard about me, TNT? My own suspension from Vegas?"

He stares at me a long moment. "Man, you was set up. I know it, lots of folks know it. Man, shit. You didn't try to sell Diggs out. You ain't that way." He starts nodding his head, his dreads dancing around the crown of his head. "Taylor, now *he's* that way. He lied, man. Lied and screwed your career all up, and for what? 'Cause he can't take losing!"

The hand comes on my shoulder again, the eyes jabbing into mine, on fire, almost. "Listen to me, Scrap. If nothin' else, this here can be your chance to get back at Taylor. Go after him through *me*. And together, we'll make him pay."

Now TNT's the one tryin' to sell *me* on us workin' together.

"How am I supposed to do that?"

TNT shrugs. "Just get me into the ring with the man. You know I can still fight." His fists, clenched, come up before me. "I hit a man just right with either one of these and they goin' to sleep."

"Yeah," I say, and my mind starts racing about ways to make this happen. My blood starts pumping and I've got this feeling again, the one I used to only get just before a fight. I know it's crazy, know folks will say it's crazy, but it just might be worth a shot. What else do I have to lose? "Yeah, TNT, we can do this."

I stand up, slap TNT on the shoulder, and think of the things the two of us might be able to accomplish. I can get TNT into the gym, get him some fights, a world rating, a fight with Taylor, too, maybe even with the world title on the line.

Money. Respect. And revenge. Oh, yeah, revenge. I do like the sound of it all.

Round Six

"Well, I think it's a fine idea," Unc says when I tell him about it. He's beaming at me, proud as my daddy probably was the day I was born. Unc says he doesn't mind a bit if TNT stays with us. By trying to develop a genuine contender, I'll be helping out his gym's prestige, because that's where I'm gonna have TNT train.

And I'm also helping myself out. It'll give me something to do and it'll also make me more marketable in the boxing world. Training fighters is an old and honest profession, a skill I can always fall back on. And it'll make me more well-rounded as an announcer. A man who's fought *and* trained surely has a lot to say about the sport.

"You know, Amos, I always knew that boy could fight," Unc says. He makes a *V* with his hands, putting them wide to begin with, then narrowing as he moves downward. "He's got the body for it and he can punch." Unc looks wistful, like he might even cry, the way he sometimes gets when talking about something as close to his heart as the fight game. "Any man who can punch always has a chance. That's what I've always said."

"That's true."

"You can't teach a man how to punch, son. It's God-given. That's what it is."

"You're right."

Unc's forehead creases for a second. "Now, about this suspension thing. You say he's in the clear?"

"As of next week, his Vegas suspension is lifted. All other states should honor that."

"What about yours?"

I knew Unc would ask me this. And I needed to know, too, so I placed a call to Douglas to check up on it.

"I'm still suspended, Unc, until they find that blackjack dealer and he can set things straight. But it doesn't keep me from managing or training fighters."

"Good," Unc says, smiling at me, arms crossed. "Good."

"I believe I can take TNT places, Unc. I think I have a real good chance."

TNT's geared up and about to start our first day of training together. I made some calls earlier in the day to folks I know in Atlantic City. There's a fight card there at the end of the month and I wanted to see if they could squeeze TNT in. The promoter, Jimmy Rocatelli, was impressed when I told him TNT was now my fighter. He said he'd call me back if anything opened up.

In the meantime, my plan is to get TNT into the best shape possible. Work him hard in the gym, watch what he eats, get him fluid in the ring, and try to maximize his strengths.

He's already warmed up and we're in the ring in Unc's gym. TNT has headgear, protective cup, and bag gloves on. The bag gloves are twelve ounces each, slightly larger than the ten-ounce gloves heavyweights fight with. I've just got on a T-shirt and shorts,

126

plus these leather pads about the size of a big pie on each hand. We're gonna work the mitts.

"Listen, now," I say. "We've got to get your jab sharp. You've got a hell of a right hand and a pretty good left hook. But your jab is what sets those punches up. And you've got what I call a lazy jab."

TNT nods slowly, like he's probably heard this all before.

"You don't like to jab, do you?"

He shrugs, so I say, "Come on, man. Admit it. You hate to jab."

"Man, fuck," TNT says, and looks to the ground.

"You know, Liston had himself a wicked jab." I don't figure TNT to be much of a boxing historian. I say this more out of the hope it'll somehow draw some shred of interest out of him.

"You mean Sonny Liston?"

"Yeah. The former heavyweight champ of the world and one authentic badass mother."

He gives me a smile as long as Liston's reach, which, at eighty-four inches, was pretty damned long.

"See, Sonny's jab didn't just set up other punches. It stopped men in their tracks. Cut 'em. Busted 'em open. Knocked 'em down."

"He knocked people down with a jab?"

"Oh, yeah. It was like . . . a battering ram."

TNT loses the grin and looks at me sermon serious. I can tell this is soaking in. "Battering ram, huh?" he says, punching his gloves together.

I hold my pads up in front of my face. He sticks out his jab, and the first one lands with force, making a crackling sound on the pad. His second one he steps in with, creating even more of an impact, and the weight of the punch knocks me right back from the balls of my feet to my heels.

* * *

Saturday night and three single men—handsome single men, if I should be so bold—are taking turns in Unc's only bathroom, slapping on cologne, checking ourselves in the mirror, making sure we look good for the evening to come.

We've decided to go into town for the night. Hit Unc's favorite bar. I'll probably only have one or two drinks myself, not wanting to be a bad example for my fighter. But it's important he get out of the house. The routine of home, gym, home, repeated enough times, can drive any man crazy.

I've got on the outfit Nylon bought me in Vegas—black slacks, turtleneck, and light green sports coat. My head's neatly shaved, with just the lightest bristle of hair. TNT and Unc have on polo shirts and slacks. We're ready to go.

"What the women like in this town, Scrap?" TNT asks as we get into the car.

Truth is, I wouldn't know, because I ain't met any yet.

"They're just fine, son," Unc tells him. "They're like women anywhere else, I suppose."

"I hope they like the ones in L.A.," TNT says. "I fought in L.A. once, years ago. Those women in L.A. had real big ta-ta's and they all looked like sex."

Unc's driving. I'm sitting next to him and TNT is in the back. I turn around and look at TNT. "Now what the hell do you mean they looked like *sex*? How can a woman look like sex, TNT?"

"Oh, it's easy, Scrap. They was all walkin' around, running their tongues over their lips all seductive like. Kind of like this . . ." TNT takes his tongue and begins to run it slowly over each of his two large lips, getting them nice and wet. It about makes me sick to watch it all.

"Damn, TNT, don't you hold nothing sacred?"

Unc's looking in the rearview mirror, laughing. "Oh, Amos, let the boy have some fun."

We go to Jimmy Q's, an Irish pub near the gym that Unc's been going to for years. Unc's not a big drinker but he likes to stop in a couple times or so a week, drink a beer, and catch up with Jimmy himself, the Irish owner.

It's not much inside—a long bar that stretches from one end of the narrow room to the other, eight or nine creaky tables, and a few dim ceiling lights that hang overhead. Still, the place is crowded. Jimmy Q's is always crowded. All the tables are taken but there's a few open spots at the bar. Cigarette smoke floods the air.

We all sit down.

A young kid, no more than mid-twenties, is working behind the bar. He's got red hair, freckles, face as clean as an unbeaten record, and hell if he doesn't look familiar. He sees us, stops dead at what he's doing, and smiles.

"Mr. Fletcher!" he yells.

I take a closer look at him. "Timmy? That you?"

"It's me, all right. But I go by Tim now." He leans over the bar and the two of us hug.

"How the hell you doing, boy?"

"Doing great. Tending bar for Dad a couple nights a week, going to law school at Rutgers during the day."

"Damn, son. I always thought you were gonna amount to something. You're telling me that you're gonna be a lawyer?"

"A rich lawyer, if it all works out." He laughs.

"Damn. I thought we could've turned you pro—an Irish kid like you with a good left hook, we could've made some money."

"Well, two New Jersey Golden Gloves titles were enough for

me." Tim points to his temples. "Wanted to have something left here, you know."

"Well, I'll be damned," I say, staring at him. Tim sure has grown. He was a middleweight a few years ago, when he was still fighting. But he's put on some weight around the belly and in his face.

"So what brings you back here?" he asks.

"Lots of things, Tim. Training this fine young fighter, for one thing." I point to TNT, who looks shyly to the ground.

Tim leans into me. "That's TNT Timmons, isn't it?" he whispers. "Yep."

"And you're training him?"

"Yep."

Tim stares at TNT, who's fiddling with his thumbs, head still down. "Wow."

I introduce Tim and TNT. Tim already knows Unc. He asks us what we'd like to drink, so we order: a Guinness for me, Budweiser for Unc, and a grapefruit juice on ice for my fighter.

"I'll go get Dad," Tim says after bringing the drinks to us. He begins to walk upstairs but doesn't make it to the top because his father—Jimmy Quinlivan himself—comes barreling down the steps like a runaway train toward us. I know it's Jimmy the second I lay eyes on him—full, red, bushy beard, chest and belly sticking out like overinflated balloons, maroon checkered flannel shirt, and faded blue jeans. A typical Jimmy outfit.

"Scrap, what the hell are ya doin' in *my* bar?" he booms, his low, gravelly voice rising high above the crowd.

"Aw, you know, Jimmy. I guess I just got a jones for poor micks like you. I wanted to go to a place where the beer is flat and over-priced, the service is horrible, and the women flat-ass ugly. Yours was the first hole I thought of."

"You son of a bitch!" Jimmy races toward me. Even though I'm a big man, he picks me up with ease. Jimmy gives me this bear hug, and half the bar's watching, seeing these two grown men embracing like long-lost brothers. "So are ya back for long?" he asks, putting me down finally.

"Could be. I got some stuff going on, Jimmy. All depends on how it pans out."

He looks at me a little sadly, his eyes lowering. "I read what they did to ya out in Vegas, Scrap. And I was upset about it—mad as hell. I know that bastard Taylor is lyin' his arse off."

"Thanks for the vote of confidence, Jimmy. But I've got some good stuff going on here now."

Unc gets off his stool and he and Jimmy greet each other warmly. They've been friends for years. Jimmy's a huge fight fan, and despite never having put on the gloves himself, he comes down to Unc's gym from time to time to watch.

"Jimmy, this here's TNT Timmons. You might have heard of him before."

Jimmy claps TNT on the shoulder and TNT steps back defensively, raising his arms.

"Easy now," Jimmy says. TNT's fists come up to eye level. "Just my way of sayin' hello." He turns to me. "Of course I heard a this guy! He's only the hardest-punching heavyweight out there!" Jimmy takes a good look at TNT, from top to bottom. "TNT Timmons in my bar—Jesus!"

TNT must think of Jimmy as harmless, because he lets his guard down and shakes his hand. "Pleasure," TNT says.

Jimmy leans into him. "So tell me, what was the hooker like?" I can barely make it out.

"Hooker?" TNT just stares at him with this dull look on his face.

131

"Yeah. Prostitute. Streetwalker. You know, the girl who you tried to get some off of that ended up being an undercover cop. Was she hot?"

Jimmy's never one to mince words. I grimace at how TNT's gonna take this. If he puts his hands up from a simple shoulder pat, there could be trouble.

But TNT just smiles. "She was knockout hot," he says. "Long blond hair and a body built for fun. When I found out she was a cop, I was like, 'Yeah, well, frisk me then. I'm guilty!'"

"I'm *guilty!*" Jimmy says, bending over and laughing.

This time, TNT allows the shoulder clap. He's still smiling when he says, "Excuse me, fellas, but I got to go drain the lizard."

Once TNT's out of hearing distance, Jimmy grabs me. "What the hell is that guy *doing* here? He's been on suspension with the Vegas commission, right?"

"Was. Now he's off suspension. He's served his time."

"Amos is training him now," Unc says proudly. "*And* managing him."

Jimmy's eyes are big as a pair of eighteen-ounce gloves. "You're shittin' me, Scrap."

"It's the truth." It makes me feel good to say it, because now I can say something about myself other than that I'm fighting. Like now there's another side to me people haven't ever known about.

"That guy's got shit-hot skills, Scrap," Jimmy says. "Power in each fist. He can knock a fuckin' rhino out with that left hook. And his right—he's got a wrecking ball of a right. How the hell did this all happen?"

Jimmy takes a seat at a now empty table and tells me and Unc to sit, too. He orders Beam Black Label on the rocks and drains it quickly.

"Long story, Jimmy, but he needed some help. I'm available and I think we can make a go of it. God knows he has the talent. He's young, you know. Only twenty-eight. Young for a contender."

"Yeah," Jimmy says. "And even though he's had thirty-some fights, he's never taken a beating, so his mileage ain't bad." Jimmy smiles and looks at the table, shaking his head. "TNT Timmons. Who the hell would've thunk it?"

I get a phone call from Rocatelli. There's good news first and even better news second. The good news is that he's gotten TNT on the end-of-the-month fight card in Atlantic City. TNT's going to fight a ten-round semifinal bout—which means he's on the undercard, but that's okay with me for now—against Monte Jones, an unbeaten prospect. A win over Jones will look good.

The even better news is that Rocatelli also has a fight card in eight days and needs a heavyweight to fill in for an eight-round undercard fight. Not much money—the purse is only fifteen hundred bucks—but, hell, a fight's a fight and we'll be in Atlantic City to boot, the second most important boxing town after Vegas.

I tell TNT the news. He's happy about it. He'll get ten grand for the Jones fight. Again, not millions, but we got to start somewhere. Just by keeping TNT active we're doing well. The bigger fights will come.

Eight days means there's not much time to get ready for our first fight. We've only been training the past three days, and TNT hasn't done any sparring yet. I was waiting until TNT got into good punching shape first—I wanted him to be able to punch hard for a few rounds on the bags before putting him in the ring with anybody. But time is short and I don't have that luxury now. We'll have to start sparring hard tomorrow.

The opponent for our first fight is Franco Hughes, a tough white heavyweight from West Virginia. He's had about fifty fights in his career and has won maybe thirty of 'em. He's durable. Usually goes the distance. Not a big puncher, but tricky. Hard to hit clean. In all, not the easiest guy to fight.

TNT and I are back in the ring. I'm briefing him on what we want to do. "Listen, TNT. This here's a good break for us. Two fights in the next month. We win both of these, we get ourselves some bigger fights against better opponents for more money."

I like to break things down real simple, let TNT know up front what's in it for him. That way, he'll have extra incentive to fight his ass off. He bites down on his mouthpiece.

"Now, you ain't in exactly the best of shape." I take a quick look at TNT's midsection. It's still about eight pounds or so over his best weight, but, hell, this is a short-notice fight. There's not enough time to get into tip-top condition. "But at least you're in some kind of shape. And that's gonna be enough to get us through the fight."

Unc's got some fighters outside the ring. They're hitting the bags, and the smacking sound when the gloves meet the bags' canvas reminds me of when I used to hit 'em. "The way I figure, you can punch hard for about four rounds. This being an eight-round fight, we gonna have to do something about that."

TNT's eyes are locked on mine. I keep down a smile, glad he's still with me.

"What we're gonna do is use the step-in jab. It's basically a dead-weight punch. You don't have to use much energy. You throw the step-in jab the first few rounds of a fight, you're scoring points, you're winning rounds, and you haven't done a damn thing. You can coast the last couple rounds on what you have left."

"All right," TNT says, and punches his gloves together. I like how he does it, like he's on a search-and-destroy mission.

I get out of the ring, and his sparring partner for the day, Dirk McBride, a thickly muscled black fighter with a goatee, gets in. "Five rounds," I say. "And remember, TNT, nothing but step-ins."

I ring the bell to start the round. TNT moves around the ring a bit, pivoting to his left, creating punching angles, something he's always done well. McBride's a fraction slow in adjusting his body to TNT's, and TNT steps off his back right foot, pushing the weight and force of his body through his left toe, thrusting him through McBride's upright guard, piercing between his gloves, knocking McBride's head back.

TNT ties McBride up, holds for a second, and spins out of the clinch. "Atta way," I say, marveling at what he's just done. Step-in jab, just like that. Takes no energy to do, none at all, but it scores points. Damn.

TNT's bouncing up and down, opening his mouth as wide as it can possibly go, then bites down hard on his mouthpiece. Jaw stretches, he calls it, though the way TNT says the word it comes out more like "jawa stretches." Good to do before a fight, I've always thought, the loosening of the jaw. Because if you get hit there while your jaw's not warmed up, you can go ahead and pull a muscle there. And nothing hurts like a pulled jaw muscle.

I got TNT good and loose in the dressing room: hand pads for ten minutes, throwing half-speed combinations to get him warm, get the blood kicking in all the right spots. Spread Vaseline liberally under and over each eye, on the nose, on the forehead and cheekbones, giving it enough time to work into the skin, letting the ointment soak to the point that it naturally lets the skin become slippery, helping punches slide off even easier. And finally, plenty of step-in jabs. Letting TNT push into my hand mitts with his left, the punches knocking me back, and me telling him that in this fight, we gonna do this same move over and over.

Now we're in the ring. I have the old feeling, the one I used to get right before I was about to fight. My stomach howls and my heart spins out of control. Sweat spills out under my armpits, soaking my shirt. The adrenaline is kicking in. It feels good to have blood rippling through my veins again in this way. It feels *right*.

I look across the ring to our opponent. TNT's opponent. My opponent. He's thick-chested. A solidly built fighter. Willful eyes. Flat nose. I hate him already. I have to hate him. Have to have feelings of fury toward him, because he's the man who's trying to keep us from moving forward in our quest. He's the one who's trying to keep us from getting what we want.

Motherfucker. Yeah, you, motherfucker. What you lookin' at, man? Lookin' at me? Lookin' at my fighter? Because we both gonna fuck you up. Yeah. That's right. Fuck you up good. Rip you apart with a body attack. That's right. Apart. Take those lungs and punch 'em so hard they don't work right no more. Leave you with punched-out lungs that don't work so you can't breathe, and then where you gonna be? You gonna be dying, man. Dying with lungs that don't work and the hope that this here man would quit punching you in your lungs, but he's not gonna because he was trained to keep punching until he can't punch no more.

It's okay to hate inside these ropes. It's necessary. You don't have your blood boiling when you step in here, when you ready to strap it on and see who's who, then you don't belong. That's what I say. Yeah, Hughes. Who the fuck are *you* to keep us from gettin' what we want? Fuck you, Hughes. You hear me? Fuck you.

Hughes looks away. That's right. He'd better. I look to TNT.

He's got some hate but not enough. His eyes are narrowed like nail holes but there's not enough fury in his eyes. We gonna have to work on that.

"He tryin' to take everything away from you," I whisper into TNT's ear. "Don't you forget that."

TNT nods. I was hoping he'd do something, like punch his gloves together and howl. We gonna have to work on that, too.

Names and records are announced. First, Franco "Tank" Hughes, thirty-one wins, eighteen losses, two draws. Twelve wins by knockout. Then, Rodney "TNT" Timmons. Funny, but I don't remember ever calling him Rodney.

In fact, don't think I've ever called him anything but TNT. The idea that he has a real name intrigues me. I wonder if his family ever called him Rodney. Maybe Rod, or Hot Rod—something like that. I don't know a thing about TNT's past—where he's from, who his family is, none of that. The fact that *I'm* the one who had to bail him out of jail in Vegas probably says a lot about his family ties, though.

TNT's record is next to be announced: thirty wins, five losses, twenty-nine of his wins by knockout. The record shows me two things. One, somebody with TNT's skills and body shouldn't have no five losses on his record. And I don't plan on him getting number six anytime soon. Not while I'm managing him. Two, TNT has dynamite in his fists. Twenty-nine wins by kayo shows that. He hits you, you explode. It's that simple.

Now that the formalities are finished, TNT walks to ring center to touch gloves and listen to the referee's instructions. I follow close behind him, a pea green Howard Johnson's bath towel draped across his shoulders. I would've liked to have had a plain white towel, but when we got up here late last night and checked in at the HoJo's, I realized I hadn't brought one. So HoJo's it is, sitting right on top of TNT's massive traps. Hell, if the fight was being televised, I'd have gone ahead and asked HoJo's for some front money, this being free advertising for them and all.

TNT smiles, which is good. I told him in the dressing room to smile, to *always* smile during prefight instructions, also known as the stare down. There's different schools of thought on this. Liston used to go up to opponents with his robe still on. There'd usually be towels stuffed under the shoulders of his robe, to make Liston look even bigger. Then he'd stare, this big-shouldered, cold-looking son of a buck, no expression on his face. None at all. Just this hollow, see-through-you look of complete indifference. Chilling.

Then there's the smile. Evander Holyfield, four-time heavyweight champ, uses it to perfection. He goes to the middle of the ring, looks his opponent right in the eye, confident grin plastered on his face, never losing eye contact or the grin, portraying confidence all the while. Telling the other guy with that grin, "I'm here, baby, and I'm gonna be here all night long. Now, how you like that?"

I thought hard about which route to go with TNT and finally decided on the smile. A man TNT's size doesn't need no towels under his robe. With his body, he doesn't need a robe, either. Just his black trunks, with TNT scrawled in red block letters, his chest hanging like a couple of country hams, biceps rippling, forearms veined, and muscles pulling. A man sees a fighter this size and sculpted grinning at him, it's gonna definitely cause some worry.

Hughes stares straight into TNT, though—keeps eye contact with him. Got to give the man credit for that, even though he likely knows just as well as I do that he's physically outmatched at five-ten and

208 pounds. They touch gloves and TNT's still got the smile going, shaking his head to the right a little, twitching almost, maybe saying to Hughes, *Man, you in for a long damn night.* I didn't say anything to TNT about the twitch, but I like it. Looks kind of crazy. Me, I wouldn't want no part of a sucker who twitches his head before a fight.

We go back to the corner. "Remember, nothing but step-ins the first couple rounds. You get him hurt, sure, unleash on him, but otherwise, be patient. Step in, move around, be relaxed."

"All right," TNT says. Aw-eyet.

The bell rings. TNT and I, we go to work.

Three rounds of step-in jabs prove to be effective. TNT's jolting Hughes with the jab and Hughes can't do nothing but take it, get rocked, and tie TNT up. After the first round, it's clear Hughes realizes he's overmatched. He clinches TNT whenever he can, trying to kill time. But he can't kill the inevitable. TNT's jab busts Hughes up, makes his right eye look like a mini-watermelon. Before round four, I tell TNT to go to work. To unleash. As soon as he's got the go-ahead to empty his arsenal, he does. I sit back and admire his work, his artistry.

Step-in jab. Hughes's head sails back, sweat flying from it, mixed with splashes of blood from his mouth and nose. Hughes tries to grab TNT, but, damn, TNT is strong. Now that he's got the go-ahead to finish things, that's just what he wants to do. TNT pushes Hughes back on his heels and digs a short, hard hook to the body. Hughes doubles over in the shape of a human pretzel.

TNT dips his knees and throws a right uppercut. Hughes's head rises. TNT feints a hook to the head and instead crushes another hook to the body, the punch landing just under Hughes's rib cage, in an area where there's nothing but skin and muscle. Hughes stands still a millisecond, pained by the blow. Then he drops to both knees, a loud grunt coming out of him. Flops over to his side, lying like a caught fish with no water, dying, but not really. This probably feels worse than death.

It's just an undercard bout, so I don't expect much of a media turnout in the locker room after the fight. But Nylon is here, camera crew in tow, much to my surprise. "Scrap, now why the hell didn't you tell me you were managing this guy? *And* training him? Why I got to find this out from Douglas instead? Man, I thought you and I were friends."

I chuckle, knowing that Nylon was going to be upset when he found out I was working with TNT. "Well, Jack, I wanted to keep this here thing low-profile. Take it slow, you know, and see where it might go. Knew if I told you, you'd be down here in a heartbeat."

Nylon grins and gives me a slap on the back. "Well, this thing ain't low-profile no more. Now that *I'm* here it isn't." He looks at the camera crew. "Start rolling, fellas." Looks at me. "Oh, Mr. Manager who's too big-time to call his friend, may I please talk to your fighter?"

"Sure." I laugh. "Be my guest." TNT's coming out of the shower now, small white towel wrapped against his body. Nylon steps toward him, mike in hand. TNT's dreads have tiny drops of water still on them, just sitting there at the tips, ready to spill onto the floor.

Nylon begins, "This is Jack Nylon with CNN Sports. I'm here in Atlantic City with Rodney 'TNT' Timmons, a bone-crunching heavyweight contender coming off a suspension slapped on him by the Las Vegas Boxing Commission. Timmons is now being managed by Amos 'Scrap Iron' Fletcher, a veteran heavyweight boxer who has recently been suspended from fighting due to a vague altercation at a Vegas blackjack table with former world champ Terrence 'T-Bone' Taylor. CNN was live in Atlantic City tonight to check out Timmons's bout with Franco Hughes, Timmons winning on a fourth-round kayo following a vicious body shot that left Hughes crumpled on the canvas, gasping for air."

Nylon puts the mike in front of TNT, who smiles and holds his towel tight. "Rodney, this was your first fight with Fletcher in your corner. How did you feel out there tonight?"

TNT looks at me. I nod. Subdued. That's the word I gave TNT in case anybody wanted to talk to him after the fight. Laid-back. Brief. To the point. Subdued. None of this "I'll knock him out to Pluto" nonsense.

"Well, I felt real good out there tonight," TNT says. "We worked on some things in the gym and tried to do 'em out here." TNT smiles into the camera, just like I told him to. Hell, a man doesn't know when an endorsement opportunity might come up. For all we know, a bigwig at Certs or Ford could be watching.

Nylon turns to me now. "So what is the next step for Rodney? He looked impressive tonight. Could a run at the title be in the works?"

I look deep into the camera. "Right now, we're just taking it one fight at a time, Jack. We have another bout scheduled here at the end of the month against Monte Jones, a hot young prospect. That'll be a tough fight for us, so we're focusing on that right now." There. That worked well enough. Keeping it simple. Keeping it subdued. No need to go out into left field with an outrageous quote.

But TNT can't help himself. I should've known better. He's fidgeting with his towel, grabbing the parts where he has it tucked around his waist, refolding it, looking distracted. I can tell he wants to say something, likely something crazy. It's in his nature. I need to wrap this up quick. "We've really got to get going, Jack." I move toward TNT, who's still fumbling with his towel. "But I'll call you tomorrow. I promise." Nylon gives me a wink, begins talking again. Just as he tells the audience that he's Jack Nylon, reporting live from Atlantic City, TNT moves past me, quick as a deer, into the camera.

"TNT, no!" I yell. But it's too late. He's got this look in his eyes, this wide-eyed, say-anything look, and his dreads bounce up and down as he moves. TNT grabs the mike from Nylon and yells, "Going after T-Bone, baby! Gonna flatten him, change his name from T-Bone to pancake!"

Nylon can't believe it. "Start rolling again," he whispers to the camera crew. "Get back on now," he says into his headset. He must be talking to studio people back in Atlanta.

"Gonna get that lyin' steak nicknamed chump back, baby!" TNT begins to throw punches, lots of punches, into the air.

"TNT, knock it off!" I move toward him, try to move him out of the camera's way, but he holds firm. He's bigger than me. Much bigger. I can't budge him.

"Get me a fight with the man. I'll douse him like A.1. sauce!" He throws more punches: hooks, jabs, uppercuts, and Nylon's camera crew is getting it all, every last word, live. "'Cause when you get in the ring with TNT . . ." He scratches his chin, thinking of what to say next. Nothing comes, I suppose, because he goes back to punching the air, making loud animal grunts as he digs the punches from his chest, saying, "Ungh, ungh, ungh!" He digs a hook. A cross. He howls.

And to the surprise of me, Nylon, the camera crew, and millions of viewers from all over the world—and quite possibly even TNT—

in the middle of all those punches, his towel falls from his waist, down, down, down. All the way to the floor.

It's later and I'm in the dressing room, alone with TNT. Nylon and crew are long gone.

"The hell were you thinking, man, pulling a stunt like that?" I'm in TNT's face, good and close, because I want him to know that I'm not here to play games. "The plan was to go low profile, remember? Build things up nice and slow, then go after the belt." I raise my hands high in the hot locker room air, which smells like week-old sweat. "Now everybody knows our plans, not to mention what else they know about *you* now."

TNT looks at me, confused. "What you mean?"

I stare below his waist. "Oh," he says.

Neither of us says anything and there's this long moment where one of us could easily just get up and walk out the room. But I don't want to. Don't know why, really, because I'm dealing with a professional screwup. What the hell do I need this grief for? My rep's been battered, sure, but if this don't go well, it could go a long way to really making me look bad to people I respect in the fight game.

TNT pinches the tip of his nose with his thumb and index finger. His eyes close. Head lowers just a bit. "Look, Scrap. I thought by sayin' some of that stuff we'd be speedin' up the process. You know, havin' television here and all, we had us an *opportunity*."

He opens his eyes and he's biting his lower lip, just like a kid. That's what I've got here. A kid. A kid the size of a man, a large man, a kid whose fists can do damage to most professional heavy-weights. A kid who, despite all the bad stuff that comes with his being a kid, wants to do right when it's all out there on the table. I see that now. I know I do. Otherwise I wouldn't have taken TNT on in the first place.

So now I got a choice to make. Do I stay with the kid, even though he's no doubt gonna do embarrassing things, things that'll make us both look like fools, even though he might mean well? Or do I see my way outta this before my reputation can suffer any more? I can just see all the boys I've sparred with in the past—Taylor and Diggs included—laughing their asses off now, enjoying many a joke at my expense, 'cause I got a fighter who can't control his mouth *and* can't control his towel.

In or out, a decision has to be made. A man has to go with his gut when it's choosing time. I get into TNT's face, so we're only inches apart, nose to nose. "From now on, I need you to stick to the plan." I grab his fists, put mine on top of his. "These here, these are our opportunity. Got it?"

He nods.

"Good. 'Cause if you keep using these, use 'em like you did tonight, and if you stick to the plan outside the ring, just like you stuck to it inside, then we gonna have ourselves opportunities galore."

He smiles, then looks confused. "*Galore* means 'lots,' TNT. Lots of opportunity." The concern leaves his face. Who knows if the boy's gonna listen? Hard to tell. One thing, though, is for sure. Nobody said this was gonna be easy.

A week later and TNT and I are working hard for the upcoming fight. TNT's hitting the mitts for a good six rounds, stepping in quick with the jab, jamming other guys' heads back like a jackhammer in sparring sessions. The jab has broken one nose so far in training and partially cracked another. It's getting so that guys don't want to work with TNT in the ring. We have to ligten up a bit.

"Aim for their foreheads," I tell TNT.

"No nose?" he says, raising an eyebrow.

"No nose."

"You the boss," he says, and hell if he doesn't start thumping that jab right at people's foreheads.

I meet with each sparring partner after they work with TNT, to get their views on his strengths and weaknesses. In my mind, feedback like this is important. Sparring partners see all in the ring. They see the punches, take the punches, and give 'em back. They're field research. I want to find out what they've discovered. Use it to make TNT a more complete fighter.

Word on TNT's gotten out. Newspapers from all over, the Newark *Star-Ledger, Trenton Times, New York Times,* and New York *Daily News,* have all come down to the gym to talk to the hottest contender around. I've finally quit trying to censor TNT. It doesn't work, and he's way too popular with the media these days to try and tone down his act. The man basically sells himself with his postfight comments, so I've decided to let TNT be TNT. He's a hard one to figure out— quiet most of the time, like Liston, but put a camera in front of him and all of a sudden my boy becomes Ali.

TNT's sudden popularity has also attracted the attention of people to Unc's gym—mainly fans, most of 'em women. And most of those women are young, single women hoping to get TNT to notice 'em while he's training.

Me, I never had this problem. It was always the men I sparred for that had women showing up at their training camp, hoping like hell to meet a hot heavyweight title contender.

But we got women showing up at the gym now in big numbers.

So many of them come by that some days Unc's got to keep telling them to get out of the way because the gym's not big and we don't got room for lots of women to be prancing about in their halter tops and tight jeans, smelling like assorted fruits. We got work to do. And as much as I *like* looking at 'em, women can cause a man to lose focus real damn quick. We got too much on the line now to let anybody slow us down.

TNT comes into the gym from the dressing room, just like he always does—in a white tank top and blue gym shorts, his biceps coiled like barbed wire, wearing a two-day growth of beard. TNT's face grows hair quickly, and if he doesn't shave every day, it looks like he's got himself a beard going.

More than a dozen ladies stand over in a corner—Unc's put them there—but when they see TNT, they race toward him. They get in the way of the other fighters who are busy skipping rope, shadowboxing in front of a full-length mirror, and working the bags.

A young brunette in a low-cut dress coos to TNT, "I saw the Hughes fight and you looked soooo mean in there. But seeing you up close, I realize what a peaceful man you really are." She tugs down on the top of her dress, giving TNT a peek of her breasts, and pulls out a blue Magic Marker. "Can you sign this for me?" she asks, handing him the marker.

TNT scratches his head and signs his nickname in big letters. He smiles and gives the marker back to the girl.

"It's permanent ink, you know," she says, sighing happily.

A black woman in her thirties, dressed to kill in a spotted yellow-and-orange miniskirt, leans into my fighter like a cheetah. She has a pair of legs that I'd die for. They're lean and muscular and could wrap around a man like a garden hose. She kisses TNT full on the mouth.

I can tell her tongue is probing inside TNT's mouth because his cheeks are swelling up in places that don't look normal. She kisses him for a good thirty seconds and only stops when I get out of the ring and separate them myself.

"That's enough," I say, grabbing my fighter. I lead him to the ring. "We got work to do."

"Gotta get her number, Scrap," TNT whispers to me, licking his lips. They're cherry red from whatever the woman was wearing. "Woman kisses like a pro."

"And how do you know how a pro kisses?"

He gives me an are-you-stupid look and shouts, "Gimme your number, baby!" A loud groan comes out of the group of hotties.

Leopard Skirt walks toward the door and turns around. I get to see her million-dollar ass that goes perfectly well with her million-dollar legs. "Sorry, honey," she says, flashing us a finger. There's a wedding ring on it. "I've been married for fifteen wonderful years. I just had to see what this hotshot everybody's been talking about tasted like. Hope you don't mind."

TNT shrugs and she's out the door, her ass wiggling all the while.

"Work," I say. "We got to get to work." I put my hand on my fighter's shoulder, leading him into the ring.

The night of the Jones fight comes and I feel pretty good about our chances. TNT's in good shape, he's working the jab to damn near perfection, and I've gotten some calls from other promoters, asking about TNT's availability for future bouts.

I know a win over Jones will bring opportunities: a possible world rating—key in getting a title shot—more fights, and more money. But we can't be caught looking ahead. Jones is a strong fighter, twenty-one and zero as a pro. Good jab. Great speed. His management likely sees TNT as a stepping-stone for Jones, a good name on his record that will elevate him to the upper echelon of the division.

My job is to make sure the only stepping TNT's going to do is over Jones's horizontal body.

Before each fight, somebody from each fighter's camp gets to go into the opposing fighter's dressing room and watch that fighter get his hands taped. It's a way of making sure the fighter has the proper amount of gauze on his hands. A small detail, but important. Too little gauze is bad because it means a fighter could basically be fighting with bare fists under his gloves. That could mark TNT up really bad. I go into Jones's dressing room, seeing how I'm the *only* member of TNT's camp, to watch it done.

Jones is sitting on a table, white cloth robe still on, eyes closed. The boy is practically asleep! Not a trickle of sweat on him. TNT's already soaked to the bone. I've had him hitting pads for the last twenty minutes, stretching out ten minutes before that. To not be "hot," to not have your body soaked with sweat and loose before a bout, is crazy to me, because once a man gets in the ring, there are no warm-ups. When a gloved fist is coming at a man's head with the intention of hitting the brain and making it shake till that brain loses consciousness, well, if that's not enough to motivate a man to get warm, then I don't know what is.

And here Jones is, dozing on the table, getting his hands wrapped. Probably hasn't even stretched out yet.

"Good to you?" says Jones's trainer, a white man in his fifties, balding, who I've never seen before.

The amount of tape on Jones's hands looks to be the correct amount. "Fine," I say, holding back a smile and hurrying back to the dressing room. TNT is throwing shots in the air, grunting, simulating hard punches to the body. Sweat and heat fill the air in the cramped room.

"We gonna switch to Reyes," I say to him, pulling out a second pair of red gloves, these being harder, more compact, than the Everlast gloves TNT has on now. Reyes are a puncher's glove.

"What for?"

I get the glove in my hand and begin to take off the Everlasts. "He's not even warming up. We're gonna catch him cold. I want you to go out there and ice him."

TNT gives me the desired response. A wicked smile. "Now you talkin' my language," he says.

TNT starts fast. Step-in jab, followed by a right. He twists it just before it lands, like he's supposed to do, because when he twists at the end of the punch, it creates a sharper finish. The right knocks Jones back into the ropes. He covers up, stunned.

"Hook to the body!" I yell, but TNT's already beat me to it. He hooks, the punch lands, Jones doubles over. An uppercut brings Jones's face up, and a TNT hook to the head slams him on the temple, the speed of the blow doing all the damage. It lands the second after TNT throws the uppercut, creating a devastating effect. The punches a man doesn't see are almost always the ones that do the most damage.

Jones loses consciousness somewhere between half a second to a full second after the punch lands, and he falls, arms first, to the canvas. Jones goes facedown, making a dull thud. There's no reason to count. The referee does anyway.

Twenty-nine seconds into the fight and it's over. TNT is the winner by a first-round kayo. He pumps his right fist into the air and looks over to me, giving me that grin. I step into the ring and hug him. "See, what'd I tell you? You iced him."

He's not even breathing heavy, really. Just sweating some, though not much more than when he left the locker room to come out here. "Yeah, I did ice him. Iced him like a cake. Like a big, thick, chocolate cake!"

"Remember, just be calm, cool, and collected."

"Right. Cool, Scrap. That's what I'll be. Cool as ice."

"That's all I'm askin', brother."

Nylon, of course, is in the locker room immediately after the fight. And why wouldn't he be? He got one of the best scenes in sports journalism history last time out. I called him up and stewed about the whole affair, but I realize he's got a job to do, just like me. Can't get on him too hard for doing his job.

"Rodney, can you explain your game plan going into tonight's fight?" TNT has the mike right next to his mouth. He's still in his boxing trunks—under my instructions—but has his shirt off. With an upper body like TNT has, we just *got* to show it off when we can. It's a hell of an upper body and folks need to see it. But for obvious reasons, I'm not gonna have TNT in a towel.

I told TNT to use Nylon's first name a lot, because this will make Nylon feel more at ease, having his first name said, maybe softening Nylon a bit, too, making him less likely to ask potentially harmful questions. Also, it'll let the viewers at home know that TNT's no spoiled athlete, he respects people, guys like Nylon, even goes to the trouble of calling them by their first name! Surely a man who calls another man by his first name can't be all bad.

"Well, Jack," TNT says, "the game plan was to start fast. Go out there and take care of him early."

Nylon nods politely and tries again. "You almost ran out there to start the fight, practically racing to the middle of the ring to meet him. Why did you start so fast?"

"We just figured that we'd jump on him quick. Finish the fight quick so we could all go home."

Nylon gives TNT a knowing nod. It's a good look: He wrinkles his forehead, as if in deep understanding, letting the public know that he not only reports the news, but he also cares a great deal about it. I got to remember to nod knowingly myself when I get back on television.

"So you're saying the plan, then, was to ambush Jones?"

Oh, shit. TNT's eyes expand and he starts moving up and down. He's gonna say something, I don't know what yet, but I've got to stop him. I place my hand on TNT's shoulder to guide him away from Nylon and the camera, but it does no good.

"Yeah," TNT says, straight into the camera, his face nearly pressed up against it. "An ambush. That's what we had planned. An ambush!" TNT starts bouncing even more, throwing shots in the air, his eyes looking crazed, like a rabid dog's. "Ambush, baby!" He throws a hard right. It just misses the camera. The cameraman ducks, almost drops his equipment, but recovers in time to keep filming. "We was the Indians, he was the cowboy! He came over the hill and didn't see it coming!"

Again, I try to pry TNT away. Nylon's got this I-can't-believe-my-good-luck look on his face again, his mouth open wide as TNT begins to slap his right palm over his mouth, doing some sort of an Indian war cry. I walk away from the both of them, thinking, *This son of a bitch is even crazier than I thought, but I'll be damned if he can't hit like a Mack truck.*

Round Seven

It's hot as hellfire in Caracas today. Says so in the paper. Ninety-two degrees. Foreman fought there a while back when he was champ. Knocked the stuffing out of Ken Norton. Why they were fighting in Caracas of all places I'll never know. But what I do know is that Foreman treated Norton like a human Ping-Pong ball. Knocked him all over the ring before the referee finally saved Norton in the second round. Norton never was any good against big punchers like Foreman. He was leery of 'em, even in training.

"Yeah?" I answer the phone. It's the day after the Jones fight and TNT and I are hanging out at Unc's, watching the nonsense from yesterday get played over and over on the television.

"It's Jack." Again, he scored big. Got another great interview with TNT. The way things are going for Nylon, the man's gonna win himself a Pulitzer Prize before too long. And he'll have me to thank for it. "You're not mad at me, are you?"

I look over to TNT, who's eating a big bowl of peach ice cream with some whipped cream on top. Since we trained real hard for this fight, I figured giving him a couple days off wouldn't hurt. Let the boy eat some stuff he likes and rest up. We didn't talk about his Custer's Last Stand comments. What would it accomplish?

"Mad at you, Jack? Naw. I guess not. If it wasn't you broadcasting it, just would be somebody else."

Nylon chuckles. "Well, Scrap, I got some news for you, something you'll like to hear."

"Tell me. I need something good in my life."

"I talked to Jake Douglas this morning. Wanted to get some information from him on the Diggs-Taylor rematch next month in Vegas. You know what he said to me? He said, 'I saw TNT fight last night. He looked pretty damn good.'"

I yawn. No big deal. Not like Douglas is a promoter.

"Then he said that Gene Davis was talking to him about having an open spot on the undercard. Said he liked what he saw in TNT. Hard puncher, great interviewer. Likes the way he's calling Taylor out. Said TNT keeps laying people out and saying wacky shit, he might have to put him on the card."

"No kidding? So he's forgotten all about TNT soliciting the police officer?"

"I wouldn't say he's *forgotten* it. But I'd say that the way TNT's been going lately, he might be willing to *selectively dismiss* it."

Even though TNT's suspension has been lifted, promoters like Davis sometimes hold grudges on certain fighters that screw up—until they become marketable again.

TNT's licking the bowl clean and is flipping channels. Turns on an old John Wayne movie. Wayne is firing his shotgun at some Indians, mowing them down, all the while riding around in circles on his horse.

"Jack, give me your honest opinion. You think I'm crazy for taking this kid on?" It's a stupid question, I know, because I *know* I'm crazy for training him.

"Well, Scrap, let me say this: You gonna get calls and protests from the Native American community. No doubt about that. And some others will say that TNT's a nut. But all in all, I'd say you got yourself one hell of a fighter. He's tough, he hits hard, and best of all, basically promotes himself. The guy's a natural on camera—a quip a minute."

Quip a minute. Yeah, I guess old TNT is. I smile as I hear TNT yelling at the set, "You gots to use your bow and arrows, Tonto! You gots to use 'em so you can scalp that cowboy!"

For better or worse, TNT is *my* fighter. That much I know for sure.

The call from Davis comes late in the afternoon. TNT, tired from the ice cream and movie, is now dozing on the couch. Unc is watching CNN and I'm trying to figure out what kind of money we want to fight in Vegas.

"Scrap, it's Gene Davis from Las Vegas. How are you?" Davis puts extra emphasis on the *Vegas,* trying to make himself sound more important. An old negotiator's trick—always make yourself sound as important as possible.

"I'm good. How you been?" I try to sound casual, like Vegas promoters been calling me all day.

"I'm fine." Davis sounds upbeat, maybe too much so. I know the voice. When it's forced like this, it means a man wants something. "Saw TNT fight last night, Scrap. He looked darn impressive."

Now who in the hell uses *darn* anymore?

"Thanks. He did look impressive, I thought. Now, what can I do for you?"

Davis pauses. All good negotiators pause at this point, because saying what you want outright is a sign of weakness, like you're a kid who just can't help himself and you've got to have it all *now*. So after the pause there's this forced laugh from Davis and I'm thinking, *Just say what you got to say and let's do some business.*

"Well, Scrap, I was thinking of using TNT on the undercard of Diggs-Taylor II next month. Wanted to see if we could work something out."

Now we're getting somewhere. Finally. "That sounds great. What do you have in mind?"

"A fight with Randall 'Rocket' Richards—I believe you know who he is—with the winner fighting the winner of the title rematch. How does that sound?"

A shot at the title if we win? Sounds phe-freaking-nominal. How could it not sound fantastic? But I don't want to show too much interest too soon. It could hurt our leverage. "Well, that would depend on the kind of money we're talking about, Gene."

Another pause from Davis. He's good at these pauses, spaces them out well. "I believe we paid you eighteen thousand dollars to fight Richards."

"It was twenty. And pardon me for saying so, but you're mistaken if you think I'm gonna take a fight in Vegas for TNT against an undefeated contender—one who I've fought and know myself how tough he is—for chump change."

"Eighteen thousand dollars isn't exactly chump change . . ."

"Again, it was twenty. And, yes, twenty *is* chump change compared to other offers I've been getting."

Now I've got Davis thinking. Of course, I haven't received any other offers for TNT yet, but, hell, what harm can it do to bluff a little? Sometimes a man's just got to throw it out there, see if it sticks. Davis doesn't say a word, likely trying to gauge what he needs to do next.

"And what offers have you been getting?"

Here comes the bluff. Hope it doesn't backfire on me. "Tony Simmons from London called earlier about fighting some British hotshot heavyweight in Wembley Arena next month. He was talking about a purse of three hundred thousand dollars with travel expenses included. And we're talking about a British fighter here, Gene!" I'm picking up steam now. "They just like London Bridge, always falling down!" I wait for a response, hoping to God that Davis doesn't call London to confirm this with Simmons, who I've never met. I only know his name from reading a recent issue of *Ring* magazine.

"If you think I can match three hundred thousand dollars then you're crazy," he says in a voice that I like, because it's not too loud and not too disgusted, only slightly so.

I'm jotting down figures I can live with on the back of an old receipt: $100,000, $150,000, $175,000. The key is to start higher, then see what happens. "I could work with two twenty-five."

"Not possible. Not possible at all. That's way out of our thinking." *Our thinking.* Like anybody but Davis is doing the negotiating for his side. Another trick—always act like there's a vast decision-making body, even if you're the only one calling the shots.

He gives me a tired sigh. "Fifty thousand. More than double what I paid you, plus a written guarantee of a title shot against the winner of Diggs-Taylor."

I'm still scribbling. I like $175,000 a lot. A whole damn lot. "I'm going with the London fight, then," I say, hoping to hell he doesn't hang up on me. "You know as well as I do that Taylor's gonna win the rematch, and the way the media's been covering TNT lately, it's gonna be the only moneymaking fight out there in the division."

"But I've got Richards to fight Taylor."

"Good. But what you got after *that*?"

Silence on both ends.

"Give me a figure, Scrap. A *realistic* figure."

The key is not to answer. Key is to ask *him* the question back.

"And what would *you* call *realistic*?"

"Say, seventy-five thousand dollars?"

"Then I guess we're going overseas."

I can tell I'm wearing Davis down, because his voice is strained as he counters with "I've got two other guys who'll fight Richards for next to nothing."

"Use 'em, then. I'd like to work with you, Gene, I really would. You're a good promoter and you've been fair with me before. But I got to be fair to my fighter."

"Ninety thousand."

"One hundred eighty thousand."

"No way."

"Have fun finding Richards a human punching bag, then."

"Ninety-nine thousand dollars. That's my final, absolute final offer."

"Is that really the best you can do?"

"Yes!" Davis sounds exasperated. I can probably push a bit more, but who knows? Don't want to risk it, especially with a shot at the title looming if we win.

"You'll have to give me a written guarantee about the title shot."

"No problem."

"Then we're going to start training for one Randall 'Rocket' Richards, Gene."

"That what I wanted to hear. I'll have my people fax over a contract to you immediately. Please sign it and send it back right away."

I give him Unc's gym's fax number and tell Davis that, yes, I'll sign the contract and send it back to him, and not to forget to send the guarantee over, too.

We're set. Ninety-nine thousand dollars sure isn't one seventy-five, but hell if it isn't a whole lot more than twenty thousand.

Now I got to come up with a game plan for the Rocket fight.

Nylon's already sent me a tape of my fight with Rocket. It came in the mail yesterday and I've already watched it three times, writing down what I see: strengths, weaknesses, pretty much anything, in a notebook. Then there's the notebook in my head, the one that still has memories of my fight with the kid. My book goes like this: Rocket has quick hands, hits hard, is in good shape. Leaky defense. Strong, but not too strong. I see some things we can take advantage of. Other things worry me, but that's what I get paid for, to find a way to fight the man.

And about getting paid. TNT and I worked out a deal when we started working together. Usually, a manager gets one third of his fighter's purse. The trainer gets 10 percent. Since I'm doing both jobs for TNT, my cut would come to 43 percent. But I told TNT that I'd save him money by doing both, told him I'd train *and* manage him for just 33 percent, letting him keep the extra 10 percent. It's worth it to me.

Why bring another person in here, be it a manager or trainer, to tamper with TNT? My way, I have complete say-so over who we fight, for how much, and *how* we fight. Total control of the camp. That's worth 10 percent to me.

Plus, the money's starting to get good. For TNT's fight against Hughes, his $1,500 purse netted me $500. His fight against Jones for $10,000 got me $3,333. And this one will get me $33,000. TNT's already paid me back half of the five grand I loaned him. The other half will come from the Rocket purse. So he's in the clear on that. It's the first time in my life I've loaned another fighter money and gotten it back.

We beat Rocket, a title fight is sure to land us millions. Millions! Good-bye, hacking it out. Hello, easy street.

Mornings is when I study TNT—really study him. Look him over, analyze his movements, his quirks, habits, try to find something fresh to work with. Mornings also happens to be when he, Unc, and I have breakfast at the Capital. Two eggs over easy for TNT, plus bacon, hash browns, whole wheat toast, OJ, and black coffee, no sugar.

TNT's a creature of habit when he eats. Hash browns first. He squeezes a bit of ketchup on the side, stabs his fork in it, then goes into the potatoes. Sip of coffee in between. Then comes the eggs, placed on the toast and eaten as a kind of sandwich. The entire glass of OJ, plus another sip of coffee, follows. Last comes the bacon. TNT chews every bite carefully, then licks his fingers and finishes the rest of the coffee.

"Like to eat the bacon last because it gives me something to look forward to at the end of the meal, having three whole strips of meat at the end," he told me once.

The way I figure, any trainer that's worth his salt needs to know what's on the *inside* of his fighter. Understanding the fighter's mind, the good and bad parts of it, *that's* what makes a trainer complete, not just boxing strategy.

I notice a lot of times, TNT doesn't look me in the eyes when we're talking. Unc and I will be sitting at the Capital, talking about some damn thing we read in the paper, and one of us will say to

TNT, "Hey, what you think about that?" He'll usually just shrug his shoulders, smile a little, and if he does say anything at all, he'll keep his eyes, for the most part, on the table. I asked him about it one day.

"'Cause I'm *shy*," he said. "That's how I am by nature."

Shy? TNT, a man who goes naked on national television? I wanted to laugh, or at least press him on the issue. But I decided not to. Though I'd like to know more about TNT's past, maybe it's best I don't. What's got him here has got him here. The smartest thing I can do now is move forward. So I keep analyzing my fighter, looking deep into him, for what to best work with.

It reminds me, though, of Sonny, who was quiet—real quiet—but around the right people, loosened up. He did Redd Foxx impersonations in front of friends, his falsetto apparently the best part. Despite his tough-guy image, those close to him said that Sonny was basically just a man who wanted to be liked.

"Many times I was around with Sonny Liston, he'd say, 'You like me, don't you?'" said one of his sparring partners. "Like a little kid would. I'd say, 'Sure I like you.' He'd say, 'You know, I like you, too.' I think because of his terrible background growing up, he was looking for someone who wouldn't criticize him or wanted to hit him without a club or a stick."

The writer James Baldwin, on assignment for a magazine, visited Sonny's camp before his first title fight against Patterson. Even though Baldwin ended up really liking—and betting on—Patterson, he felt like he understood Sonny.

"He reminded me of big, black men I have known who acquired the reputation of being tough in order to conceal the fact that they weren't hard," Baldwin said. ". . . For Liston knows, as only the inarticulately suffering can, just how inarticulate he is. But let me clarify that: I say suffering because it seems to me that he has suffered a great deal. It is in his face, in the silence of that face, and in the curiously distant light of his eyes—a light which rarely signals because there have been so few answering signals. And when I say inarticulate, I really do not mean to suggest that he does not know how to talk. He is inarticulate in the way we all are when more has happened to us than we know how to express; and inarticulate in a particularly Negro way—he has a long tale to tell which no one wants to hear."

Johnny Tocco, one of Liston's old trainers, said that Sonny was basically just a loner.

"He always came to the gym by himself," Tocco said. "He always left by himself. The police knew he'd been in prison, and he'd be walking along and they'd always stop him and search him. So he went through alleys all the time. He always went around things. I can still see him, either coming out of an alley or walking into one."

Hand pads. Working the hand pads. Smacking the pads, sweating it out, getting in shape. Good punching shape. Getting ready for Rocket. Gonna kill Rocket. Gonna be all over him, throw punches from every angle, every angle humanly possible, overwhelm him, make him hurt, make him grunt, make him cry out, make him want to quit.

Rocket's gonna be sitting on his stool after one of the rounds, telling his trainer he can't take no more, because the freewheeling badass on the other stool is making his life living hell. He can take some heat, but not the kind of heat you're throwing at him. Regular heat he can take, but not top-notch, furnace-level heat that *you're* gonna be giving him.

Working those pads. Punching. Yeah. Keep punching. Keep

working. Don't stop that there punching, TNT. Fatigue makes cowards of us all. A famous football coach said that once. But it's true. Suck it up when you get tired, baby, make yourself do it, because if you don't, nobody else will.

Feel the burn. Feel your arms boiling with pain. Your body's crying out. Telling you to stop. Telling you it needs rest. Fuck your body. Yeah, man. Fuck it. Don't worry about your body. Don't listen to it. Overcome it. Keep hitting those pads, TNT. Force yourself. Force yourself and keep your arms moving, because when your arms are moving, you're scoring points, and when you're scoring points, you're winning rounds. Feel the burn, man. Yeah. Feel the burn and make yourself keep punching and fuck what your body's saying because you want this bad enough, don't you?

Feel the burn, hear the sound of your glove smack into the pad, hear it echo throughout the gym, tell your body to shut the fuck up because your body isn't shit compared to what you really want and that's a win over Rocket and a title shot with Taylor.

I want TNT to focus on a grueling body attack. I had some luck hitting Rocket with body shots and figure that TNT can do the same. Maybe focus on the body early in the fight, wear Rocket down, move up to the head in the later rounds.

I'm having TNT work on throwing lots of straight rights and left hooks to the body, bending his knees as he gets inside to really get leverage on the shots. He's plastering away on the mitts at a good pace. We go six hard rounds, and satisfied with the day's work, I tell TNT to go take a shower.

"Good job," I tell him. "Remember our saying."

"Kill the body and the head will die." He smiles, looking at the floor. "We gonna jump rope?"

TNT, a true creature of habit. Just like his eating the bacon last,

I always have TNT jump rope last, because he's good at it. Which means he likes it. I found that out one of the first days we started training together. He'd always be saying, "Scrap, how 'bout we start with the rope?" Came to find out, he's fast as blazes on that rope. By making it the last exercise we do each night, TNT tells me it motivates him through each gym session, to know he's got jumping to look forward to last.

And the *we*. I really like the *we* TNT always uses, like the two of us are a team. Truth is, we *are* a team, have the same mission, it seems. Revenge and respect, together.

While he gets out of the ring and begins jumping, the leather rope going whirl-a-whirl on the hard gym floor, I towel the back of my neck and lean against the ring ropes, feeling the tightness of the ropes hard against my back, just like the many times I was in the ring myself. I close my eyes and visualize myself back in there, in front of a large crowd, hearing the noise but not really, more a background sound than anything.

My hands rise instinctively to their proper position: right hand on chin, left up high, chin tucked in, legs bent slightly. I spin quickly off the ropes in a pivot, the soles of my shoes squeaking against the canvas. I throw a five-punch combination at the imaginary opponent on the ropes. I always spin off smooth, with never a hitch in my step, and the punches are always the way they should be—always short, always compact, always accurate. I end with an imaginary referee stepping in and stopping the fight. I grab the towel, place it around my neck, and leave the ring victorious to the thunder of cheers—the crowd chanting my name, loving the fact that they've seen me fight.

As I'm climbing down, I notice TNT's about done with his rope skipping. People in the gym have thinned out. It's just me, TNT, and a couple other fighters finishing up some stomach crunches.

TNT goes through a final series of double jumps, where the rope whirls twice while his feet are in the air, making whipping and slicing sounds. He shows great speed and balance and does ten such jumps in a row. Satisfied with the explosive bursts, I tell him to stop.

"You sure?" he says, face dotted with beads of sweat from the effort. "I can jump some more."

It's one of the many things that makes training TNT so easy. He doesn't ever seem to get tired or complain when we're in the ring. It's like this place is a home to him—a place he naturally belongs.

"I'm sure. You done good for the day. Go grab yourself a shower."

TNT looks over to the gym entrance. "Uh, Scrap, you might want to shower, too."

"Why's that?"

"Well, because I told June and September and Katrina to meet us. We all going out tonight."

"Who's *we,* TNT?"

TNT wipes his brow with his shirtsleeve and grins. "You, me, and Unc."

"Thanks for tellin' me sooner."

"Aw, come on, Scrap. It'll be fun, man. June and September are twins. They good-lookin' twins, too. We gonna have a real nice time."

"I suppose their mom is named April or August or something like that, right?"

"Naw. I don't think so, at least." He looks puzzled.

"So who's this Katrina?"

"A friend of they mom's."

"You tell Unc about this?"

"I told him to meet me at the gym at eight. Didn't tell him we had dates, though. I was afraid he might not come."

It's five till eight now.

"How the hell you set all this up, TNT?"

His T-shirt is soaked so he takes it off, revealing his mighty upper body. TNT's pecs hang like boulders over his chest, biceps flaring with thick, fresh veins. "I was leavin' the gym the other day. You was still here because you and Unc was taking care of some business." Ewe an' Unc was takin' ca-ya a sum bidness.

"So I'm about to get on the bus when I see this real pretty woman standin' outside the Capital and she's crying. She's got her head in her little hands and she's crying real hard so I go up to her and I says, 'Hey, there. What's the matter?'

"She tells me that she went to pay for her meal and she couldn't find her purse. Said she'd lost it and couldn't pay for her meal or for a bus ride home. So I told her, 'Don't cry, pretty lady. I'll help you out.' So I went inside the Capital and paid her bill, and then I said a girl as pretty as you shouldn't be riding no public bus anyway. That's for damn sure. Then I apologized for saying *damn,* because you're not supposed to use profanity in front of classy women, are you, Scrap?"

"No, you're not."

"So I told her that my name is Rodney Timmons, and if you don't mind, I would like to put you in a cab and pay for it so you get home nice and safe. I didn't have a hankie or nothin' so I couldn't give her one but I would've if I did. But I didn't. I'm gonna carry hankies around from now on, though. I can see now how they'd come in handy."

"So that's how you met her then. By putting her in a cab?"

"Yeah. And yesterday, on my way out the gym, I go by the Capital again and she's in there. She waves at me and I go in and she gives me this big hug and says thank you and won't you join me for a cup of coffee, and I said sure but I just take mine black with no cream and no sugar because that's the way we always take it, ain't it, Scrap?"

"It sure is."

"And she says okay, let me pay for it, though. And I says are you sure and she says yes. And I wasn't sure about that because I always thought the man should pay for the meal, and even though coffee ain't no meal, it's still somethin'."

This is the most I've ever heard TNT talk. Till now, I've never heard the boy put together more than a sentence or two. And here he is, babbling on all because of some woman. I guess I can't let him down now.

We meet the women at Melito's Deli, a great place right near the gym. Though it's technically called a deli, Melito's also has great pasta—they make their own tomato sauce and throw in large chunks of hot salami, even. Since I'm training a fighter now—not doing the actual fighting myself—I can eat whatever I want.

September and June are beautiful young women in their early twenties. Both are black, have long, thick hair, the color of chestnuts, and smooth, clear faces that remind me of china dolls. Both are wearing sweaters and jeans tight enough to show off their wonderful bodies.

Their friend Katrina is no slouch, either. She's in her mid-forties and has nice dark skin, a fit figure, and big brown eyes. I can tell right away Unc is attracted because he starts talking in this upbeat voice, like everything is great—he's great, I'm great, the world is a great place, and let's all have us a real good time.

"They all pretty, ain't they, Scrap?" TNT whispers to me as old man Melito himself leads us to a table in the back of the small restaurant.

"Sure are."

Despite his earlier gabbiness, TNT is quiet during the meal, preferring to occasionally shovel in a scoop of rigatoni and stare across the table at September instead. She's quiet, too, I notice, and in between sips of Melito's homemade wine gives occasionally shy glances toward TNT, her cab-fare savior.

It's up to me and Unc to do the talking. Unc's particularly jazzed and it's good to see him enjoying himself in the company of a nice woman. I'm glad that he's come out and joined us. June and I haven't said all that much since we've been seated, but she gets things going by talking about my job.

"When September told me that you were a fight trainer, I didn't really want to come along," she says. "She doesn't have a problem with boxing, but I find it extremely hard to justify grown men getting paid obscene amounts of money to beat each other senseless."

"So why *did* you come along?" I say. Hell, in my experience, some women don't mind the fight game. Some do. Nothing can really be done about it either way.

"As a favor to her. She said Rodney was nice to her the other day so I thought I'd come out."

"What do you do, June?" I say, trying to change the subject.

"I'm a law student. Third year."

I laugh at this. "And *you're* telling *me* you have a hard time justifying getting paid for what I do—when you're in a profession that has an even worse reputation than boxing?"

"Easy now," she says, fingering her drink.

"Hey, if you can come down hard on my job, why can't I do the same on yours? Can you dish it out but not take it?"

"Say what you want about the legal profession, Amos. Call it crooked if you'd like. It's a fair assessment. But I'll tell you this— our goal isn't to intentionally hurt other people."

"You sure could fool me."

Her forehead tightens up and she glares at me. "What I mean—and I think you know what I mean but I'll say it anyway—is that our goal isn't to intentionally physically hurt another human being, like you do in boxing. How do you justify that?" She's talking in this low voice, probably so her sister and mother's friend don't hear her arguing with me.

"Justify what?" I say.

"Boxing. Deliberately giving another man a beating for money."

"Listen, this isn't the time or place to play Ms. Morals. I came along as a favor to TNT. I don't need to sit here and defend what I do for a living."

"I'm not asking you to defend anything. I was simply making a point."

But now she's got me riled and thinking. And when that happens, I usually take to mumbling to myself. "It's the art of self-defense, anyway. If you knew the first damn thing about the sport, you'd sure as hell know *that*."

"What did you say?" she asks.

I shake my head and start to mumble some more. But I remember where I am and stop myself. "Nothin'," I say to her. "I didn't say a thing."

June gives me a long look, stone-faced. Then she cracks the tiniest of smiles. "I guess we're both in relatively sketchy professions, aren't we?"

"The sketchiest, I imagine." I take a good look at her, figure June for the no-nonsense type who scares men off with her aggressive personality and confidence. Give me a couple months and I could make her one tough fighter. "But let me ask you something—how do you feel about what you do, or what you are going to do, once you finish law school?"

Her eyes widen. "I love it," she says, her voice going lower. "I love, absolutely love the law. I can't believe when I'm done with school that I'm actually going to get paid to do it. I really can't. It's hard to put into words but it's something that I think I was meant to do."

"That's exactly how I feel about the fight game, June."

And as far as talk about our careers go, that is that.

The evening ends with all three of us outside Melito's, exchanging small talk.

TNT leans into September and gives her a quick kiss on the cheek. Unc and Katrina makes plans to see a movie they've both been talking about wanting to catch. And me—I just stand next to June, not knowing *what* to say. There's this awkward silence between us and it's finally broken when Unc grabs me by the elbow.

"You ready, lover boy?" he says.

"Yep."

I give June a wave and she nods as Unc, TNT, and I walk toward the car.

"So how'd it go, gents?" Unc says. I've never heard him say the word *gents* before. As he drives us back home, he can't keep from smiling.

TNT's quiet face is plastered with a big smile, too. Eyes closed, he takes deep breaths occasionally, telling me all I need to hear.

"How about you, Amos?" Unc says. "You and June hit it off or what?"

"Real big, Unc. She hated the fact that I'm in boxing."

He slaps me playfully on my knees and laughs real loud. "Well, I thought you two had good chemistry. She's probably just trying to play hard to get. I could tell just by looking down the table that ya'll had some good chemistry going."

"Really?"

"Sure." Unc thumps his chest with his index finger. "I got an eye for this type of thing, son."

"Sexual Healing" by Marvin Gaye comes on the radio and Unc begins belting out the song in his deep baritone. So he's got an eye for these types of things, does he? The way I see it, Unc needs to go and get himself some glasses.

Unc and TNT get along fine. TNT, despite Unc's saying not to, has given Unc some of his purse money—a couple thousand bucks—for room and board. TNT told him to please take it. Even though Unc protested, I knew he could use the money for the gym. It's where Unc puts most of his money these days, upgrading equipment and making building repairs.

TNT listens to Unc, too. When I told TNT he should take some of his purse money and put it in a mutual fund, he turned right to Unc and asked what he thought of the idea.

"My nephew's no financial genius, son, I'll tell you that," Unc said. "But he's always done okay for himself, because he's always been disciplined with his money. So if I were you, I'd take small chunks here and there and invest. Because you never know when you might need that money."

TNT listened and we started him up an account.

It's funny, too, because I see TNT act differently outside the ring, especially toward Unc. Outside the ring, TNT is more subdued. Quiet. He always seems to be thinking, to be taking things in, seeing where those things might fit into his world. In this sense, he reminds me a lot of Sonny. There's this quiet wit to him that most people don't get to see.

But with Unc, TNT is always questions. Like the other night,

171

when the three of us were watching an old World War II movie. Something sparked in TNT's mind, I think, because he leaned over to Unc and asked, "Mr. Fletcher"—Unc has repeatedly asked TNT to call him Unc, but he won't yet—"you ever been to war?"

Unc nodded, half watching the movie, half dozing in his favorite chair, which he does on most nights.

"What was it like?"

At this, Unc opened up both eyes. He was quiet for a moment. Thoughtful. "I suppose I could say it's the kind of feeling you have when you walk down that aisle into a fight. You know the feeling. Butterflies dancing in your gut, heart beating faster than a race engine. Only thing is, you feel that way pretty much all the time." Unc had been in Vietnam for a bit. He's never said much to me about it before.

TNT said nothing, just rested his chin on his knuckles. After a good while, he shook his head. "That must've been awful."

"War's no good on any man. Anybody who speaks fond memories of war is just fooling himself."

"Did you hate it?"

"No, son. I didn't hate it. But I disliked it. There's a big difference between the two. Hate is channeling all your energy, all your being, into wanting one particular thing or person see destruction. In the end, if destruction comes, you still haven't really gained all that much, except for a hardened heart. Never get so hung up on hate that it hardens you."

Later that evening, when Unc was dozing in the chair and I was nodding off a bit myself, ready to call it a night, TNT shook me lightly on the shoulder. I woke up, startled.

"Yeah, what is it?"

"Your uncle," TNT said. "He's really a smart man."

I rubbed my eyes and ran my hand over my mouth, stifling a yawn. "He's seen a lot of things."

TNT's dreads danced in the shimmer of moonlight that came through the windows. All lights were off, save the television set, which is how we always watch it at Unc's.

"What he's sayin' about hate, that is, that it can be a cancer . . ." TNT stopped, let his chin rest on his knuckles again, a position I began to notice he took whenever he was thinking hard about a particular thing. "Scrap, do you think that maybe how we going after Taylor, you know, after all he done to you, do you think maybe *that's* a cancer?"

I pinched my eyes, surprised at the comment. I didn't know what to say. It was late, I was tired, Unc was dozing, and I'm getting asked questions about *hate*. I told TNT no, that hate wasn't necessarily involved in our going after Taylor, because if Diggs held on to the title, we'd be fighting *him* and not Taylor. I told TNT that I wasn't particularly *happy* with Taylor, certainly not fond of the man, but that, in the end, no, there was no hate involved, so there wasn't a cancer to speak of.

This seemed to satisfy TNT, who then gave Unc a gentle nudge and said, "C'mon, Mr. Fletcher, time to retire for the evening." Unc smacked his lips two or three times, like he always does, stretched his arms over his head, let out a groan, and went on to his room. TNT pulled out the cot we bought and put it in the kitchen, where he sleeps, and I went and made up the couch for myself.

The house was quiet. Only problem was, when I lay down on the couch, I made the mistake of looking into the window, and there I saw my reflection. What I saw in that reflection was something unmistakable. It was the face of a liar.

* * *

Despite my obsession with Taylor, I know that I've got to get TNT ready for the fight with Rocket first.

Training's been a breeze so far. TNT's now in top shape, at fighting weight, lean, body hard as a diamond, sparring ten rugged rounds with several different sparring partners, working and digging to the body with zeal. Physically, he's right where I want him. Mentally, he's almost there. Each day before we start training, I have him do mental exercises, envisioning himself walking into the ring on a hot Vegas night, seeing Rocket in there, staring him down, the bell ringing, and the two of them colliding. All of this is important because it'll help desensitize TNT to the actual event. Once a man has played a certain situation over and over in his mind like a tape, constantly playing and rewinding, he's ready for that event when it occurs.

But there's something special I want to share with TNT.

It's a Monday evening, four days before the fight. We had a short workout today, our last, and we're leaving for Vegas tomorrow.

TNT and I are in front of the television. Unc's still at the gym and I figured I'll show this to TNT with just him and me here, between the two of us. I didn't tell him what's on the tape. After the tape is finished, I said, I'd explain.

The tape begins to play. It's Liston–Cleveland Williams, their first fight. Williams was a heavyweight contender in the early to mid sixties. Cleve, they called him. A bone-breaking puncher. But against Liston, Cleve was the one getting broke. Liston knocked him out in the third. TNT watches Sonny pulverize Williams, watches Liston's jackhammer jab jolt into Williams's head, watches Liston's left hook crackle and spit on Williams's body. During the massacre, TNT is silent.

Next up are the two Liston-Patterson fights. Both end in one round and neither are competitive. Sonny drives Patterson around the ring with heavy, thudding shots, and in both bouts, Floyd drops to the canvas like a sack of wheat.

I watch TNT for a reaction. He just stares at the tape, though, seemingly engrossed in the footage, knuckles under his chin.

"What do you know about Liston?" I ask him. "Besides being champion of the world and all."

TNT watches Sonny send Floyd staggering with a wicked body shot that looks like it could've permanently bruised Floyd's insides. I wouldn't have wanted Floyd's body after those beatings. "Well, besides being champ, what else *is* there to know?" he asks me back.

Next up on the tape is Liston-Martin, the fight at the end of Sonny's career where he gets knocked out. I have it on because I want to show TNT that no man is invincible. The way Sonny gets pummeled in the ninth from a Martin right hand proves that.

But I don't show the Ali fights. Because to me, that wasn't really Sonny. Not the Sonny I know, anyway.

The first round of the Martin fight is beginning. There's Sonny, on the screen, sticking his jab out, looking as menacing as ever. "My man," I say. "There's a lot more to know about Sonny Liston. A whole helluva lot."

I tell TNT. I tell him what else there is to know about Charles "Sonny" Liston. Tell him about Sonny's hard upbringing, him not knowing his own birth date. Tell him about Liston's climb to the top of the division and his long wait for a title shot. Tell him about how Sonny was harassed by police in different cities, about Sonny finally getting his shot at the title and winning it, tell him about the cold reception in Philadelphia, his losing the belt to Ali, Geraldine, the reporters, about him in Vegas, where it all ended for him, and about Paradise Memorial, under the airplanes, and a headstone that says "A MAN."

When I'm done, I have this feeling of relief, like a weight's been lifted, because finally there's somebody I can tell about my thoughts on Sonny without having them think I'm crazy.

"I'm not saying Sonny is a saint, now," I say to TNT. "The man obviously had some crooked dealings in his life. But I guess what I wanted to do is just share this with you, because to me Sonny is a motivation in lots of ways. He showed me that no matter how hard or how bad things can get in life, good things can happen if you let them." I shiver, realizing that I've quoted Sonny verbatim.

It's now round six in the Martin fight. Sonny's not getting the better of it. He's older, slower, and not doing the things in the ring that he did, say, five years before.

"He doesn't win this one, does he?" TNT finally says.

Liston gets hit with a right and Martin moves out of the way before Sonny can retaliate.

"No, he doesn't. He gets knocked out in this one."

Sonny jabs, but the punch is blocked.

"Why the headstone, Scrap? Why 'A MAN'?"

Sonny gets hit with a jab now, square in the nose. He's too tired to bend his knees so he's getting nailed with punches that have no business hitting him.

"Because that's what he was."

The bell rings to end round six.

The tape doesn't show commercials. Instead, we both sit and watch the corner men go to work on both fighters. Sonny's taking air in large gulps in his corner, trying to regroup. "Scrap?"

"Yeah?" Martin's getting his head soaked with a wet sponge, the water trickling off him like a tiny stream.

"Thanks for telling me all this, man."

"Don't mention it."

Both men rise off their stools for round seven.

"This isn't Sonny at his best," I say. "I just happen to have this fight on here with his others. Kind of a reminder that any man can lose on any given night."

"Yeah, I hear that."

Sonny's visibly tired, trying hard to keep his hands up. Martin looks much fresher.

TNT coughs, then says something in a low voice. I can't hear what he's saying so I ask him to speak up.

"Nothin'."

Sonny's throwing the jab but it's slow. Martin slides his head to the side and the punch goes right on by.

"Come on, man. What'd you say?"

Martin's jabbing and landing. The two men clinch. Sonny looks bone tired, like he'd rather be on a Vegas craps table, rolling some dice and seeing his money multiply instead of getting pasted with jabs from his old sparring partner.

"Just wonderin'," TNT says, still staring at the screen, "if when we get to Vegas, if we could maybe pay a visit to Sonny's grave. You know, pay our respects and all to the man."

Martin's jab is landing more frequently now, pretty much every time he throws it, and it's obvious that Sonny's run out of steam. It's clear he's not anywhere near the fighter who once destroyed Williams, nowhere near the fighting machine that twice took apart Patterson.

But that doesn't seem to matter now. Because not every man has a time to shine. If a man *does* get the opportunity to shine, though, it's cause for rejoicing, however brief that time is.

I lean over and put my hand on TNT's shoulder. "I tell you what. I think Sonny would be mighty pleased to hear that. Mighty pleased indeed." And I go on upstairs to retire for the evening, leaving TNT to watch the rest of the fight by himself, because him being alone with Sonny, even if it's only for a couple of rounds, is important.

Round Eight

We get to Vegas two days before the fight. Me, Unc, and TNT are staying in the Riviera. Training expenses take care of it. It's desert hot, the sun beating down hard on the city like a sweaty threat. Despite the weather, the town is jammed with people wanting to see the fight.

They're calling Diggs-Taylor II "Repeat or Redemption?" It's on fight posters all over the city. My prediction is on the side of redemption, though I wouldn't mind a little redemption with the bastard myself. Get him one-on-one in a room and I'll show the man what redemption is all about, in the form of lefts and rights. Doesn't matter how fast he is or how hard he hits, either, because revenge is a damn powerful motivator, can make Supermen of us all.

The first night we're in town, we go to Caesars Palace, where they're having a press conference for the rematch. Since we're the main undercard bout and the winner of our fight gets a title shot, Davis wants us there, too. I'll get to see both Taylor and Diggs for the first time since I left Vegas.

The conference room is packed with media from all over the

country. Television outfits from everywhere, so many acronyms that it makes my head throb to try and remember them all.

Diggs and Taylor are center stage for the media session, while TNT and Rocket sit to their sides. I had TNT put on a basic white sweat suit for this. Nothing too flashy. Nobody's dressed up, so it doesn't make sense for TNT to have on a suit. Have him wear a suit and the next thing I know, reporters are saying Scrap Iron and TNT are *pretentious* now that they've achieved some success.

And sitting here, in Vegas, before the media, watching this take place, four of the best heavyweights in the world battling it out for the right to be called the "baddest man on the planet," I tell myself that, yes, despite it all, despite all the shit that's happened these past few months, I've got to admit that I've achieved some level of success. I'm managing a top-ranked heavyweight contender and I'm proud of that.

"David, what is your game plan concerning Taylor's cut from the last fight? Will this be a target for you again?" It's Sampson, from the *New York Times*. Sometimes I can't believe this guy. *Of course* the cut is gonna be a target for Diggs. Once a fighter gets cut, the scar tissue is always fair game for future opponents. Been that way for years. Now, if Sampson was a bit smoother, he might've said something like "Tell us about Taylor's tendency to cut." That would be *leading* Diggs instead of *telling* him, letting him explain to every-body that, yes, the cut *is* a target in this fight.

"Everything's gonna be a target," Diggs says. "His head, his body, his left arm, his right arm. He one big bull's-eye and I one big dart."

Diggs looks like he's in good shape, cheekbones flaring through his face, training having melted off all the fat. His jab's probably as quick as it's ever been, and I bet he's been running like a gazelle. I wonder, though, if he's been getting quality sparring.

"Terrence," says Rudy Battaglia, from the Newark *Star-Ledger.* "Your response to that challenge?" Taylor is wearing a maroon sweat suit, white lines running down each side, ball cap folded narrowly at the brim, dark sunglasses. He looks agitated even though I can't see his eyes—lips pursed together, mouth tight, face blank.

"Man, all I got to say is gonna be said in the ring with *these.*" He holds up two large fists. "Ya'll trying to hype something that ain't there, trying to act like this man has a chance when all ya'll know that nobody on this planet holds a chance against me. Last fight was a fluke. A complete fluke. Everyone knows. And now we talking about cuts and darts and all this bullshit. Let's just cut all the crap out and I'll do my talking in the ring."

"How do you feel about Amos 'Scrap Iron' Fletcher—the man who was once your sparring partner and the man accused of asking you for money in exchange for information on David Diggs in the last fight—being back in Vegas?" It's good old Nylon.

Silence fills the room. Taylor clears his throat, then waves his hand out to nobody in particular. "I think I said I didn't want to talk about no more *bullshit,*" he says forcefully.

Nylon stands his ground like he always does. "Well, bullshit or no bullshit, there has never been any substantiation to your claim that Fletcher offered you money. None at all. And Fletcher was suspended because of your claim, to the disappointment of quite a few folks in the boxing community. Your response to this, please?"

Taylor keeps shaking his head and he's got this I-can't-believe-you-have-this-much-audacity look on his face, his mouth curled up. I'd love to wipe that smug expression off with the back of my hand.

"Like I said, I ain't in the mood for bullshit. This is bullshit and if you want to talk about it, talk about it to somebody else." He stands up. "This interview session is over."

Taylor begins to walk down the podium, and as he does, I notice TNT moving his seat back. My heart races. I know I need to stop him before he does something that we'll all regret. But he's quick. TNT may be large, but he's cat quick and he pounces out of the seat and toward the podium stairs. He blocks Taylor's exit and calls him a name.

"Who you callin' punk ass?" Taylor demands, his arms crossed tight across his chest. Security, thank God, comes racing over and gets between the two men.

"I'm callin' *you* punk ass, Mr. Ex-Champ," TNT hollers, his chest heaving mightily. "You runnin' around lyin' about folks, good folks, and it just ain't right."

Taylor pushes away two guards who are standing in front of him and charges toward TNT, who's being restrained by three men. Seeing the disadvantage and not wanting my fighter to get hurt, I run over to him. *Good folks*. TNT, I realize, is talking about *me*.

I step in front of TNT so I'm between the two fighters. Taylor's got a vein bulging out his forehead and his teeth are bared. But I don't care. *Good folks*.

"You wanna throw a punch," I say, pushing my face close to Taylor's, "then be man enough to throw it at me. Least I can properly defend myself from a punch, not like these lies you've been spreadin' about me."

Before Taylor can do anything, more security piles in. The whole place is a mêlée, with all of us getting restrained. Davis watches with a mixture of horror and joy, the horror coming from such a scene, which will no doubt be shown on television networks tonight all over the world, giving the sport of boxing yet another bad name, one more it certainly don't need. The joy comes from the ratings that will no doubt increase from such a scene. That's boxing—a sport always in conflict with itself.

Since TNT's name has been getting bigger and bigger with all the media exposure, we've got a new set of problems to deal with: women.

They hang out in the lobby of the Riviera and swarm us whenever we come into the building—women of all kinds, black, white, Mexican, Asian. TNT gets asked to sign objects ranging from a full-size poster of him with his boxing gloves on to a pair of black lace panties that, one woman says, "I just took off a little while ago."

When we get up to our rooms, it doesn't get much better. A dozen women cram into the elevator with us, crowding around TNT and squeezing tight against me and Unc.

"Are you a fighter, too?" asks a young brunette in a black cocktail dress so tight the material might be mistaken for Saran Wrap.

"No. I'm the trainer," I tell her.

"Ohhh . . ." She lays a heavily tanned hand on my arm and leaves it there.

We get off the elevator and they follow us. A few doors before we reach our rooms, I come to a full stop and turn around to face them. Three women are clinging to TNT's elbows, and Unc's being propositioned by some blonde who could be his granddaughter.

"Listen," I say in as authoritative a voice as I can come up with, Nylon-like in its directness. "We got a fight coming up, a big fight, which means we need to focus. I would appreciate it greatly if you ladies would leave before we're forced to call hotel security."

The sighing that results sounds like a million pounds of air being let out of a tire.

"I'm not joking, ladies. I want y'all off this hallway now." And

I stand in front of them defiant—arms crossed, badass-mother look on my face, with my eyes narrowed.

A few of the bolder women mumble under their breath. But I stand my ground. A couple others force-feed quickly scribbled phone numbers to TNT before trudging back to the elevator.

Soon we're in the hallway, alone.

"That was pretty damned impressive, son," Unc says. "You did a fine job taking control of that situation."

"Thanks, Unc. Control of the camp. That's all it is."

TNT puts one of his large hands across my shoulder. "Good thing I got you here, Scrap, to keep Brenda and Tiffi in line," he says, staring at the paper and starting to laugh.

The door across from ours opens up and a tiny old man comes out in the hallway. He's wearing a pair of red-white-and-blue boxer shorts, a wife-beater T-shirt, and navy socks pulled up almost to his knees.

"I flew in all the way from Miami today to see this doubleheader," he says in a creaky voice. "And I just wanted to shake your hand, young man, for the job you've done."

TNT smiles and steps in front of me, his hand outstretched. "Thanks, sir—" he begins.

"Not you," the old man says, shaking his head. He's deeply tanned but that's no surprise. It's what old people in Miami probably do— get too much sun. "You," he says, and points directly at me.

"Me?" I say.

"Hell, yes. Amos 'Scrap Iron' Fletcher. Heavyweight boxer who just turned trainer. And a damned good trainer you've made so far, in my opinion. This guy"—he points to TNT—"couldn't jab for shit before you got ahold of him. And his bodywork! Jesus, his body-work—it's like he all of a sudden went to graduate school in how to work the body."

184

Unc's turning the key to the door and TNT's following him in. "I'll just be a minute," I tell them. "Me and . . ."

"Stanley."

". . . Stanley gonna talk here for a little bit." I look at Stanley, the tan man from Miami, and beam. *A damned good trainer*. How about that! I got to talk to Stanley at least a little bit about the fight game. It'd be rude not to. After all, who are we without the support of the fans?

I told TNT that we should talk to Sonny separately, but he doesn't want to do that. "Naw," he says, flowers in hand, some mix of reds and yellows we picked up at this florist's on the Vegas strip. "You got to be there *with me* when I'm talkin'."

"Why?"

"'Cause you done this before. Me, I'm new at it and I might mess it all up."

I don't really want to be in front of the grave while TNT is talking to Sonny. What he says to the man is between him and Sonny. I tell him as much but TNT will have none of it.

"Just stand near me, Scrap," he says, eyes pleading. "It'll make me feel better, knowin' you around."

And so I agree. No sense in saying no when we've already come out here to visit. There's clouds all in the sky at Paradise Memorial today, some looking like stuffed mushrooms, hovering over the sun, dropping the temperature down a bit. I smell freshly cut grass, and some rogue blades sit at the base of the headstone. TNT is on his knees, something I've never done, and he places the flowers he brought in the vase. It shakes when he moves it.

I take a couple steps back, for proper respect and distance. TNT is talking in this low voice, in something that sounds like a man talking to a child, but I can't quite make it out. I hear assorted words, only in bits. "Sonny . . . fight . . . Scrap."

He looks back at me a couple times, but I look away, not wanting TNT to know I'm watching. I let him finish, and when he does, he walks past me, tortoiselike, and pinches the tip of his nose with his fingers. His eyes are moist. TNT walks about twenty yards away and stares into the cloudy sky, thinking, I believe, fighter's thoughts. Thoughts of punches, both giving and taking, constant soreness, the slow oxygen burn of the lungs in a tough fight, the weighted stumps that your legs become with each passing round.

Maybe he's thinking there's a connection now between him and Sonny, the way I did the first time I came out here. I realized I might never be champion of the world that day, might never become immortalized in fight history, but at least Sonny and I had this in common, something nobody could ever take away from either of us: We were both fighters. Nothing, nothing at all, could ever change that.

My turn. I take a step toward the grave, a familiar friend by now, get down to a knee. The ground is Vegas hard, parched from the sun and baked like clay under the green grass. With no flowers to occupy my hands, I fiddle with them and decide to place them behind my head. It feels different, but at the same time, reassuring. "Got a big one tonight, Sonny. We win, we get a shot at the title. Can you believe that?"

I envision Liston, up in the sky, looking down, saying, *Yeah, kid, I sure do believe it. Ain't life crazy?*

"Just got to get past this one is all we have to do. Then we home free."

My eyes closed, I picture Liston saying, *Hey, man, I agree you got to take care of this one first, but there ain't no such thing in the world as* home free. *Home free don't exist, my friend. You best remember that.*

I chuckle and then mutter, so only Sonny and I can hear, "Ain't that the damn truth."

When I'm done saying what I need to say to Sonny, I get in the car. TNT's already in the passenger side and I give the engine a good rev.

"Nobody's ever cared about me the way you have, Scrap," TNT says.

I look over at him. He's got his hands out in front of him, studying them the way a math teacher would look at a calculator.

"What you talkin' about, TNT?"

"You feel about me the same way you do about Sonny, don't you?"

All I can hear is the purr of the engine and the silence of the graveyard.

"What makes you say that?" I ask him.

"Because you *know* about me, man. You know about me without having even to ask." TNT keeps his hands out in front of him, knuckle-side up. The knuckles are red from punching. They'll stay that way forever. The raw redness that never leaves a fighter's hands. "You know I ain't gotten many breaks in my life. You know that my family don't want nothin' to do with me. You know that I'm a screwup, man, but you still treat me decently. Just like a normal man."

"You *are* a man, TNT."

Fight night. TNT and I are in the dressing room, this enclosed little room with a table TNT can sit on while I roll gauze on his huge hands, one line of tape stretching tight, him making a fat fist, squeezing, me putting another roll over on him. Mindless work, but the kind that lets us both think instead of talk, lets us visualize in our heads what's to come once we get in the ring.

"Feel good?" I ask him once the wrapping's finished. TNT has made two fists, his knuckles bulging.

"Yeah, feels real good. Feels tight." TNT punches his right hand into the palm of his left, creating a thick, slapping sound that fills the room.

I get a couple things ready and put them in a bag: styptic pencil, to close cuts; Enswell, a small metal device that compresses cold onto the face, reducing swelling; Vaseline; mouthpiece; bucket of water; Q-tips. "You remember the plan?" I ask him.

"Yeah. Body. All body. Dig hard, under the ribs, hit him on the hips, too. Bruise them hips so he can't move later in the fight."

The bag's filled up with what I need. We're ready to go. I smile at my fighter. "Yeah. That's good, my man. Just make it happen, okay?"

"Sure thing."

I study my fighter's face as he gets off the table, his upper body stretching the fabric of his new dazzling white robe. Trails of sweat pool down TNT's sideburns, ending at his chin and dripping onto the floor, from a rugged fifteen-minute warm-up just minutes ago. His eyes are vacant. Willful. I like what I see. We leave the room and head for the ring.

It's round four and I don't know what the hell TNT is doing. He came out for the first like a man on speed, throwing leather like quicksilver, jabbing, ripping shots to Rocket's body, almost lifting the boy off the canvas with some of his blows. Rocket's eyes were wide as meteor craters, wondering what he'd gotten himself into, fighting this freewheeling dynamo.

For some reason, early in the second, TNT slows down. It's not that he's tired, either, because I *know* the boy's in shape. I trained him, after all. Still, he slows down. He stops punching as much, lays listlessly on the ropes, letting Rocket string together a series of combinations.

Jab, right, hook to head. Hook to body.

TNT on the ropes, covering up.

Rocket teeing off. Me yelling. Us losing rounds.

TNT in the corner after each round, saying it's all right, Scrap, I'll catch up. I'm just waiting for the sucker to make a mistake. But he keeps waiting and we keep losing rounds. Come round five, we've lost three of the first four rounds and can't afford to lose another one if this fight goes the distance. I know we can't wait any longer.

"Man, shit," TNT says, slumping on the stool, spitting his mouthpiece, blood and spit caked on it, into the water bucket. "He got himself a lot of energy. But I gonna wear him out." TNT's panting as he speaks, sucking in large lungfuls of oxygen, his chest going up and down like a mountain range, and I'm thinking, *This here's the man who's worn out.*

"He throwing a lot of punches, but he's gonna get tired," TNT says. Which may or may not be the case. If TNT's right, then great. We catch Rocket tired late in the fight and nail him. But if he's wrong? We play a waiting game where our waiting is never justified. Rocket wins on points and our title shot is gone. Urgency is what we need and we need it in our corner *now*.

My hand raises as I think back to a story a trainer of mine once told me about. It was a welterweight title fight between Emile Griffith and Benny "Kid" Paret. Gil Clancy was training Griffith. It was just before the thirteenth round and Griffith had been listless the past few rounds. Clancy knew something drastic had to be done.

He slapped Griffith—slapped him hard—across the face. Told Griffith to wake the hell up, to get out there and finish his business before it took care of him.

Griffith responded to the slap. Knocked Paret out in the very next round.

Time rolls quick in the corner, moves faster than an Ali jab. A man's got to make each second count because there's only sixty of them to work with. My hand comes up toward my waist and I open my palm as I'm thinking, *Do I need to slap TNT?* I've never slapped nobody before, but this is for his own good here. The man needs to be woken up because he's blowing a title shot.

TNT's panting and my arm is rising. He's looking off somewhere, beyond the ring, maybe, could be into another world. It's what happens in those fast sixty seconds between rounds. The mind floats, goes in a million different directions, seeing a million different images, not settling on even one.

My hand comes up to TNT's face, palm still open. I touch his chin with my index finger. He has sweat and stubble there, feeling like wet sandpaper.

"Listen to me, now," I say, keeping hold of his chin. His eyes meet mine and he looks at me with trust, with confidence, a clear-eyed look that is both tired and hopeful at the same time, and I know I can't do it. But I can do something else. "What do you think Sonny's thinking right now? You think he's proud of the fact that you waiting around, hoping to catch the man later on. *Later on!* Like you got time to waste! Like Sonny ever had time to waste! You know how old Sonny was when he died?"

TNT's attention has turned to me now. "How old?" he asks, taking in a deep breath. Sweat trickles down each temple, soaking my finger.

"Thirty-eight years old. You think he lived like he had time to waste?" Silence. "Do you?"

TNT stammers and looks to the ground.

I tilt his chin, move my face closer to his, go eyeball-to-eyeball so there's nothing to distract us. "You damn right he didn't have time to waste. Nobody does. Now get yourself out there and handle this man like I know you can."

TNT gets off the stool. I take his mouthpiece, soaked clean with fresh water, and place it in his mouth. He bites down and I rub his shoulders. Precious seconds tick by. "He's watching you. He's watching me, too. The *both* of us."

My fighter hits his gloves together hard. "Yeah," he says. The bell rings and he's on his toes for the first time since the beginning of the fight.

TNT gets going. Starts stepping in with the jab, ripping shots to the body, digging his punches with leverage, grunting as he throws. A jab here, a body shot, another jab. TNT mixes it well and Rocket is confused by the sudden aggression.

We win the fifth and sixth just by being busier. Going into the seventh, I figure the fight is even. Rocket hasn't slowed down, necessarily, but TNT's burst of energy has taken some steam out of him. "Stay busy," I say before the seventh begins. I'm smearing Vaseline under TNT's right eye, just a glob of the stuff so he doesn't get a welt there. "Keep those little punches coming. Rat-a-tat-tat. You got it?"

TNT gives me a look that tells me, yes, he knows what to do.

"Sonny always fought well in the seventh," I tell him. "It was usually a real good round for him."

The seventh round begins with Rocket jabbing, keeping his distance from TNT, who has shown over the past few rounds to be a superior inside fighter. Rocket sticks his jab out hard, but TNT's hands are up and he picks them off with his gloves. I see a pattern develop: Rocket jabs twice, both punches landing on TNT's left glove, then Rocket dances away. He does it time and time again. Why didn't I notice this earlier? Two jabs and he moves away. So simple.

No matter. I'll just tell TNT when he gets back to the corner. Rocket's moving laterally, left to right, on his toes, staying out of TNT's punching range. TNT follows. Rocket plants his feet and jabs once. Blocked. Jabs a second time. Blocked. Just as Rocket begins to move out of the way, TNT unloads a right of his own over the top of Rocket's jab, blasting him on the jaw. TNT times it perfect. Rocket never sees the punch coming. It twists the left side of Rocket's chin, twisting his face at an inhuman angle. Rocket's knees sag and he falls into TNT, who takes a step back, slightly confused. Rocket drifts to the canvas.

I can tell right now Rocket ain't getting up. No chance of that. He just got coldcocked by a beautifully timed punch. The referee doesn't even bother with a count. TNT leaps into the air, waving his fists over his head.

Looks like we just landed ourselves a title shot.

"I did it, Scrap. I nutcracked him."

"You did *what*?"

"Nutcracked him." TNT holds up his right, now bare of glove and wraps. We're in the locker room. He's going to shower quick so we can watch Diggs and Taylor go at it. "This here the cracker. His head, that was the nut." TNT's got a smile as big as Nevada drawn on his face.

"Yeah, well, don't use that nutcracker nonsense with the media, okay?"

TNT gets this semipouty look on his face.

"But you did a fine job tonight." He recovers a little. Smiles. "Sonny, he would've been proud of you."

"You think so?"

"Hell, yes. You went out there and took charge. Earned your title shot, just the way Sonny would've done it."

TNT holds his right up to his face, inspecting it. He's got a huge hand, almost as big as Taylor's. "You hear that," he says to his hand. "We took care of business. Now what you think of that?"

I hear a door open, then footsteps. TNT starts to walk to the shower, a white cotton towel covering the lower half of his body. His upper torso is a mixture of sweat and veins, big wet beads of perspiration forming in the areas where I'd spread the Vaseline most liberally.

I hear the footsteps now just around the corner, moving faster. A head pops over. It's Nylon, almost out of breath.

"Jack, what's going on?"

"Hey, Scrap," he pants. "I was hoping I'd catch you before you went into the arena."

"Come on, now. I already gave you two of the best interviews of the year—at me and my fighter's expense. TNT's not gonna talk to the media till *after* the Diggs-Taylor fight." I hate to be blunt with Nylon, but I can't afford another embarrassing incident on television. Not with a title shot coming up.

"That's why I'm here. I was hoping I'd catch you because I just got clearance from the higher-ups."

"Clearance for what?"

Nylon fingers his chin. "For *you,* Scrap. Helping me call the fight tonight. What do you say? You and me, calling Diggs-Taylor II? You know that CNN doesn't show live fights, but I've been asked to do the call for pay-per-view, live, and I could use some help. We'll get the trainer of the hottest heavyweight contender around—that's you, of course—and see what he's got to say about the two men in tonight's title fight. We'll pay you the going rate, of course."

Shit. I didn't expect *this*. "I'm not prepared, Jack. Don't have any notes on either fighter . . ."

Nylon points to his temple. "Scrap, you don't need notes, man. What you got stored up in there on both these guys, *those* are your notes." He gives me this big smile and stands in front of me, waiting for an answer.

Nylon and I are ringside, me in a tux that's a little too tight, but what the hell. Diggs and Taylor have both entered the ring and the introductions are about to be given.

Diggs takes his robe off. "Diggs looks good," I say. "He weighed in at two hundred and fifteen pounds yesterday at the weigh-in, two pounds lighter than the first fight. That tells me that he's still going to be quick, if not a little quicker than the first fight. Speed is Diggs's game, and it looks to me like he's trying to give himself every possible edge in that department by coming in a little bit lighter."

Nylon gives me the knowing nod. "What's your theory on a fighter and his weight, Amos?" Nylon asks, giving me the lead-in to expand on the subject.

"Well, Jack, my theory is that a fighter should be allowed to gain a pound a year as he matures, as his body fills out more. So by that formula, David Diggs can gain some weight in the coming years as his body hardens. But by coming in light tonight, he's showing that he considers his quickness a valuable weapon, one he wants to be working at peak efficiency."

Taylor already has his robe off and is ripped as ever. Chest bulging over his stomach, the two pectoral muscles hanging like a couple of ham bones. Midsection divided into six hard cubes, three on each side, the six-pack effect of countless stomach crunches. Forearms swollen, ready for trading concrete-block blows. Taylor actually weighed in three pounds less than the last fight, which tells me he's in great shape and he's focusing on speed even more in this fight, possibly hoping to catch Diggs early.

"Taylor looks very good, too," I say. "The lightest I've seen him in years. He always trains hard, but it looks like for this fight he took it to another level." Much as I hate the man, I got to respect the pain he went through to get into the shape he's in. It's a professional's respect.

The introductions are made and I tell Nylon and our worldwide audience the keys to the fight: Diggs to use his jab and move, Taylor to start fast and take away any momentum Diggs has from the last fight.

The bell rings. The crowd lifts into this titanic roar, and it's then I realize that we'll be doing battle with one of these men *real soon*.

Diggs pumps out two jabs in rapid-fire fashion. The first is blocked. The second connects, but only barely. Taylor rolls with the punch just as it lands, moving his head fractionally, away from the direction it was thrown, diluting the effect of the punch. Taylor hooks to the head in immediate response, but misses. Still, Taylor looks quick, quicker than I've ever seen him. Diggs has to be careful.

Diggs is moving left to right, drawing Taylor to him. Taylor follows on his toes and Diggs throws a combination—jab, right to body, hook to head. All land. Diggs scoots to his right. Taylor shakes off the punches and goes after him again.

Taylor jabs and Diggs blocks it. But the jab diverts Diggs's attention for a fraction of a second and Taylor comes in quick underneath with a heavy hook to the body. It lands just under Diggs's rib cage and I can literally hear him go, "Ooomph." The air sags out of him.

"That was a great body shot, Amos," Nylon says. "I think it might have shook David Diggs up."

"Yes, it was a good shot. Taylor is a good inside fighter who will brutalize your rib cage if you let him. Diggs needs to tie him up right now to kill some time and recover."

Diggs does. He grabs Taylor's arms and holds them tight. The referee comes in and breaks them apart. Diggs gets back on his toes and jabs, but misses the punch. He tries a quick sneak right—leading with the right instead of jabbing to set the punch up. Taylor bends his knees, though, and the punch sails harmlessly over his head.

"Taylor's defense looks good, Amos. Better than I've seen in a long time. Diggs is having a hard time connecting with anything so far."

"Yes, he is, Jack." I remember to say Nylon's first name, which will remind the viewers that he's not some nameless, faceless announcer who's just jabbering away. "Diggs is throwing a lot of leather, but you have to give credit to Taylor. He's making Diggs miss."

Diggs shuffles right. Taylor follows, jabs, moves to his left, cutting Diggs off. Diggs is in the corner, a place he doesn't want to be against Taylor. Diggs tries to tie Taylor up—just what I would do—but Taylor must have seen this coming, because he gives Diggs a forearm shiver that distances the two men.

Taylor lands a right to the body. Diggs tucks in his elbow to block the blow, but something is wrong. It happens so quick I almost don't see it. In dropping his left to block the body shot, Diggs has also lowered his right, not by much, but enough to create an opening. Taylor's left hand is planted on his own chin and he twists his hips. His left thrusts out, and traveling less than six inches, the punch finds Diggs's jaw. The short punches are always the ones that kill you.

"David Diggs is down!" Nylon yells. He hits me on the elbow. "Dropped by a hard left hook from the ex-champ!"

"Diggs dropped his guard for a moment and Taylor capitalized on the mistake! Can Diggs get up?"

The count reaches five, and Diggs, who has fallen onto his back, is still in the same position, eyes vacant. At seven, he sits up groggily, like a man severely drugged, and shakes his head. At eight, he gets to a knee, his mouthpiece half out of his mouth.

"Diggs is up!" Nylon yells. He hits me again. "He's on rubbery legs, but he's up!"

I look at the clock. "Twenty seconds to go in the round. The question is, can Diggs survive the round and make it back to his corner?"

The referee waves Taylor back in. Diggs tries to move around, but his legs are still shaky. He moves with the grace of a crippled swan trying to fly. Taylor lands a short right to Diggs's jaw and follows with a left hook that finds Diggs's temple, sending his mouthpiece flying out in a spray of murder red, and as he drops to the canvas in an unconscious heap, there's not even a count. The referee, using good sense, has called an end to the fight.

"I came here on a mission and I did what I said I was going to do. And that was execute that lucky no-hoper. I told everybody the man was lucky the last time out. Tonight, I proved it. I hope now there's no disputing my greatness." Taylor's at the postfight press conference, tooting his own horn. He looked good, for sure. We're gonna have to draw up a good game plan to beat him.

"Terrence, let's talk about your next fight, against contender Rodney 'TNT' Timmons, who looked rather impressive tonight in knocking out—"

"What, you talking about the Dynamic Duo? Scrap Iron and

197

TNT?" Taylor gives the crowd a sneer. "You got the fighter who can't think and you got the trainer who can't fight." It's all I can do to stop myself from going over there and smacking him in the mouth. "Fact is, if you put the two of them together, you might get a fighter who'd cause some problems. But even then I wouldn't be too worried."

I can't help it. I got to say *something*. "I'd be a little worried if I were you," I say into my mike. Diggs, who should be sitting next to us, isn't since he was taken to the hospital for a concussion right after the fight. "Because when we get into the ring, we're going to expose you as a fighter and also as a liar, the kind of man who makes things up about other men when the going gets rough." I give the media a quick glance to get their attention. "Ought to change your nickname from T-Bone to Tin Man, because if you had a heart, you might have never lost the title in the first place."

Taylor lets this set in, then steams. I can see his eyes light up. "This here heart just won back the belt," he says, punching his chest. "Good enough to do something a second-rate fighter like you never could."

"Just wait until we get in the ring. And we'll see who's second-rate then."

Strangely enough, TNT's quiet during all this. He's just looking down at the table at his hands, studying, it seems, the knuckles. If he hears anything Taylor or I am saying, he doesn't acknowledge it. Occasionally he's asked a question from the media but dismisses it with a wave of his hands, saying, "No comment. My manager can answer for me."

Taylor and I go back and forth on a good many things: which one of us don't have heart, who's gonna do what to who come fight time, who's more of a man. No conclusions can be reached by just talk—only Taylor and TNT in the ring together, man-to-man, bone-on-bone, can decide the answers.

TNT continues to sit like a gentleman, passing questions off to me, suggesting to me that maybe the boy has finally decided to listen. Instead of running off at the mouth all the time, he's finally thinking, doing the bulk of his work in the ring. And of that—of the ring work—TNT's doing a fine, fine job.

"Diggs, it's me, Scrap."

Diggs is lying in a hospital bed. I can't tell if he's asleep or not because the lights are off. I sneaked in by telling the person at the hospital front desk that I was Diggs's trainer. They didn't check ID or nothin'. Ex-champs fade from the scene pretty damn quick—even if it's a matter of hours.

"Ummh . . . ," Diggs mumbles. He turns over and opens his eyes. "Scrap, that you?"

"Yeah, man. It's me."

His face doesn't look that bad, but I bet he's got a hell of a headache. Taylor hit him like a lightning bolt tonight.

Diggs sits up a bit and reaches for my hand. It startles me. He holds my hand for a second and gives me a light squeeze. "Thanks, man," he says. "You know, outside of Renetti, De La Rosa, and some reporters, nobody else came to see how I was."

"Yeah, man. I know how that is. A man gets beat and everyone forgets about him all of a sudden."

"Thanks for coming, Scrap."

"Yeah. Well, I just wanted to let you know, man. Straight up, I didn't do what I was accused of."

"I know, man."

"You do?"

"Hell, yeah. Renetti don't see it that way, but I do. I know you didn't try to screw me out of nothin'."

He lets go of my hand and I give him a smile. Just a little one. "You gonna be all right, man," I say. "Take a few months off. Rest up. You got a ton of money now, you know."

"Yeah, I know."

"Well, we gonna be next in line for Taylor. And I'll promise you this: We're gonna give him a beating he won't soon forget. We'll beat that bastard into submission and win the belt back. Hell, you might want a crack at it before too long."

Diggs coughs and gives me another little smile. Even in defeat he's a warrior. "Yeah, man, I just might want another crack at that thing." He coughs again and I know it's time to go.

After Liston lost to Ali the second time, Sonny sat alone in his dressing room.

Patterson, who'd twice been knocked out by Liston and was at this point an ex-champion, came into Sonny's locker room to pay his condolences. He didn't know what to expect, but thought he'd tell Liston he knew what he was going through.

"I said to him, 'I know how you feel. I've experienced this myself,'" Patterson said. "And he didn't say one word, he didn't say anything. He just kept looking—because he had that mean look on his face. But I kept on talking anyway . . . and finally I said to myself I don't think I'm reaching him. I went to walk out the door, and before I could get out to the door, he ran up and put his arms around my shoulder and he said thanks. I turned around. And that's when I knew I reached him."

Back in the room and I'm tired, bone tired, from the evening's events. I can only imagine how TNT feels. I stretch out on my bed and relax for the first time in hours. Until I hear a knock at the door.

When I open it, standing before me is a sight: one brunette, one blonde, both with bodies that have more curves than a racetrack, barely concealed under tight black cocktail dresses.

The brunette stands to the left of the blonde and gives me a sinister smile, her mouth curling as she eyes me. "Hi," she says. "We're here to see Mr. Timmons."

"Look now," I tell them. "TNT, he's just had himself a hard fight. He's resting up and doesn't want to be bothered."

But they walk right past me, rubbing against me as they walk into the room. The blonde goes over to the window that overlooks the glitzy Vegas skyline, all lights and oversize buildings sweeping the landscape. She just stands there and stares out the window like I hadn't said a damn thing.

"Listen," the brunette says, walking up to me. "We're completely legitimate. We really are." She stops, puts her hands on her hips, and gets her purse. She pulls out her wallet and shows me an identification card. "This is me. My Wall Street identification card. I trade commodities on Wall Street. So does my friend."

The blonde comes over, fishes a card out of her purse, and shows me the same thing. Both pictures match.

"We have HIV results, too," the blonde says, and pulls that out. "Both negative. We practice safe sex and expect our partners to be safe, too."

I'm trying to take this all in. They can sense they have an advantage over me so they press it.

"We're intelligent, adventurous women who like to have good times with famous men. We're not prostitutes and we're not going to run to the media or anything like that. We're just here to have a good time."

The brunette strokes my arms gently. "A good time," she purrs.

"Let me make a quick phone call," I tell her.

The phone rings five times before a groggy TNT answers. "Yeah," he says sleepily. "What is it?"

"Get over here now, TNT," I whisper.

"Why?"

"Now's not the time for questions. Just get over here."

There must be urgency in my voice because TNT's at the door less than a minute later, hair sticking up every which way, like a half dozen sticks of dynamite, sleep crusting his eyes. I have the door just partly cracked. "What is it, Scrap?" he says, rolling his right arm over his head a couple of times real quick. "Damn shoulder's sore from all that punchin'," he mumbles. I open the door wider for him to see what's inside. He continues to stretch.

He sees them. I *know* he sees them because his eyes get bigger and lose their sleepy look. He gives his shoulder another roll. Shakes his head.

"They said they wanted to see you, TNT," I whisper into his ear. "Said they wanted to see you, and there they are, boy, right there, in those cocktail dresses tight as a fist in a glove."

TNT continues to stare at the two women. His eyes are vacant.

"They came here to see the man, TNT. And that, my friend, is *you*." I put a finger on his chest. "I know you're tired—dog tired— but you got yourself a chance to get yourself exhausted in a completely different way now. Because these women, they want to see what it's like to be with the next heavyweight champ of the whole wide world."

"Scrap, I . . ." TNT tilts his head toward the door. "Can I talk to you outside for a second?"

"Uh, sure." I take a look at the women. They're squirming out of the cocktail dresses now, stripping down to black lace lingerie. "Would you ladies give us a second, please?"

We go outside. "TNT, they're legit, my man. They showed me Wall Street ID cards, showed me HIV results—they're negative. They just a couple of beautiful women who like to live on the edge and want to sleep with a man of power." I give him a shrug. "You ask me, you got yourself the opportunity of a lifetime here."

TNT waits silently until I finish, nodding a little here and there. "Scrap, man, I don't mean no disrespect or nothin', but I already got myself a lady."

The hallway's empty. Which means I *can't* be hearing things. "Excuse me?" I put my finger in my right ear and turn it a couple times. "Did you just say you got yourself a girl already? TNT, come on now, you got two gorgeous women in there—legit as all get out. If there's a heaven, man, you just stepped into it! And you're talkin' to me about *another woman*? *Please* tell me I'm hearing things, because otherwise I'm gonna think I gone and lost my mind!"

TNT lets out this sigh that's a combination of fatigue and frustration, his chest heaving under his too tight white T-shirt. "It's September, Scrap. I really like her, man." Ah-real la-kuh, may.

"TNT! You only been out with her one time!"

"I can't help the way I feel, Scrap. I been thinkin' about her a lot lately. We just got off the phone when you called."

I put a hand on my fighter's sore shoulder. "The way I see it, she's there, way on the other side of the country." I wave my hands for emphasis. "You, you're here right now, my man." I point at the door. "See what I'm sayin'?" I lean into him. "TNT, Sonny wasn't *always* faithful to Geraldine. He fooled around on her, man. Right or wrong, good or bad, that's what he did, with all sorts of women. White, black, you name it, he did it. And he was *married* . . ."

TNT shakes his head and looks down at me. "All I'm askin', Scrap, is for you to respect what I'm sayin'. What Sonny did, man, that's his business. What I do is my business." He rests his hand on my shoulder gently. "I appreciate you callin' me over here, Scrap, I really do. You think about me more than anybody I ever known, man, and I can't ever thank you enough for that. But I think I might even love September, Scrap, and all I'm askin' for you to do is *appreciate* that."

A fighter-trainer-manager relationship is nothing without respect. Without respect, it cracks, crumbles, goes to shit. You got to believe that no matter what else, each part of that relationship has the other part's best interests in mind at all times.

"Okay, man." I give TNT a solid hug. "Why don't you go back to your room and get some sleep."

"All right, Scrap." TNT begins to walk toward his room, then turns around to look at me. "What you gonna do with those ladies?"

"Gonna go back to the room and see if they still in the mood for some fun." I smile at him. "Because I ain't in love with *nobody*."

Round Nine

Training for a title fight is new to me. New to TNT, too. But seeing how we're new at it together, we should be all right. The fight date has been announced. To capitalize on the momentum created from the postfight press conference, it's set in four months. Caesars Palace, outdoors, on pay-per-view. Taylor's getting twelve million for the fight, plus a cut of the pay-per-view sales, while TNT's getting two million. My one-third cut comes to $667,000, by far more money than I've ever had.

In fact, it's so much money I don't quite want to think about it right now. We got too much at stake with the upcoming title fight. The money's still gonna be here after the fight, I reason. No need to let it distract us.

I thought of taking TNT somewhere with me, Unc, and a few sparring partners, maybe a place like the Catskills, where the air is clean and there's nobody around to bother us. But then I thought, why go changing it all up on TNT, messing with the boy's routine? He's big on routine, and seeing how well we've done so far, I don't want to change our training for the biggest fight of our lives.

Unc and I begin training camp by watching tapes of old Taylor fights. He's a tough customer to be going to battle with. Has the same size as TNT, rock-solid power in each hand, iron chin, and good speed. At first glance, the only thing Taylor isn't really good at—besides keeping his mouth shut—is foot speed. Diggs gave him some problems with movement in the first fight. That's something to begin with, at least. It's what I like to do when sizing up an opponent. Find out his weakness and exploit it.

In the end, boxing comes down to styles. The old saying "styles makes fights" is the truth. A man can be the most gifted fighter in the world, can have bunches of speed, range, and power, but if he can't handle a certain fighting style, he's gonna get beat. That's why it pays to break down each opponent's style, figure out what that person is good—and not so good—at.

Maybe the fighter drops his left just a bit after he jabs. No problem. Counter with the right hand all night long. Maybe the fighter's great on the outside, but get in close and he can't do a thing. Simple. Stay on his ass the entire night, never letting him get more than a few inches away.

Style is what gives a fighter with less ability the chance to beat a guy with more natural talent. A tactical advantage, I call it. And for $667,000, I'm gonna find every tactical advantage in the world.

We head over to Jimmy Q's to get our minds off the fight. It's early in the week so we figure that not many people will be around to bother TNT. My fighter has been on the cover of the local sports section every day since we've been back.

Jimmy himself is tending bar tonight and his eyes light up like a full moon when he sees us.

"Guys, how ya doin'?" He ducks under the bar and shakes each of our hands warmly. He shakes with TNT last, putting his hand on my fighter's sturdy shoulder. "Most importantly, how are *you* feelin' these days, Mr. Soon to Be Champ?"

"Strong," TNT says, then holds up his right, balling it into a meaty fist. "The nutcracker, it feel good, too."

Jimmy gives me this it-ain't-all-there-is-it look and I just kind of shrug. You got to be a little crazy to be the best in anything, I guess.

"You're ready for Taylor, then?" Jimmy asks.

"Yeah, I'm ready. Scrap and Unc been workin' me hard in the gym and we been strategizing, too. We all about business, Mr. Q. All about winnin' that belt." All 'bout win-ahn dat bet.

"That's *Jimmy* to you!" Jimmy laughs, then looks at me in amazement. "Mr. Q! Can you believe that shit, Scrap?"

"Jimmy, or Mr. Q, or whatever the hell your name is, how about you get back to the other side of the bar and refill my drink?" I turn around and it's some guy in a red-checkered flannel shirt, faded blue jeans, and a baseball cap. In his thirties. A couple of his buddies sit next to him at the bar, all with empty mugs of beer.

Jimmy, no stranger to bastards like this, yells over his shoulder, "Yeah, yeah. Be there in a minute!" He asks TNT about how sparring's been going, says he saw Skeeter "Vampire" McCroy fight once in Atlantic City and Skeeter bled so much that his cutman up and walked out of Skeeter's corner after the seventh round because Skeeter's right eye was such a mess.

I feel a hand on my shoulder. I turn around. It's the guy in the flannel shirt. He has this big, bushy beard and yellow, crooked teeth. Jimmy gets a lot of blue-collar types in here.

"Excuse me, pardner," Flannel Shirt says gruffly, moving me to the side. I can't believe he's put his hands on me, because even though he's big—maybe six foot one, two hundred pounds—I'm bigger. He gets right on up in Jimmy's face and holds out his mug, which has only the remains of some foam on the bottom. "Now, do I have to hit you over the head with this here mug or are you gonna fill this fuckin' thing up?"

Flannel Shirt's two buddies, I notice, have come up behind him, arms crossed, doing their best to play the role of badasses.

Jimmy stares at Flannel Shirt for a second, eyes piercing. "Nobody's gonna be breaking *anything* in here," he says. "I don't know who you are, friend, haven't seen you in here before, but I'm the owner here. That means *you* don't talk to *me* like that if you wanna get served. And you certainly don't interrupt me while I'm talking to my friends. Now go sit back down over there—take your boys with you—and I'll serve you all once I'm finished."

One of Flannel Shirt's buddies gives TNT a long look and says to his friend, "Doug, ain't that the guy who's fightin' for the title?"

The friend shrugs his shoulders. Flannel Shirt stares at TNT and, recognizing him, says, "Yeah, that *is* him. Damn. Thought he looked familiar."

TNT gives Flannel Shirt a shy smile and nods his head a little.

"You're the fucking nut whose towel came off on national television." Flannel Shirt looks at Jimmy. "I didn't know you served *retards* in here."

The two buddies laugh. TNT gets a scowl on his face but also drops his head a bit. I think I can see his Adam's apple move.

I grab Flannel Shirt hard around the scruff of his neck. I squeeze his throat with such force that his knees automatically dip.

"Listen here," I say, trying not to raise my voice and alarm the rest of the customers. "I'm a peaceful man. But when you insult my fighter, you stupid son of a bitch, you insult *me*." I strengthen my grip and hear Flannel Shirt choking and it feels good to have him powerless.

But I'm grabbed from behind before I know it. An arm reaches around my chest and pulls me back. I spin and ball up my left, ready to step-in jab, then batter whoever's stupid enough to grab me, work the poor fool's rib cage until there's fractures.

"Easy now, son. Just take it easy." It's Unc. He's got this calm look in his eyes and the slightest of smiles on his face. Flannel Shirt is behind me and bent over, sucking in air from my choke, and Jimmy and TNT are inches from the two goons, I suppose just in case they try anything.

"Unc, why'd you grab me?"

Unc leans into me and whispers, "Either you or Rodney hit one of these men and everything we been working for could go down the toilet. You're both licensed professional boxers, and under the law, your hands are considered deadly weapons. So you just stay put." He slaps me on the shoulder and moves toward Flannel Shirt, who's since recovered, more or less, from my choke hold. He points a threatening finger my way.

"You!" he yells. Now we've got the entire bar's attention—maybe twenty people in all. "Me and you! Outside! Now!"

He has to be *crazy* to challenge me to a fight. I'd kill him!

Unc gives me a dismissive wave. "I think it's time for you to leave," he says softly to Flannel Shirt.

Flannel Shirt gets within an eyelash of Unc and I'm about to spring in between them myself, but TNT thrusts his large hands on Flannel Shirt's chest and gives him a light push, sending him stumbling backward.

"That's enough, son!" Unc reprimands. "Let me handle this."

Unc keeps eye contact with Flannel Shirt and says again, very calmly, "I think it's time for you to leave now."

Jimmy seconds him. "Yeah. Get outta my bar and take your buddies with ya. You're not welcome here."

Flannel Shirt's got fire in his eyes, though. "I ain't goin' anywhere till I get a piece of his ass!" He points at me.

The goons stay where they are, giving a healthy respect to the man who will soon be fighting for the world title.

"Got news for you," Unc says. "Only person getting a piece of his ass is a good-looking woman."

TNT smiles but doesn't laugh.

"But I tell you what," Unc says, moving closer to Flannel Shirt. "If you absolutely can't leave here without a fight, I think I can accommodate you."

Unc turns around and begins to head out the back door. Flannel Shirt follows. So do the rest of us. Some of the bar crowd begin to follow, but Jimmy stops them.

"First person to go out this door never gets served in here again," he says. Since this is the kind of place longtimers frequent, they take him at his word. "This here's a *private* matter."

The back of Jimmy's bar empties into an alley. A couple of green, industrial-size Dumpsters sit on both sides of the narrow passage, and a thick fog rises up from the ground. All of us are outside—me, Unc, TNT, Jimmy, Flannel Shirt, and his boys. Unc's rolling his arms over his head and twisting his hips from side to side.

"So, you like goin' in bars, demanding things, calling people names, do you?" Unc says to Flannel Shirt. Unc starts running in place real fast.

Flannel Shirt licks his teeth and grins. "Old man, I do *what* I want *when* I want to *who* I want. And I don't give a fuck about you, this bar, or the big dummy over there."

"Well, we gonna see about that," Unc says. He gets into his boxer's stance.

"Unc!" I yell. He hasn't *fought*—actually gotten in the ring with a man who was trying to hurt him—in at least twenty years.

"Quiet, Amos. Let me do my thing here."

I move toward him but Jimmy gets in front of me. "Let him, Amos. Let him handle this guy."

Flannel Shirt starts the fight by throwing a wide, screaming right at Unc's head. Unc cleverly ducks under it. Flannel Shirt falls off-balance from the miss and stumbles. Unc smiles as Flannel Shirt gets back on his feet, eyes burning.

"Kick his ass!" one of the goons yells.

Flannel Shirt throws a left and misses, but instead of stumbling, he kicks Unc hard in the knee. Unc immediately bends down to grab it and Flannel Shirt takes advantage by throwing a looping right that catches Unc on his lip, slicing it. A small stream of blood drips onto the ground. Flannel Shirt is about to kick Unc again when TNT intervenes. He shoves Flannel Shirt so hard that he goes flying into the ground, and when he lands, he does a backward somersault.

Unc hobbles on the injured knee and pushes TNT away. "Dammit, let me handle this!"

"But, Unc, he just gone and kicked you!" TNT stammers.

"If you don't let me finish this on *my* terms, I'm gonna kick something of *yours*."

TNT looks over to me and I wave to him to come over my way. "Man, fuck," TNT says, sighing.

Unc's got a look in his eyes I ain't seen in a long, long time. A look of unchecked fury. Flannel Shirt gets back on his feet. His buddies dust him off. "You all gonna step in every time I knock this old fucker around?" he smirks.

"They ain't gonna do a damned thing," Unc says. He glares at us. "It's just you and me and an ass whipping that you're due for."

Flannel Shirt shakes his head and smiles. "Old man, you must be about as stupid as they come."

Unc's back in his stance, hands high, chin tucked in, but he's favoring his right leg. Flannel Shirt tries to jab but it's obvious from the way he throws the punch that he's just a street fighter, a barroom brawler, undisciplined in the ways of a true boxer. Flannel Shirt's shoulder gives everything away by moving a full second before the punch comes. Unc moves his head to the side and the left storms by.

Unc's circling on his left toe, keeping Flannel Shirt within punching range. He lets loose a quick jab and the punch splits between Flannel Shirt's guard, tagging his nose. Flannel Shirt blinks. His eyes water. Unc shifts a little more to his left and jabs again. Same result. Flannel Shirt's eyes are welling up now from the nose punches and he's fast losing composure.

"Keep that jab in his face," I holler. "Keep sticking it!"

Flannel Shirt grabs Unc's left arm and tries to wrench it at the elbow. Another one of his street-fighter moves. Unc's face twists for a second but he backs up a step and straightens his arm out. Unc takes his right and drops it on Flannel Shirt's temple. Flannel Shirt's legs dip and he staggers backward from the blow, releasing Unc's arm.

We're all standing against the side of the alley, and even though Flannel Shirt's buddies aren't making any moves, TNT says forcefully, "Y'all stay right the fuck there. Or I'm gonna open up a big old can a whip ass on both a y'all!"

They don't move a muscle.

Flannel Shirt grimaces and moves close to Unc once again. Unc's lip is fat and bloody, knee's hobbled, but he's got this look of confidence on his face anyway, kind of like Sonny used to have before

212

his fights. The confident smile, just a tiny upturn at the lips that says, "I'm here, baby, now how you like *that?*"

Flannel Shirt tries to jab again but Unc parries it with his right palm, slapping it away. Unc jabs in reply. Flannel Shirt's head rockets back as the punch lands. Unc jabs again and there's a stream of blood oozing from Flannel Shirt's nose—his hands are wiping the blood away when Unc hooks off the jab, the punch landing on Flannel Shirt's eye, right on the socket. The area begins to swell almost immediately.

Unc shows he's got a little street fighter in him, too. He steps hard on Flannel Shirt's left toe and Flannel Shirt yells like a wounded animal. Unc takes advantage. As Flannel Shirt's chin lowers to look at his foot, Unc gives it to him. A snarling right uppercut that begins with Unc dipping his knees, getting his body underneath Flannel Shirt's. Unc's right explodes toward Flannel Shirt's nose, the punch getting most of its force from the burst in Unc's legs.

Flannel Shirt's head cannons back as the punch connects. His arms flail helplessly by his side and Unc stands silently, admiring his work. Flannel Shirt's legs are going every which way, like there's a wire that runs from his brain to the rest of his body and Unc's punch has snapped it.

And without moving forward another inch, Flannel Shirt falls right on his ass, blood spilling from his nose, eyes glazed, face battered like raw meat.

Unc's breathing heavy and he's sweating. But his voice stays calm.

"From now on, young man, I'd advise you to be careful of who you call a *retard*. You just might piss somebody off."

Flannel Shirt don't say a word. He just runs his hands across his face and comes up with smears of blood. TNT tilts his head to the goons and they cautiously approach their beaten friend.

"You guys try to spill any of this to the police or media, just know that I got witnesses inside that bar—regulars a mine—who'll back us up in a court of law," Jimmy says. "Now take your buddy, what's left of him, and get the hell outta here."

They help Flannel Shirt up and begin to walk a lonely path down the alley.

I walk over to Unc. He's bleeding from his lip still, limping from the kick, but he's got a million-dollar smile on his face. TNT beats me to Unc, though, and embraces him.

"Thanks, Unc," TNT says. "I 'preciate what you done, but you didn't have to go and get yourself hurt."

"The hell with hurt," Unc says. He takes a step back and fires his still useful jab in the air. "Nobody's gonna talk about a two-time navy boxing champion's friend and get away with it, now are they?"

I see TNT mouth the word, mouth it slowly, but he's doesn't say it. *Friend.*

I begin sessions with TNT by getting in the ring with him myself, working on a move specifically designed for Taylor. Today's move is what I call a quick spin. Taylor's a hell of an inside fighter—good body puncher, good leverage, short, crisp punches. Inside, I think he might even be better than TNT. So we've got to offset that. Where Taylor isn't as good is on his feet. It takes him a second to adjust when moving his body angles—if he plants his feet in one spot, then has to change his feet in another direction, it takes him a hair longer to adjust than the average fighter.

Most of Taylor's opponents know he's good inside, so what they try to do is just tie Taylor up. Grab his arms and hold on until the referee breaks 'em. But Taylor's strong. He usually breaks free with that strength, pushes his opponent off him, creating a gap, then starts

214

punching. Just like that, he's back on the inside, doing damage. I've seen it on tape dozens of times.

"All right," I tell TNT. "We gonna work on spinning off today. You remember what I told you, right?"

"Yeah, Scrap," he grunts. TNT's got on dark blue headgear, blue gloves, and a red protector cup sits on his hips. I'm wearing blue headgear as well—just in case TNT lands a stray punch—and red gloves with a white cup. "When we inside, I spin left. And while you catching up to me, I punch. Then I spin again and do the same thing. After two runs, I move right and get back outside."

The boy is listening good these days. "You got it. Get on over here and show me now."

We simulate the move of two men in close. I lean my left shoulder on TNT, feeling just how big a man he really is, his weight solidly rooted on the floor despite my heavy leaning. I say go. TNT spins to his left, moving his body away from mine, at the same time creating a punching angle for himself. Where my body is now located, I can't reach TNT with any punches. I have to adjust my own feet and body position to do this. As I'm moving, TNT lightly fires a three-punch combination at the top of my head. Ping, ping, ping. And as I throw back, TNT's already spun again, firing again, ping-ping-pinging again, and I'm moving my feet again, but TNT's danced away, out of my range.

"You got it, my man," I say as TNT continues to move side to side, waving at me playfully with an open glove. "But we need to keep working this here move. Time and again, till it becomes habit. We got to not just do it now, but in sparring, too, all the time. Got to make it like second nature."

"I hear you."

"You know why we want it to become habit?"

"Yeah, Scrap. Because habits, man, they like my head, man."

"How's that?"

"They hard to break."

Sonny trained with attitude. Hell, the man *always* had an attitude about him. Even though she often talked about what a gentle man he was, Geraldine also said, "He don't set up and grin at me all day, either. I ask him a question and he gives me an answer and he's through. He's not a grouch, he's just got that look on him."

Sonny could be brutal on his sparring partners. His training camp manager, Archie Pirolli, had himself a tough time just finding live bodies for Sonny to work with. "These fellows get fifty to sixty dollars a day, they have no expenses, they get the best of food," Pirolli said. But when Pirolli would call to inquire about their availability, many would tell him to just drop dead. You couldn't pay a man enough money to take the beatings that Sonny would give in sparring.

While in Denver training for the Ali rematch, Sonny was sparring with a big young heavyweight from Pittsburgh. Sonny made the kid's nose bleed all over the floor and, wanting him to stay in camp, made sure the kid held his head under cold water to stop the blood.

Sonny asked Teddy King, his timekeeper, if the kid was going to leave camp.

"Well, he wants the doctor to look at his nose," King said. "He could have a doctor here look at it, but he wants to go back to Pittsburgh."

"Did you tell him it was the altitude?" Sonny said.

"*I* told him," said Chauncey Hudson, a 170-pound sparring partner Liston was using to simulate Ali's speed.

Geraldine heard about the kid's nose later that night. "Charles, you hitting him too hard?" she said.

TNT and Unc have just gotten back from dates with September and Katrina. Unc comes in first, humming a Temptations song he said he just heard on the radio. He's dressed up more than he normally is—light blue shirt, first couple buttons opened at the neck, pressed white slacks, and brown loafers. He's still humming when he takes a seat in his easy chair, not smiling outwardly, but from the upbeat tone of his voice I can tell he had himself a fine evening.

I checked the weather earlier and saw that it's seventy-eight degrees in Nairobi. I ain't never probably going to visit Nairobi, but you never know. If TNT wins the title and Gene Davis offers us enough money, I suppose we'll fight anywhere. Besides, it would be good to take the title over to Africa. Give the folks over there a show. I wonder if Sonny ever thought about going over to Africa to fight?

"What you doing, son?" Unc asks, pointing at the television.

"Watching tapes of Taylor's two fights with Diggs. Looking for things here and there." Diggs jabs, lands, and Taylor shakes his head at the punch, like it didn't faze him. "You have a good time tonight, Unc?" I know he wants to talk about his date.

Diggs jabs again—this is the first fight—and Taylor parries the punch with his right hand, then steps inside and unloads on Diggs's body.

"Yes, I did. I had myself a fine time." I click on the remote to pause the fight. I look at Unc, who's leaning back in his chair and smiling like some kid who's just been told every day from here on out is a Saturday.

"What'd ya'll do?"

Unc's hands are resting behind his head. "Just had ourselves a nice time, Amos. A real nice time. That Katrina," he says, and thinks for a moment. "She's good company. You know what I'm saying? That's what she is. We went out for some dinner, had some nice conversation, then went back to her place for a while and just sat around, talking." He takes a deep breath. "Just nice to sit around and talk to somebody for a change, and enjoy their company."

I give Unc a smile. "So did you just talk, or was there something else going on?"

"Nah, son. It's not like that. We just talked is all."

"That's *all*?"

"Yes, that's all." He sounds agitated and gets up from his seat. "She did give me a good-night kiss on the cheek, if you got to know," he says, walking into the kitchen. "She's just a good, clean girl and I enjoy talking to her. You got to realize, son, you don't have to do the nooky knockin' with every girl you meet."

"Okay."

"And you too damn young, Amos, to be sittin' around here night after night, cooped up like some animal, obsessing about this fight. You're a young man. You need to be getting out the house and enjoying yourself from time to time."

My cheeks get hot and I stand up. "I enjoy myself, Unc. I'm just making sure I know as much about Taylor as possible. I want us to be ready when we fight."

Unc turns on the faucet and pours himself a big glass of water. "Ready?" He laughs. "You know Taylor so well by now from all you studied that you more ready than any trainer I ever seen. And you gonna sit here and tell me you *too busy* to do anything tonight because you needed to study Taylor's tapes." He laughs. "You watched his damn fights so many times you should have 'em memorized by now in your brain."

"There's always more to learn . . ."

Unc swallows half the water and throws the rest into the sink. "Of course there's always more to learn. Yeah, you could sit here every damn night, watching every tape of every fight Taylor's ever had, and you could probably pick up new things. But you got to get out there some, son, meet some people, have a life away from the ring. Hell, look at Rodney. He's out tonight, having himself a great time. Sometimes I think *you're* the one fighting Taylor, the way you stay cooped up. You so focused sometimes, Amos, it scares me."

My eyes are hot, hot as my cheeks, but I'm cool. I know Unc just wants to help. "I just need to be ready for this one, Unc. I really do. It means everything to me."

We're both quiet.

"I just worry about you is all," he says.

"I know, Unc." We hug. "I know."

He steps back. "You find anything good on those tapes?"

"Couple things. We can go over 'em tomorrow."

"Good." He walks to his room but stops at the door. "Katrina said June asked how you were doing."

"She did?"

"Yep. I told Katrina to tell her you were doing fine." He pauses, smiling. "June also said that you were 'ruggedly handsome.' You believe that, Amos?" He begins to laugh. "Ruggedly handsome!"

"Shut up, Unc."

"All right." He goes into his room.

I look out the window of the living room. It's dark out. None of those flashy Vegas lights dominating the sky here—just a blackness

219

that settles the surroundings, making the night quiet. Peaceful. A feeling of calm comes over me.

I wonder if Sonny ever felt this way, looking out his window, the feeling of the challenge of his life staring him down, and for the tiniest of moments, felt peace with it, enough peace to sit back and breathe deep, even while knowing there's still hell to go through.

TNT does his roadwork early—around six—with me and the other sparring partners. I don't much mind the running, been doing it all my life anyway. We do around five miles a day at a pretty brisk pace, starting slow, then picking up speed between the second and third miles. By the fourth we're really cooking, legs pumping high in the air, lungs expanding, strides lengthening, legs feeling the burn usually only felt in the later rounds of a tough bout.

By the last mile we're all exhausted, running on nothing but guts and a vision of what the opponent's doing, and that vision almost always includes an opponent who runs that final mile hard, harder than you do, and that vision makes you run with even more urgency, till the legs are ripping with acid buildup and the lungs are gassed out to capacity, looking for nothing but rest. It's in the last mile, the one that's run more in the head than in the body, that a man really gets himself in shape. Not in the body—the mind.

After the run we all eat breakfast over at the Capital. Me, TNT, Unc, and the sparring partners. Machine Gun, who I just hired now that his ankle's healed, Primo Garcia, a veteran Mexican heavyweight who's durable and provides good work, and of course Vampire McCroy, whose tendency to bleed in his biggest fights earned him his nickname. All three work like hell in the ring, giving TNT valuable sparring rounds in the gym.

And sparring's where fights are won or lost—where things get real as possible, two men going at it, head-to-head, trying to take the other out. We don't play around in sparring. This is serious business. I've even offered ten thousand dollars of my own money as a bounty for anybody who can knock TNT down during training, hoping the cash reward will be incentive enough for the sparring partners to do their best to try and work TNT over, which he's gonna need if he's gonna get into the kind of fighting shape he needs to be in to beat Taylor.

Nobody's collected so far on the bounty, and as far as I can tell, nobody will. TNT has a rock-solid jaw. He's never been knocked down as a pro, and I've rarely seen him seriously stung by a punch. Some fighters, they're just born with a strong jaw. There's lot of theories why. Maybe the fighter has a strong overbite and that makes his chin stronger.

Could be that the fighter's wisdom teeth were pulled. Supposedly, pulling these weakens a fighter's jaw. Maybe their jaw muscles, which are as dense as muscles come, aren't fully developed. Me, I was never down as a pro either and can't explain why. I got my bell rung a few times, sure, but never did hit the canvas. But some fighters, they just have this tinkle in their chin, and when a punch comes their way, it's even money whether they're gonna drop.

Patterson explained getting knocked out about as well as any man ever did: "It's not a *bad* feeling when you're knocked out. It's a *good* feeling, actually. It's not painful, just a sharp grogginess. You don't see angels or stars; after Liston hit me in Nevada, I felt, for about four or five seconds, that everybody in the arena was actually in the ring with me, circled around me like a family, and you feel warmth toward all the people in the arena after you're knocked out. You feel lovable to all the people.

"And you want to reach out and kiss everybody—men and

women—and after the Liston fight somebody told me I actually blew a kiss to the crowd from the ring. I don't remember that. But I guess it's true because that's the way you feel during the four or five seconds after a knockout . . .

". . . But then this good feeling leaves you. You realize where you are, and what you're doing there, and what has just happened to you. And what follows is a hurt, a confused hurt—not a physical hurt—it's a hurt combined with anger; it's a what-will-people-think hurt; it's an ashamed-of-my-own-ability hurt . . . and all you want then is a hatch door in the middle of the ring—a hatch door that will open and let you fall through and land in your dressing room instead of having to get out of the ring and face those people. The worst thing about losing is having to walk out of the ring and face those people . . ."

TNT and I are walking over to September and June's house. Stars fill the New Jersey sky tonight and the moon's half-out, giving the evening the feel of its own Vegas glitter.

The women don't live far away so it's a short walk. We had ourselves a good workout today. TNT's jab was ripping into McCroy's face for three rounds, causing the Vampire to bleed. Then he dug sharp hooks and tight right crosses into Primo's rib cage, making the tough Mexican scream *"Alto!"* at one point, as he was doubled over by the body blows.

But I been worried about TNT. Sure, he's been training hard as ever, sparring like a warrior, running swiftly in the mornings, watching fight tapes whenever I ask him to, but he's also been spending every free moment outside the gym with September. Every night since we been back from the Rocket fight. TNT always comes home by midnight, but he's always over there, hanging out with her.

"Just like bein' around her" is what he tells me about it. "I'm still focused on what I need to be focused on."

Still. I don't want other things to be occupying my fighter's mind this close to the battle. We need total focus on Taylor.

"So you excited to see June again, Scrap?" he asks as we head down their street.

I stop walking. "TNT, I ain't excited to *see* anybody. I'm just coming along because there ain't nothin' else to do tonight."

TNT smiles. "Unc told me she called you 'ruggedly handsome.' That why you comin' over?" He just recently started calling Unc, Unc.

"Man, you can just forget the whole thing if you gonna go on like that." I turn away from the house but feel like a fool.

"Come on, Scrap. I was just playin'."

I stand my ground a moment longer and eye my fighter top to bottom, forearms bulging, neck thick, face lean from the training. He looks like a killer. "Just knock off the goofy stuff," I say as we walk together toward the house.

We get to the door. Their house is similar to Unc's—older, made just after World War II, light green on the outside, small front yard, nice narrow porch in the front of the house with a couple rockers on it, overlooking a suburban street.

TNT, with handpicked flowers at his side, knocks and stares at the door like a gentleman. "She always come by the second knock," he says, and gives me this gleeful look that makes his eyes crinkle.

Sure enough, September opens the door just before knock number two. The flowers take the breath right out of her. "Oh, Rodney," she says, and gives him a big hug. "You *shouldn't* have."

I'm just standing around, hands in my pockets, when September pushes TNT away and says, "So nice to see you again, Amos." She extends a delicate hand and we shake. I give her a soft shake on purpose—not something I'd do with an opponent or promoter, where the shake is everything, what defines you as a man.

"Nice to see you, too, September."

She grabs TNT by his elbow and motions for me to follow. "Come on inside," she says, and we do. "I'll let June know that you're here." She yells upstairs, then looks down at the flowers in her hands. "Let's go to the kitchen, Rodney. You can help me put these in a vase." TNT nods and they're gone. I'm left standing in the living room and damned if I don't feel like I've just been ambushed.

June comes downstairs moments later, wearing a maroon sweater and blue jeans. She has a little bit of makeup on, blue eyeliner just above her lids. She looks pretty.

"Hi, Amos," she says, as I get up from the couch. There's this awkward moment where I don't know whether to shake her hand or hug her, and in the end I do both, give her a half shake that ends up being a quick hug, which, I have to say, feels nice.

We both sit and I tense up a little, remembering our last conversation about boxing and the law. I get ready for some verbal sparring.

"So, I hear you're all leaving in a couple days?" she says. "How do you like it out there in Vegas?"

"Vegas is great," I say, trying hard to enunciate each word, just like in my announcer's voice. Something about June being in law school makes me want to elevate my word choice, so I add, "Vegas is actually quite splendid." I cringe after saying it, though, realizing that me using the word *splendid* just don't sound right. "I like it a lot is what I mean."

"It's where all the big fights have been over the last twenty years, I've noticed," she says. "Hagler-Hearns, Holmes-Cooney, Holyfield-Bowe."

I pull back some in my seat. "How you know all *that*?" She smiles. Her lips must have a hint of gloss on them because they're shiny in this good way that makes 'em sparkle.

"I've been reading up on the sport. In fact, I read a book about boxing this past week. Joyce Carol Oates wrote a book called *On Boxing*. It's a collection of essays. Very perceptive writing."

Joyce Carol who? "Yeah, she's good," I say. I don't know who the hell that is but don't want to seem ignorant.

"I found *Them* to be one of her best novels. Though she's quite the short story writer, too."

I know I'm in over my head but I ain't ever gone down without swinging first. "Yeah. *Them* is pretty good, but not as good as my favorite book, *They*. Now that was one good book."

Thankfully, June laughs and I'm off the hook. There's no more talking about Joyce Carol Quaker Oats.

"We gonna take a walk," TNT says. He and September appear in the doorway. "Ya'll mind?"

"Fine with me," June says.

I shrug my shoulders. "Knock yourself out." TNT gives me a look, a fighter's superstition. "I mean, have fun."

"What I'm saying is that I still don't approve of boxing as a form of entertainment," June says. She's gotten us both cold bottles of beer and we're drinking and talking on the couch. "Two men pummeling each other for sport, for entertainment, for money. It just seems warped to me."

I sip my beer and nod. "It's an old argument. People are always going to be opposed to boxing. The truth is that once you get hit, you lose brain cells. And brain cells don't ever come back."

"So how can you justify doing it?"

225

"June, I can't sit here and explain it to you. Not in any words you'd understand. All I can tell you is that you have to know what it feels like to hit and be hit to fully understand. You have to be in there to know what it really feels like to slip a punch, to know how damn good it feels to move your head to one side when another man's throwing a punch at you and, because of what you did, that punch sailed on by. You have to be in there to know what it feels like to have another man, with his guard up, expecting you to hit him, yet your jab is so quick that when you fire it at him, it still surprises him and hits him because it's so fast.

"And to fight in Vegas, under the bright lights, before a big crowd, with the entire world watching . . ."

"I'd have to be in there to really know what it's like," she finishes.

"Yeah." I take a deep breath. "Sorry about that. I didn't mean to ramble on."

"No." She pats my hand lightly. "You're passionate about it. That's a good thing. I don't fully understand what you're talking about, Amos, and I certainly don't like it. That's just me, though. But it's good to be passionate about something. Most people go their entire lives without any kind of passion."

We talk about June's passion next—the law—and her plans to practice once she finishes school. She says she'd like to stay in town and work for a small firm where she can actually go to court and practice law, instead of being a highly paid paper pusher for some hotshot New York City firm.

I finally tell her it's about time for me to get going, and she walks out to the porch with me.

"Thanks for having me over," I say. "I enjoyed it."

"I did, too. Good luck in Vegas."

"Does that mean you're going to be watching our fight?"

She sighs. "I can't see paying forty-nine ninety-five to watch two men beat each other, but September's already ordered the fight. She promised Rodney she'd watch him."

There's silence for a moment.

"Since she'll have it on already, I guess I'll watch," June says. "I'll look for you in the corner."

I give her a smile. "And I'll make sure to give you a wink from that corner. All the way from Vegas."

"You do that."

There's another odd moment where we're both quiet again, and so I step into June and give her a hug. I hold her close to me and smell her neck. The scent reminds me of country apples.

"I hope to hear from you when you get back, Amos. With or without the title."

"Hopefully with," I say. We pull apart. I lean into her again and give her a quick kiss on the cheek. She shyly grins and turns away. I see TNT and September coming up the street as I walk down the porch steps.

The next day, after sparring—we usually work at least six rounds a day, sometimes as many as nine—we go back to Unc's and watch tapes of Taylor for a half hour or so, then discuss strategy. Sometimes the sparring partners join us. Sometimes they just do their own thing. Unc's house is always open, he tells them, so every now and then they drop on by.

Tonight, TNT, Unc, and I are watching a couple of Taylor's fights and talking about a particular hitch in Taylor's step that Unc has spotted. Every time after Taylor punches, he does a short one-two, left-foot, right-foot shuffle, with his feet. It's how he sets himself to punch again. Time and again, we watch it. Taylor punches, plants his feet, puts his left forward, moves slightly, puts his right forward, moves ahead a little, punches, then sets again.

Once or twice we notice that something Taylor's opponent does interrupts the two-step, as Unc is calling it. A jab from his opponent while in midstride. Just moving out of the way. Or pushing into Taylor, disrupting the flow of his mechanical movement.

"That's what we got to do, then," Unc notes, jotting it down in a notebook he keeps for moments such as this. Unc's always doing this when watching fights on tape. He writes down his observations and then uses them at the gym the next day, teaching them to other fighters. "We got to mess with that two-step. It's the whole basis of his offense. We screw that two-step up, we mess up Taylor's entire game plan."

I see what Unc's getting at and am glad to have him help. He's got a talent for finding tiny glitches in good fighters. Chinks in an otherwise sturdy armor. "It's a shuffle is what it is," I say, slapping TNT on the knee and motioning toward the set. "See there. He goes one-two, one-two. Then he punches." We watch as Taylor fires a heavy-duty combination at some helpless soul's head, then does the shuffle, one-two, punches, one-two, punches again.

Unc rewinds the tape. Both fighters rapidly move backward on a shaky screen. The tape resumes.

"Watch here," Unc says. "Now."

Taylor punches again—double jab, right hand. He lands all the punches. As he's in the middle of the two-step, though, his opponent sneaks in a jab of his own. Taylor stops the two-step and, disoriented from the annoyance, shakes off the punch and tries the two-step again. Shuffle, shuffle, but before Taylor can complete it, his opponent has moved to his right, out of the straight line Taylor's walking in. The opponent lands another jab, then a right. Taylor shakes his head again and tries the two-step once more.

This time, the opponent is standing still, giving Taylor the chance to complete the movement and land the punches that follow after.

"When you give him a little something different, it messes him all up," Unc says, looking at both of us. "You see what I'm saying? His little hitch step gets all screwed up when you do something to stop it. Throw a jab, move out the way, whatever. The key is that it stops him from punching."

"And when he's punching, he's most dangerous," I add.

TNT sits up in his seat, moving closer to the television, his large, round eyes focused heartily on his opponent. I like seeing TNT intense like this. "When he ain't punching, I *am* punching," he says. "And that, my brothers, is gonna be plenty dangerous. Believe you me, it *will* be dangerous."

We got but a week to go before the fight. We're leaving tomorrow for Vegas—me, Unc, TNT, and the three sparring partners. Affairs for the bout are pretty much tied up. We got the plane tickets, rooms at Caesars, a workout schedule at a Vegas gym for the last few days before the fight, and a daily media interview session, so we can continue the fight buildup. Everything appears to be taken care of.

We're at the gym and TNT is on his sixth round of sparring. Machine Gun worked with TNT the first two rounds, McCroy the second two, and now Garcia is finishing up the day's work.

Garcia jabs and the punch lands square on the top of TNT's headgear, the glove smashing into the leather as it connects. TNT dips under Garcia's following right and hooks to Garcia's rib cage. When the punch lands, I hear air come right on out of Primo.

"Dammit, you got to get underneath that jab *before* it lands!" I yell. "Taylor's jab will bust you up if you don't slip it!" I'm up on the ring apron, looking for weaknesses in my fighter—any final flaws that I can correct before the fight. There haven't been too many.

Garcia spins to his left, fires a jab, and mimics Taylor's two-step. One. Shuffle. Two. TNT throws a forearm out at Garcia, disrupting the stutter step, then fires another hard hook to the body, same spot as before. Garcia doubles over at the waist, hands down, and TNT throws a short, corking right hand to Garcia's now-exposed head. Dozens of other fighters are watching this, our last workout session here at Unc's before we go to Vegas, and what they see is Garcia, a sturdy heavyweight with a reliable chin, get drilled with a right hand that looks so perfect in delivery that it could knock out any man, and I do mean any man, on the planet.

The right travels four, maybe five inches, steam practically coming off it, and TNT rotates his wrist before the moment of impact, his entire arm rotating as well with the movement, creating more force, more sharpness to the blow.

Garcia's knees buckle and he falls backward, into the ropes. The bottom rope sags low to the canvas and holds Garcia's barely conscious body up. His eyes are glazed and senses impaired as TNT, who I've told to act like every sparring session is the title fight—and as a result, never to let up, even for a second—races over to finish the job.

"Stop! Stop!" I yell as TNT has already fluidly moved with the grace of a jungle cat toward the ropes that are keeping Garcia from touching the canvas. "That's it for today!"

TNT, his right cocked to deliver a final, mind-numbing blow, looks back at me. Garcia is still on the ropes, tangled and helpless. "We done for today," I say again. "Good work, baby. Good work."

TNT stares at me, holding his gaze, his right still primed to fire, eyes bulging like satellite dishes. It's a look that is both disturbing and, at the same time, almost joyful, for me to see. Right now, TNT would hit his very own mother if she was in the ring with him. He is in a pure warrior state. Anger, motivation, raw energy, and fury have blended together to form a man whose primary goal is to go out into a Las Vegas ring, in front of millions of people watching across the world, and shut another man's brain down for money.

It's a look that's achieved after months of grueling training, the same brutal torture in the gym day in and day out, the body breaking down and building up with each passing day, until the only thing that keeps a man sane is the opponent. The vision of the opponent, that is. Seeing him in your head every moment, what he's doing to prepare for the fight, right at the exact moment you're thinking it. What he's gonna do to you in the ring, what punches he throws your way, and what his power tastes like, when his glove smashes you in the mouth, ripping open your upper lip and all you taste is a mixture of his leather, the salt from your sweat, and blood.

You go to bed each night, exhausted from the training, back locked up, muscles pulled but still functional, welts and bruises on the face, raw to the touch, legs on fire from the daily running and rope skipping, and even then, asleep, he haunts you in your dreams, stands before you in a recurring vision. Mocking you and taunting you, letting you know that even asleep, you still haven't escaped him.

It's what keeps a man sane during the training for a fight. The vision of the opponent. And you grow, after a while, to dislike that vision very, very much. You grow, after a while, to *hate* it.

I should know. Because I've been there. I've had those visions, and I've grown to hate them very much.

By the look in TNT's eyes right now, I can tell that he, too, has that vision. Taylor has been haunting him long enough, in his waking hours, and in his dreams. Taylor's been there, gloves raised, mocking him, taunting him. I've seen Taylor, too, both awake and asleep, the visions growing stronger as fight time approaches.

The weather in Vegas is oven hot and the sky is clear when we get off the plane. Slot machines flood the terminal, the neon lights flaring up and beckoning. I resist the urge, as does Unc, but not TNT. He rushes over to a dollar-a-pull machine and puts in a ten. Pulls down on the lever five times at two bucks apiece and comes up empty each time.

"Man, shit." TNT looks at me with disappointment. "Didn't get lucky even one time."

Unc, ever the practical one, shakes his head. "Boy, what I tell you about gambling? It's like taking a wad of money and just giving it to the casino. The odds are always with them, son. How you think they stay in business?"

"Man can still get lucky every once in a while," TNT mumbles.

We all walk off to get our luggage.

There's two pictures of Sonny that stick out for me. One is when Sonny posed for the cover of *Esquire,* December of '63, back when he was champ. He's dressed in this Santa Claus outfit and has his famous scowl on his face, looking, as a writer once said, like "the last man America wanted to see coming down its chimney."

Corporate America sure didn't like having Sonny-as-Santa on the magazine's cover. *Esquire* ended up losing nearly one million dollars in pulled advertisements.

The other picture is of Sonny sitting down in a casino. Behind a roulette wheel, or blackjack table, shirt off, sullen look on his face, staring at the camera. I wonder what Sonny was thinking at that moment.

Probably was wishing the camera would leave him alone so he could gamble in peace.

Now that we're in Vegas, all we got to do is count down the days to the fight. But for a fighter, the days and hours before a fight stretch long, like the Nevada desert, sprawling and vast, never seeming to end. Time becomes the biggest enemy. Time just sits, sits in the hotel room while the television's on, drowning out the noise. Time sits over a meal, overpowering the taste of a steak, until the juiciest piece of meat is tasteless in your mouth.

Time just sits and stares, waiting for a man to go crazy.

I know time and know what it can do to a man. Outside of the last couple workouts, all we got to do over the next four days is the interview sessions with the media. So Unc and I do our best to make it go faster.

TNT's a big fan of movies, and we have him make up a list of ones he's dying to see. The list includes *Star Wars, Jerry Maguire* (TNT loves screaming "Show me the money!" when he's in one of his moods), *Glory,* and *The Great White Hype,* a boxing comedy. Movies help wear down time, help ease TNT's mind, the two things we need most before the fight.

"Terrence, Rodney 'TNT' Timmons is an explosive puncher who has been on a hot streak of late. In fact, ever since Amos Fletcher has taken over management and training of his career, Timmons has been moving steadily up in the rankings. Could you give us your opinion of the job Fletcher has done and the threat Timmons presents to your title?"

The question is similar to that of hundreds asked in the past week here. All the questions more or less stack up the same: You've got a past with Scrap. Tell us about it so we can keep the controversy coming.

I can't say I fault the newspaper and television folks. Controversy sells. People got an interest in genuine bad blood between folks—it's always been that way. For the most part, I try to keep my mouth shut and focus on the fight. Don't want to take away from the fight, which people should be paying attention to, because it's gonna be a good one.

"Man, it's the same thing again and again with you people," Taylor says, face souring. "I've done said it a thousand times already, but hell. If I got to say it one more time for you deaf reporters, I'll say it."

Sampson, the geeky *New York Times* reporter who asked the question, nods meekly, pushing his glasses up his thin, pointed nose. He holds his pen and notepad in front of him like a shield.

"Timmons, he's a good fighter. Good power. Takes a good shot. He's looked tough lately. I'll give him that." Taylor gazes down the podium over to where we're sitting. "So obviously the man's a threat. Any man who's big and can punch with authority is always going to be a threat."

Sampson scribbles this down furiously.

"But Timmons is also lazy in the ring." Taylor points to his temple. "Not all there sometimes, if you know what I mean. What, he's *Native American* now, talkin' about how he's gonna ambush me?" The media laughs. TNT looks confused.

"And for Scrap." Taylor looks my way. "Shit, we used to spar together. When you train with a man, you think you *know* him, and I'll tell y'all what, I sure thought I knew Scrap better than I did. There's a code among sparring partners, one you never break if you want to stay in the biz: Never, ever offer up camp secrets to the opponents. Not for free, not for cash. 'Cause once you do, your cred's gone."

Nylon speaks up.

"So you *still* maintain—despite the lack of any witnesses other than yourself and the fact that the Vegas commission lifted their suspension of Fletcher along with the conclusion that there had been no wrongdoing on his part—despite all this, you *still* maintain that Fletcher, as you've said several times before, offered you money in exchange for camp secrets of David Diggs, who Fletcher was working for at the time?"

"Most definitely."

Nylon looks my way. "Amos, your reply?"

I consider taking a deep breath, to get time to clear my head. But then I decide against it. It might look like I'm nervous or fidgety, and I don't want to give off that impression, because I'm not. At this moment, more than anything else, I'm just *tired* of all the bullshit surrounding my suspension.

"Jack, I've always maintained that the exact opposite happened, and many people who know me in the fight game have proclaimed my innocence. I thank those people for that." I stare at Taylor during all this, wanting every word of mine to sink in. "What it all adds up to is that I feel sorry for Terrence. I feel sorry for him because any man who has to make up such an outrageous story to cover up for that fact that he'd just been beaten—well, it doesn't say much for his self-respect. Because me, I'm a man, Jack. That's all. I do my work honest, and at the end of the day I can look myself in the mirror and know I see a man there that I respect and that *I'm* proud of. And to tell you the truth, I think other people do, too."

Taylor's face turns dark and the media has this calm about them. All is quiet, except for some scribbling that creates a light, drifting sound in the room. My fighter looks at me, places his hand on mine, and smiles. Unc is in the audience, too, nodding his head, and rubbing an eye. Later on, I know Unc will say he had something in that eye rather than admit anything else. I feel good about what's been said, like for once in my life I've said what I've wanted to say well, said it *right,* and to say anything else right now would only damage the moment.

I stand, my fighter's hand still on mine, and raise both of them into the air, our fists high, triumphant. We hold them there. I feel the bright flashes of cameras, hear murmurs from the crowd, see the wicked intensity of Taylor's face. None of this matters to me now. What does matter is me and my fighter, Unc in the audience, June back home, and Nylon, smiling, shooting me an upward thumb.

TNT and I walk off the podium, out of the room, while questions, many questions, are fired our way. But we leave, having answered all the ones that mean anything.

TNT's last sparring session before the fight. We got ourselves a gym here in Vegas to train in and I've closed it off to the media. Don't want them around for our final workout because I don't want the writers printing anything that could give Taylor an edge. I also want this last training session to be just between us—me, Unc, TNT, and the other camp members.

My fighter's gonna go hard today. Real hard, but only for three rounds. I don't want him overtrained.

"Listen now, TNT," I say to him, buckling up his chin strap on his worn brown leather headgear. "I want three fast rounds outta you today. Throw lots of punches, my man. Hard punches. Simulate the first three rounds of the fight in your head—make yourself believe it's Taylor in there you're fighting today. You got it?"

"Yeah, man," TNT says, his mouthpiece half hanging out his mouth. But I'm not convinced.

"Close your eyes," I tell him.

He looks at me.

"Close 'em," I repeat. He does. "Now clear your mind. All I want you to see is black. A big blank wall of black. Nothing else. Tell me when you got it in your head."

TNT's eyes are shut, his headgear's buckled, and he's breathing in real deep. "Got it."

"Good. Now think of Taylor for me. Think of him with his shirt off, gloves on, sweating. Think of him with a snarl on his face, TNT. A nasty snarl, see him with his right hand cocked, ready to throw it at you. See him, TNT."

"Yeah. Yeah, I see him."

"Good. Keep your eyes shut. Now hear him. I want you to hear him, okay? I don't want you to hear anything in this gym . . ."

TNT partly opens his eyes.

"Keep 'em *closed,* dammit. You think I'm playing around?"

He shuts them again. "Naw. I don't think you playin'."

"I want you to block out all the sounds in here until all you see is Taylor and you don't hear a damn thing."

TNT's eyes peek open again for a second. "I keep hearin' the bags getting hit, Scrap."

I turn around. The sparring partners are shuffling around, loosening up. "Next motherfucker to hit a bag gets fined ten big ones!" I shout.

We get instant silence.

TNT shuts his eyes. "Okay. Forget blocking out the sounds. Now keep your eyes closed and think of Taylor. See him. You see him, TNT, don't you?"

"Yeah, man. I see him."

"All right. Now I want you to hear him, TNT. Hear his voice. Hear him saying, 'TNT Timmons, man, he ain't never been shit and he ain't never gonna *be* shit.'" I pause to let it all sink in. "You hear him?"

TNT nods, eyes still closed. "Yeah, man. Yeah. I hear him now."

"Yeah. And how that make you feel?"

TNT's quiet a moment and I'm about to interrupt him when he says, "Gets me mad, Scrap. That's what it does. Makes me want to be in the ring with him *now*."

"Good. That's what I want. Now open your eyes."

He does. I stare at him. "You *are* in the ring with him now."

TNT looks confused. He glances over at the sparring partners, who are now stretching in silence. "Naw, Scrap, I'm gettin' in the ring with *those* guys," he says, pointing.

"That's where you wrong, my man. Close your eyes again."

He does.

"I want you to see him, TNT. Focus. Clear your mind and see him. See him in the ring, just before the bell is about to ring. See him with a nasty look on his face and all he wants to do to you is knock you out, punish you, make you look like a fool in front of the entire world. You know that's what he wants to do, don't you?"

"Yeah."

"You see him now, don't you?"

"Yeah."

"You don't like what you see, do you?"

"No."

"So what you gonna do about it?"

I'm saying all this real quiet, so nobody but TNT and myself can hear.

His eyes are still shut. Face serious as a mortician's. "Gonna crush him. Gonna make him pay."

"You gonna deliver a world-class beating to him, ain't ya?"

"Yeah."

"Open your eyes."

He does.

I move in close, closer than I already was. "It don't matter who's in the ring with you for the next three rounds. Don't matter one bit. Hell, I don't care if Liston *himself* came through those ropes, ready to duke it out. Because it's *Taylor* in there you fighting. You got me?"

"Yeah."

I point over to the sparring partners. They're all still loosening up, because they never know who's gonna spar until just before the rounds start. I like running my camp this way. Keeps everybody on their toes.

"Now who you fightin' today?" I ask my fighter.

"Taylor."

"And who are they?"

"Taylor."

"And what you gonna do to him, TNT?"

"Destroy his ass."

"Unc, put this on for me, will you?"

Unc gives me an odd look. "Amos, what the hell you doin', son?"

"We got three rounds to go today. TNT needs good work and I plan on giving it to him."

Unc holds the headgear awkwardly. "Son, you haven't sparred in months. And Rodney, he's been in there damn near every day. Why don't you let one of the regulars go in there for his last workout?"

"Naw, Unc. Come on now. Put the headgear on me. If you don't, I'll just get Skeeter or Primo to do it."

Unc lets out a big sigh. "What are you trying to prove?"

"Ain't nothin' to prove, Unc. TNT, he got something to prove."

"The hell are you talking about?" Unc fastens the chin strap. The headgear feels snug around me.

"I need to know for myself that he's ready, Unc. And the only way to do that is get in the ring with him myself and test him out."

"You make him sound like a new car," Unc grunts. "Testin' him out."

"It's just somethin' I need to do. He goes three hard rounds with me and then I'll *know* he's ready."

Unc sprays a generic mouthpiece with a blast of cold water and sticks it in my mouth. His face looks serious. I can see wrinkles forming in his forehead.

"He ain't gonna kill me, Unc. Don't you worry about that."

TNT's already in the ring. His eyes are shut and he's talking to himself in this low voice, walking to each of the four corners of the ring and bouncing his back hard against the ropes. I step into the ring and throw a quick combination in the air—jab, right hand. I nod to Unc. He looks at the clock next to the ring and waits for a fresh minute to start.

"Time!" Unc yells, and I race to the center. My fighter's head lifts up and he opens his eyes. He stops and stares at me.

"Scrap!"

"Naw. I'm Taylor."

He looks confused. Precious seconds go by. "You Scrap."

"No, I'm not. Who did we say you were fighting today?"

Silence.

"Who, damn it?"

"Taylor," he says, voice just barely above a whisper.

"All right, then. Now who am I? Remember, TNT."

His eyes get dull and narrow, like he's figured out something complex. "You Taylor."

"Yeah. Yeah, that's right. And what you gonna do to Taylor right now, TNT?"

He sniffs in some air through his nose. "Gonna take him out."

"Hell, yeah. Now let's get to work. We already wasted enough time here."

It feels *good* to be back in the ring again with a live body, good to be on my toes, dancing, shuffling around side to side, seeing an opponent with dangerous fists cocked, primed to throw deadly blows at my head.

TNT must take me for a sucker because he leads with his right and misses. Hell, lead rights rarely work. Ali managed to land some on Foreman in their 1974 title fight, but Foreman was slow as the mail.

The punch whizzes by my ear and I counter with a short left hook that lands on TNT's nose. His head jars back and I skip to my left to avoid his counter.

"Jab, son!" Unc yells outside the ring, advice for TNT. Can't blame Unc for doing that. TNT is the one, after all, who's fighting for the belt, not me. "Step inside him and jab!"

TNT does a half nod and I know what's coming. He plants his weight on his back foot and springs off it, moving straight toward me, full speed ahead. I time the move perfect, spin out the way just as the punch comes, and TNT falls into the ropes.

He quickly turns and I greet him with two short uppercuts that

clip him on the chin, each punch lifting up his massive head. I drill
him with a hook after the right uppercut, the punch landing on the
side of his headgear, moving it over his eyes.

"Time!" Unc yells. He gets into the ring and positions the headgear back into its proper place.

My lungs are starting to burn some even though we haven't
worked a full round yet. Shit, this is tiring. I spit my mouthpiece
into my glove, partly to suck in some fresh air, partly to talk to TNT.

"You got to set that jab up, baby! You can't be telegraphin' it like
that! Taylor'll see it a mile away!"

TNT just stares at me, sweat starting to trickle down his chin.

"And *lead rights*? You got to be kiddin' me with them lead rights!"

Unc slips back outside the ring. "Time!" he yells again. TNT
comes at me hard, jabbing. I dip under his jab and hook to his body,
twist my fist in his gut. He grunts, pushes me off him, sending me
back on my heels. The boy is strong. Quick, too. He's on me fast,
closing the gap, and he fires a short right to my body. I lower my
elbow just as it lands and my arm takes the brunt of the blow. Still,
my elbow feels like a lead pipe's just hit it.

I spin out of the way and throw two jabs. TNT parries both away
with his glove and hits me with a sweeping hook. The punch lands
on the side of my jaw. My head rockets back and I can just make out
the right hand that follows—it comes sizzling at me and I bend under
it just in time, tie TNT up, and hold on tight to get my head clear.

TNT won't let me hold long, though. He pushes me off again
and I go back on my heels once more. He's on me, throwing body
shots with bad intentions. The punches sting like hell as they rico-
chet into my ribs. I keep my head lowered and hit TNT with a
sharp right uppercut, then a hook. He shakes his head no, telling
me without saying a word the punch wasn't worth shit.

I jab as the bell rings. It lands. I jab again. TNT blocks it, fires a corkscrew right that crashes into my side. I double over briefly, and as TNT's closing inside, I hit him with a left uppercut.

"Time! Time! Time!" Unc's in the ring, in between the two of us, prying us apart. "What the hell's wrong with you guys?"

Unc's got his arms under TNT's shoulders, leading him back to his corner. TNT fires a wild right at me anyway, but the punch misses badly. Unc shakes his head in disbelief and bear-hugs my fighter.

"What the hell is wrong with you, son? The bell rang damn near a minute ago! Now get the hell back to your corner." Unc eyes me. "You, too, Amos! The both of you are crazy!"

I stand my ground in the center of the ring and keep eye contact with TNT. His eyes are wide and red, filled with a mixture of rage and pent-up fury that now, after months of training, is coming unleashed in its rawest form.

I punch my chest with my right fist. "T-Bone Taylor, baby!" I yell across the ring. The rest of the fighters stand on the outside, likely thinking that I've lost my mind. But I don't care. "That's who *you* motherfuckin' dealing with!"

Round Ten

TNT's prefight meal consists of pasta, grilled chicken, mustard greens, bottled water, and grapes for dessert. The pasta provides complex carbohydrates, which TNT will need for tomorrow's fight, since the evening meal before a bout is usually the one a man fights on. Chicken has protein, greens are a good source of vitamins, and bottled water helps red blood cells quickly convert oxygen. Grapes have the best sugar for energy, and I'll also make sure TNT eats a couple bananas tomorrow morning. It'll give him potassium, which will help him retain water under the hot ring lights.

I eat the same meal as my fighter. Together, in silence, we feast, me conjuring visions of TNT in the ring, imagining what he'll do, how he'll handle certain situations. What if Taylor catches him with a thumb early on and TNT's eyes swell up like a balloon? How does TNT react? What if TNT knocks Taylor down early? Does he get out of control afterward, looking for one big shot to end the fight, or does he take his time and pick his shots?

I have no doubt that TNT, in these last twenty-four hours before he steps into the ring with millions of people watching from around the world, is thinking similar thoughts. And also the final, chilling thought that every fighter has just before he's about to step into the ring: When the bell rings, it's just me and him.

When the bell rings, I'm alone.

At nine, I'm back in my room. TNT's in his room, watching a movie.

I plan on dozing a bit, though I doubt I can. Just like fighting, this training and managing business seems to have the same effect on my sleep before a fight—it don't exist. Maybe I'll catch an hour, two, if I'm lucky, but most likely it'll be a long, long night. I'll continue to see Taylor in my mind, ready to do battle. He'll be there till the fight starts. Taylor jabbing, throwing the punch with bull's-eye accuracy, jackknife sharp and strong as steel. Taylor crossing with his right, the punch landing on my fighter's jaw, twisting his face as it lands, changing TNT's very features before my eyes.

In my mind, Taylor does everything right, moves in and out of TNT's punching range, hitting and not getting hit, his face clean as a fresh snowfall.

These are the visions that keep me awake, that keep me thinking. And my boy, TNT, he's in the next room, thinking, without a doubt in my mind, these very same thoughts. Because when the time to go to war with another man draws near, that other man is all you think about. He and you, alone in that ring, and you pray to heavenly God that you got enough, that you *man enough,* to be able to fend him off.

I hear a knock around four in the morning. I got the television on but the sound is low. Sleep hasn't come. Just thoughts of TNT and Taylor, playing the fight out in my mind like a tape, over and over again, hundreds of different scenarios appearing.

It's TNT. He looks groggy. Eyes puffy from needing—but not getting—rest. Dreads pulled back neatly, white T-shirt and gym shorts on. "Hey, Scrap, you got a minute?"

"Yeah. Come on in."

TNT looks around the room. "Man, it's about impossible to get any sleep on nights like this." He looks at me and laughs. "*Especially* on nights like this."

"Well, you know I know all about that." I point to a chair and motion for TNT to take a seat. He does. "What's on your mind?"

He runs his hand over his face, wiping his eyes, and sighs. In about seventeen hours, he'll be fighting for the heavyweight championship of the world, the chance to become a member in a very exclusive club. World champion. Just those two words, the sound of them, bring shivers. To be the best in the entire world at something. Most men would give years off their life to be able to say that just once.

"Got a lot on my mind, I guess. Mainly Taylor, though. Trying to keep the plan in my head, trying to think what I'll do in certain situations. Trying to see myself walking down the aisle to the ring, with all those people screaming." TNT laughs. "Probably so I don't get all freaked out when the time comes."

"Well, I know you done that many a time before. This here's exactly the same, except the stakes are raised a bit."

"Yeah, that's the truth."

Now it's quiet in the room. A good quiet, though. I know what my fighter's been thinking these past few hours. The same thoughts as me. It's like we're *one,* almost.

"How about we get out of here for a little while?" I say to him. "I know a place that I think we ought to go."

* * *

247

The sky is beautiful this time of the morning—a dark, bruised purple, dotted with grayish clouds that look like swans, and though night still reigns in the sky, daylight is fast coming.

The cab drops us at the entrance and I tell the driver to wait, keep the meter running. We'll be a half hour or so, but there's a good tip in it for him if he hangs around. He says he will. Then TNT and I head on over to see Sonny. Pay our last respects before this evening's fight. No planes coming in overhead at this hour, so Paradise Memorial is spooky quiet, maybe the only time and place that Vegas actually sits still.

The headstone's the same. Always the same. The name—"Charles 'Sonny' Liston." The dates—"1932–1970." And underneath: "A MAN."

The coming morning is cool. A slight wind is swirling, just enough to cut into the inevitable heat, making it pleasant to be out of the air-conditioning. The blades of grass are dew-soaked, but TNT and I both take a seat, right on our behinds, on the grass in front of the headstone.

"Thought we'd come out here and just talk, TNT." I notice he's sitting Indian style, legs crossed, hands folded across his chest. "About whatever comes to mind. Don't matter what, just whatever it is you think of."

"Yeah, sounds good to me." TNT fiddles with his thumb while staring at the headstone.

I close my eyes to create the proper mood. "Sonny, I hope you can hear us, man. Me and my fighter, Rodney Timmons, well, we both out here this morning because we got us a big fight this evening. It's for the title, and, well, I know you know all about that." I quickly open my eyes and see that TNT has his eyes closed, arms still folded, legs still crossed. Good. "We just out here to talk, Sonny, because

248

we just need to blow some steam off, I guess. You know how it is right before a fight. Can hardly sleep and all you see is who is gonna be in the ring. I guess that's about where we both are right now— me and Rodney, so we thought if we could come on out here and be near you, that maybe we could clear our heads."

When I finish, quiet takes over. Some birds chirp, light, fluffy little sounds, background noise, really, while we continue to sit. The sky's still purple, the clouds still shaped like birds, and TNT and I are still thinking, I believe, about Taylor.

"Hey, Sonny," TNT says, quaking the silence. "It's Rodney here." I open my eyes slightly and notice that TNT's smiling. His eyes are closed, but he's smiling. I close mine again. "Scrap's right, Sonny. We got a big one tonight. Biggest one of my life." TNT laughs, a short laugh that's more of a grunt than anything else. "Kind of like when you worked so hard to get that first Patterson fight. And you finally did. Man, I bet you was going crazy before that one, thinking how you was gonna *have to win* after working that hard, after waiting that long. Hell."

My fighter breathes in deep, and without even looking, I can tell his chest is swelled up cavern big. "Guess when it comes right down to it, a man's got to take care of what's in front of him. That's the measure of a man, isn't it?" TNT doesn't wait for an answer. Not from me, not from Sonny. "It helps, though, Sonny, knowing that you here. That you with me. I gonna be thinking about *you* tonight, before I go out there. Hope to make you *proud*."

I hear my fighter get up. My eyes are still shut but I can hear it perfectly: TNT stands, runs a hand over his now damp pants, clears his throat, and begins to walk off toward the cab. He says nothing to me—leaves me alone with Sonny for some final words, something that he and I need to discuss before I go. For this, I am grateful to TNT. Because my fighter, at long last, has now truly known what *I* was thinking.

The end came in December of 1970. Geraldine, who'd been out of town visiting her mother for the holidays, came back to their Vegas home in early January of '71 and found Sonny lying dead near the kitchen, an apparent victim of a drug overdose. His body had been there, authorities later said, for about a week.

The police officially ruled out a murder possibility, but some close to Sonny weren't sure. They said they never saw Sonny take drugs and that he might have gotten caught up in the Vegas underworld, done something wrong, and was killed.

The real story may never come out. But Sonny's final wish, as he told Geraldine, was to go down The Strip one last time. Geraldine granted that final wish for her husband, and gamblers in the casinos came out to watch Liston go by in his steel coffin. "People came out of their hotels to watch him pass," said Father Edward Murphy, a Jesuit priest who became friends with Liston in Denver. "They stopped everything. They used him all his life. They were still using him on the way to the cemetery. There he was, another Las Vegas show. God help us."

So what was the real story? Of Sonny's happiness? Did it exist?

I know there were moments when the man was happy. I see victory smiles on videotape after he won fights, or when a kid was sitting on his knee and Sonny resting there, all calm and carefree, like he didn't have a worry in the world.

But I also know the other side. Sonny and Philadelphia. Sonny and Denver. The police. The mournful look on his sometimes sad, tired face.

Near the end, Sonny often drove out to Lake Mead. There, he'd sit alone in a small motorboat, with a fishing pole, and drink beer. Thinking fighter's thoughts, I'm sure. Even when the fighting's over, the thoughts of the game still linger.

"But the thing with Sonny was no matter how close you got to him—and we were close—you always got the feeling that there was this sadness there that he wouldn't talk about," said Davey Pearl, a Vegas boxing referee and close friend to Sonny.

This sadness. I stare at the headstone, the trimmed grass around it, the vast Vegas sky. *This sadness.*

If Sonny's sad, I don't want him to be sad no more.

I don't say anything to him this time. Don't think I need to. I know he's here, close to me, thinking what I'm thinking. I've got a chance tonight—a good chance—to make him happy. I believe I can do it. Me and TNT, together, we can provide Sonny with some happiness.

It's the least we can do.

Round Eleven

I'm putting some final dabs of Vaseline on TNT's face, spreading the jellylike mixture under and over both eyes, adding to what I placed there an hour earlier. TNT's sweat has mingled with the Vaseline, creating small pellets of sweat on his cheekbone.

TNT's good and warm, courtesy of a fifteen-minute session we just finished with the hand pads—him throwing various combinations, me catching. His punches were sharp, fast, and accurate. My boy is ready.

Our music, the music I picked out just earlier today, after I finished my private discussion with Sonny, begins to play. Unc opens the door to our room and I can feel the fresh Vegas air drift in, helping to replace the stench of sweat we've created.

"Showtime, gentlemen," Unc says, winking at us both. TNT gets up and I lead him to the door. I grab my supply bag and put my hands on my fighter's shoulders, giving them a good squeeze. Our song continues and through the entrance of the door I can hear the crowd roaring, waiting to see the challenger appear before them after so much waiting.

I look to the night sky as I listen to the music and smile. Somewhere up there, among the stars and moon, he's listening. I don't know where exactly, couldn't fingerpoint the spot, but I know he's there and I know he's smiling.

"It's *our* song, Sonny," I say as we head into the crowd.

Me, TNT, and Unc walk down the aisle and move our heads slightly, side to side, to the rhythm of the song, "Night Train," what Sonny used to skip rope to when training for fights. He even went on *The Ed Sullivan Show* once, jumped rope to "Night Train," like a show pony for the entire world to see. "It's for you."

Taylor's entered the ring, blue velvet robe snugly fitted across his shoulders, something that doesn't surprise me. Taylor always wears tight robes. When he comes into the ring, he likes his opponent to see how big his shoulders look, so he likes to have fabric stretch real tight up against them. Doesn't bother me, though. What matters is what you do once the robe is *off*.

He throws a spurt of punches in his corner with his robe still on, sweat spilling from both temples onto his unshaven jaw, drops of it meeting on his chin and falling on the robe, creating spots of wetness around his chest. Me, TNT, and Unc just wait in our corner for the introductions, TNT bending over at the waist every once in a while, moving his hips side to side, loosening himself up.

"Nice, deep breaths," I whisper into his ear. "Jab with authority right away, stepping in with that jab all the time. Get out of his way once you're inside. Remember, don't stand straight in front of him, either. When he sets his feet, either move out of the way or disrupt his punching patterns." I feel like a man sitting before a priest for the very first time, confessing all my sins. Right now, I want to give TNT every bit of knowledge of the fight game I've ever picked up.

"All good, Scrap." TNT bites down a couple times to get his jaw loose. "Everything's real good."

The weather's about what I expected. Clear night sky. Hot as hell. The ring lights, shining down hard on us to give the millions of pay-per-view viewers a better view, make it about ten to fifteen degrees hotter. It's probably more than a hundred degrees in the ring. Men have been known to get blisters on their feet after long, grueling Vegas fights—from all the heat.

I think of all the places I've checked the weather these past few months: Caracas, Ho Chi Minh City, Buenos Aires, Zurich, Munich, London. Now Vegas. Vegas. We're here. I'm here. TNT's here. Unc's here. We're all here. We're in Vegas, in the ring, fighting for the world title, people from all over watching. Vegas.

People can say whatever they want to about me now, they can say that Scrap is this or that, put me down. Whatever. The truth is that I'm in Vegas *now,* on important business. I'm not anywhere else. I'm *here*. Nobody can dispute that.

The introductions come and go quickly. I feel like time has fast-forwarded me and only snap out of it when TNT's record is announced: 33–5, with 32 KOs. Cheers come when both names are announced, though, I believe, more come for TNT.

The ref wants both fighters in the center of the ring. It's Joe Terrino, a bald, heavyset Italian with lots of experience—he's refereed a bout or two of mine before, even. He's good. No-nonsense, doesn't let fighters clinch or clown around. Real businesslike.

TNT and Taylor stand face-to-face, noses inches apart, and I take a long look into Taylor's eyes while standing by the side of my fighter.

Taylor won't look at me—he won't look at TNT and his knowing smile, either—and I realize now, standing here before the biggest event of my life, that I really don't hate the man. I want to beat him, sure, but I don't hate him. At this moment, in Vegas, fighting for the belt, with everything I ever wanted from the game sitting here before me, I don't think I can hate any man.

The night has turned hot and I know it's going to be a hellacious bout. It's made even hotter by the way Taylor starts the fight—by coming out fast, fists flying.

He jabs, and even though the punch falls on TNT's gloves, Taylor advances, burying his head into my fighter's chest. A left hook to TNT's body follows, as does a right. TNT dips his knees and grunts, both body shots landing with thuds.

TNT spins to his left. Taylor stops, sets his feet, and begins to move forward.

"Break it up!" I yell from the corner. "Break up his pattern!" I know TNT likely can't hear my voice, any voice, but it feels good to yell instructions anyway.

TNT stiff-arms Taylor with his left, his arm thrusting out to the champ and pushing him back, almost on his heels. My fighter fires a right to the body of his own just under Taylor's rib cage and the punch finds a home. Taylor winces. I can see his eyes squint and TNT follows with a short left hook to the head.

It lands, snapping Taylor back into the ropes, and my man is on him like a vulture, his head now buried in Taylor's chest, both hands working machinelike on Taylor's body, every repetition of sparring, every drop of sweat spilled during training paying enormous dividends for us now. Taylor covers up well, hands high, elbows in tight. He's rolling with most of the shots.

"To the side!" I yell.

Unc leans into me and whispers, "Boy can't get cocky. Taylor's good off them ropes."

"I know. He's got to work the angles. Spin and make Taylor miss."

But TNT, caught up in the moment, the crowd screaming and on their feet, sensing an early knockout, doesn't move. He stands in front of Taylor, the last place he should be after he punches. And Taylor takes advantage.

TNT gets caught with a right—a wicked right that lands just above his temple, on the top of the head. Taylor churns a left hook quickly after, the punch finding TNT's nose like a baseball bat, the glove smashing into it, and I hear a squish as TNT's nose responds by leaking streams of blood from the left nostril, redness coming down onto his chin, over the Vaseline, spilling onto his naked chest.

TNT grabs hold of Taylor, his arms wrapping tight around the champ's upper back. The bell rings. My fighter must be hearing two bells, especially after taking that last punch. He gladly drifts over to the corner and plops down on the stool, a survivor of round one.

Unc's got a styptic pencil shoved up TNT's damaged nostril. It's still bleeding, splashes of red covering the base of the white stick. I see some red marks under TNT's right eye that'll probably develop into lumps in later rounds, a result of his facial bones being hit with more pressure than they're used to. I run a wet sponge over TNT's head, steam rising off him.

"You can't stand there in front of him!" I say, making sure to keep eye contact, so he can absorb every word of what I'm saying. If he gets one thing—just one thing—from what I tell him in between rounds and then goes out and uses it, I'll consider that a victory. It's hard for a man to make too much sense of what's being told to him in the corner.

Thoughts come in fragments in between rounds. There's sixty seconds on a stool to comprehend what just happened, there's the crowd noise, a cameraman in your face, and your opponent sitting on a stool on the other side of the ring, ready to come out firing when the bell rings again. It can get pretty damn confusing. To top if off, your lungs and legs burn like hot coals and there's nothing more you want to do than suck in as much air as possible so you got something to offer in the next round.

Unc greases up TNT's face. "You hit him with some good shots, son, then you stepped back to take a picture—admire your work. You can't do that with this man. Angles, son. What Amos talked about in camp. Hit and slide."

I soak TNT's mouthpiece in our water bucket. A tiny film of blood has seeped into the numerous tooth marks. I wash it clean and place the hard plastic back into TNT's mouth.

"Jab with authority, work the angles, and break his pattern," I say, my face just inches from my fighter's. I simulate what I want him to do, stepping back a couple of feet. "He goes one-two step, you push him off." I thrust my arm out. "You jab." I release a quick jab from my hip. "You step into him." I move forward, back into TNT's face. "Do that, and he's ours. You got it?"

TNT breathes deep, sweat coming down his face like a river. I take the styptic pencil out and throw it into the water bucket.

"Got it, Scrap," he says. TNT stands up, hits his gloves together, and jumps up and down as the bell sounds for round two.

In the ring, fights can last an eternity. Thirty seconds into a round, a man can think that round is near over, even though there are two and a half more minutes to go. Time can drag in the ring, especially when faced with an opponent who hits like a wrecking ball, or when you can barely lift your legs because they feel like dead weight.

But on the outside of the ring, when you're involved with a fighter, time flies. Lord, how it flies. It's a distinct pattern of sound, images, and flashes that hit the mind hard, some staying, some going, till you don't know where the hell time went.

In round two I see TNT stepping in with the jab, knocking Taylor's head back and sweat spraying from Taylor as the punch lands. I see Taylor grimace, bite down on his mouthpiece, and jab back.

I hear Unc beside me, hollering at TNT to move away as Taylor fires a combination at TNT's midsection. I see TNT's face sag as the shots land.

I see Taylor one-two-ing and TNT moving in with the jab before Taylor can punch.

I hear Unc yelling, "Yeah! That's what I'm talking about!"

I see a Taylor right come over the top of my fighter's jab, see the punch land with crushing impact, actually hearing the glove crunching the side of my fighter's cheekbone and see TNT's head go rocketing backward.

I hear myself scream, "No!"

I see TNT grab on tight to clear his head, see the referee breaking the fighters up while they're clinching.

I smell cigar smoke from the high rollers in the front row, movie stars who paid up to two grand apiece for ringside seats, puffing on giant cigars, the fiery orange ash lighting up the night.

I see TNT on his toes, sliding at different angles, and when Taylor sets his feet to punch, see my fighter firing at him with both hands, quick combinations that back the champion up and put him on the defensive.

I hear the bell, metal on metal, a dull ringing that means sixty seconds rest and then you're back in hell, and I see my fighter coming toward me, having likely just won himself a round on the official scorecards.

After six rounds, Unc and I have the fight scored three rounds apiece. Our votes don't count, so we're trying to be as objective as possible. For the hell of it, I paid Garcia five hundred bucks to watch the fight on pay-per-view in the hotel room, and he's calling me on my cell phone after every round to let us know how the pay-per-view's "unofficial ringside judge" is scoring the bout. He's got it 4–2, in favor of my fighter. Still, it doesn't mean much, considering the history of Vegas fight judges.

There's an old saying in the fight game about leaving any fight up to the judges: Don't do it. Hell, Larry Holmes beat Gerry Cooney with everything but the Bible in their '82 title fight. Knocked Cooney down in the second, jabbed him pretty much at will with his spearing left, scoring points all the while. But the judges had the fight close—real close—even though Cooney had been penalized a couple points for low blows. That Holmes was black and Cooney white made this closer-than-expected scoring even more interesting—seeing that a white heavyweight champion would be a much bigger draw than a black one.

Holmes made the scoring academic. He stopped Cooney in the thirteenth. But that fight was a lesson for anybody who goes the distance in Vegas. The answer, it seems, is to knock out your opponent so what the judges have to say don't matter.

But that's easier said than done, especially when the opponent can take the full brunt of a steel wrecking ball on the head and keep on coming. All we can do is fight the fight one round at a time. Focus on it like that and hope we come out okay.

TNT's features begin to change after the seventh, a rough round for us that sees Taylor land several hard rights to my fighter's face.

Taylor's right keeps landing high on TNT's left cheekbone, which has now swelled up the size of a tiny golf ball, the flesh knotted and hard, raised under the eye. TNT's upper lip has also been sliced open from repeated jabs. His nose is still bleeding and his left eye is puffy and closing fast. It's horrible, in a way, to see this transformation, but there's a disturbing beauty to it, too.

Taylor's face is changing, also. Both his lips are raw from round after round of taking hard jabs. His forehead is a series of welts and bumps, the area inflated like a tire, and his left eye is badly bruised, a dark purple outlining the attacked area.

The beauty—if you can call it that—comes in the history the two men are making, the legacy they're leaving here in Vegas, in the night desert heat, in front of all these people. Years from now, folks will remember seeing these features change, these badges of honor. And the core of TNT and Taylor will live on, in the memories of others, long after they've stopped fighting. The leaving of a legacy. That's the beauty, the terrible beauty, of the fight game.

My fighter begins the eighth willful, with fury in his eyes. It's as if he decided that the seventh was just one round, and now that it's over, he can write it off the books. He backs Taylor up with his jab, the punch spraying blood from the top of the champ's lower lip. TNT lands a hard right to the body, exactly on Taylor's rib, and I hear Taylor, obviously pained by the blow, moan. TNT spins to the side and Taylor punches—but hits nothing but air. When his fists come back to him, the champ is treated to a jab-right combination.

Both punches land on Taylor's chin, the right fired quickly, not really hard, the speed of the punch coming from its being planned to fire in TNT's head before he even threw it, the jab clearing the way for my fighter's right to come through Taylor's guard and make an impression. By the looks of things, he's made one.

TNT moves to his right, away from grabbing range, and connects with a monstrous right hand, the punch slamming into Taylor's temple. The champ falls back into the ropes on rubbery legs. TNT advances.

"He's got him hurt!" Unc yells, glaring at me. "Taylor's out on his feet!"

He may be. Queer street, I call it. But a man's always got to be careful when he has another man on queer street—'cause the man who's wobbly will do anything, and I mean *anything,* to stay on his feet. It's the fighter's instinct.

And Taylor is resourceful, which is why he's champ in the first place.

TNT strings a volley of punches at his dazed opponent. Jab, hook to the body, right uppercut, left hook to the head. Taylor rocks unsteadily along the ropes, moving his shoulders and head with each blow landed, more as a reflex than anything else, denying the punches of some, but not nearly all, of their force.

The crowd is standing, cheering, whistling, shouting. Going wild. Movie stars who make more per picture than most fighters do in a lifetime have their heads raised back, watching two men beat each other senseless in a Vegas parking lot, and they are loving every minute of it. Tomorrow morning they'll be sipping cappuccino in a Vegas five-star, thinking about taking a box-aerobics class, because of the brawl they've seen from the two men here tonight. Maybe they'll even use a power jab in one of their next movies.

They're all on their feet, TNT punching, Taylor taking, Terrino watching closely. I hear the sound just as TNT fires one more right to Taylor's body, the punch crunching into the champ's side. It's the bell. The damn bell. We had ourselves a chance to finish the champ, but the bell has gone and saved him.

"He's hurt," TNT pants on the stool, blood flowing freely from his mouth and nose. Unc wipes his entire face with a sponge and dips it into the water, which is now dark red. "I got him teetering."

I smear more grease on TNT's face. He looks like a pumpkin with dozens of ridges sprouting out in various places. His eye's near closed, an easy target for the champ's vicious right.

"Yeah, he's hurt, but the man's still dangerous. Don't you forget that."

I look to Unc, who's shoving a wad of tissue up TNT's nose, to stop the flow of blood.

"Side to side," Unc says, looking at me while doing the work. "Keep him confused with angles and hit him when he's turning to catch you."

"How you feel?" I ask. It's a stupid question, but in my mind, necessary. I know what TNT feels like: like a rack of raw meat that's been hit a couple dozen times with a baseball bat.

"Legs are tired. Can't see the right no more. Otherwise, I'm okay."

Shit. Can't see the right. Taylor's best punch.

"Keep your left up, son," Unc advises.

"Yeah, keep the left up," I repeat. "Remember, you got the momentum now. Don't let him take it from you."

After eight rounds, Unc and I have it scored at four rounds each.

Garcia calls right after the bell rings for the ninth and tells us they got it 5–3, us. But who the hell knows how the three ringside judges have it scored?

My fighter circles cautiously in the early stages of round nine, protecting his eye with his left, raised up high near the cheekbone, the fist open, ready to parry any blow coming its way. Taylor plods forward, jabbing, trying to get inside.

TNT feints a jab, putting his left shoulder in a short, quick, jolting motion, then throws a right to the head instead. The punch nails the champ flush, and again, he staggers backward.

"Get to it!" Unc yells. The crowd once again surges to its feet, a collection of suits and gowns and cigars that cost more than I care to imagine coming together in this primal roar, sensing the kill, like animals.

My fighter wades in, head planted firmly on Taylor's chest, hands moving rapidly, taking pieces of the champ apart. Hooks and rights dig deep into Taylor's belly. The champ howls and grabs at TNT. He ties my fighter up.

"Spin off, son!" Unc yells, his face so sweat-soaked that I consider getting *him* a towel, but the only one we have is covered in blood.

Too late. TNT doesn't see the first right coming, and he certainly doesn't see the second right, either, both thrown from the ropes, both desperation-style shots, thrown from the champ's hip, and thrown with power. The first crashes into TNT's unprotected jaw and his jaw twists from the blow. TNT's legs turn to jelly, moving every which way, his eyes wide and unfocused. He's stunned by the punch.

The second right is wide, looping, and if it had a straight arc to it, the punch would most certainly have deposited TNT on his back. But thank God for us, the punch isn't straight—so it doesn't do maximum damage.

"Hold, TNT! Hold!" I scream. His legs are still moving everywhere, left to right in a cyclone shift, his brain temporarily unable to signal to his body, the two now working as separate parts.

TNT grabs out of reflex and latches onto one of Taylor's meaty arms. My fighter's mouthpiece hangs half out in the clinch while the champ tries to continue punching with his freed-up right, but he's too close to do any damage.

Terrino, who's been in the middle of many of these clinches tonight, looks tired. And why wouldn't he be, having to repeatedly push apart two men who total nearly five hundred pounds?

"He's got to stay away and get his head cleared," Unc says to me, his brow creased with worry.

"I know." I have no idea of what else to say. It's one of those moments that is purely the fighter's. It's up to TNT now to survive. There's nothing more I can do for him. He has to keep clear of danger until the bell rings. And he has to do it alone.

TNT, on legs that still aren't working properly, tries to get on his toes. He stumbles while trying to move to his left. Taylor jabs, moves inside, and punches fiercely. I hear a man in a voice that sounds like crushed rocks scream, "Kill him, T-Bone! Finish the job!"

My fighter grabs, spins, and jabs. Taylor lands another right. Cameras flash everywhere, lighting up the arena with their repeated clicks. The smell of liniment, sweat, and leather mingle together and TNT falls into the ropes.

"He's hurt," I say to myself, so low that even Unc can't hear. "My man is hurt."

TNT raises his gloves to protect himself and Taylor responds by stepping back to create proper punching distance, about six inches away. With the proper spacing, Taylor bends his knees and lets rip a thunderous hook to the body—the punch heads straight for my fighter's rib cage.

TNT steps forward at the same moment, pushing off his back heel, where all his weight was. The punch collides into Taylor's left eye before the champ's body punch lands. TNT, now on the inside, holds on for all he's got and waits for Terrino to break them. During the clinch, the bell rings. We get out of the ninth alive, but just barely.

"Jab and move!" I scream, squeezing the soaked sponge, letting the freed water spray all over my fighter's battered body. Drops of moisture cling to him loosely as he leans back in the stool. "You got to stay away from him until you clear your head. You hear me?"

TNT's eyes are still glazed, like he's had six or seven beers. Pupils dilated, eyes not fixing on one particular point. "Damn, he can punch," TNT offers, the highest form of respect, I suppose, that can be given in the ring.

"So can you!" I plead with my fighter. "Stay away from his right." I shake my head, realizing that what my man needs right now isn't fight advice—hell, he knows how to fight. He's been doing it all his life. No, what he needs is something else.

"Stay the course, now," I tell him. "This next round, I want you to fight it for every person who ever told you that you were nothing. That you'd never be nothing but some joker, somebody people would laugh about. Well, everybody who ever made fun of you is watching *now,* TNT. They *all* watching now. They all glued to their sets right now, watching you in a life-and-death struggle with the world champ, and one of two things gonna happen here in the next few rounds: They either gonna say, 'Damn, he came real close.'"

"Or?"

"Or they gonna say, 'That motherfucker has himself a pair of steel gonads, the way he came back tonight.' And then they gonna say to their friends, 'I used to know that man.'"

TNT gives me a smile, only a tiny one, but that's enough for me. Shows he's listening. And if he's listening, he's got enough left to come back. Terrino comes over to our corner, customary after a fighter has suffered through a particularly rough round.

"He okay?" he asks me, giving my fighter a hard, close look. TNT matches him pupil for pupil and smiles again.

"I'm going to be watching very carefully," Terrino says to me, meaning, if my boy gets in trouble this next round, he won't hesitate to stop the fight.

"Thanks. We gonna be okay, though."

I nod and TNT stands up. He's still on unsteady legs, but he's here, he's willing, and, hell, I can't ask for much more. "I want you to remember all those people, TNT. Each and every person who ever doubted you. And then I want you to remember one more person while you're at it. A friend of ours, from here in Vegas. I think you know who I'm talking about."

The look on my fighter's face—one of perfect calm in the heat of this battle—tells me that, yes, he knows who I'm talking about.

We survive the tenth. But we don't win it. At best, the round's a draw, with TNT starting the round shaky from the shelling he took in the ninth. His legs return, though, halfway through the tenth, and his jab starts landing. By the end of the round, he's hitting Taylor with it pretty frequently, and the champ's right eye is practically closed, looking like a hard-boiled egg with a tiny knife cut through the middle.

After ten rounds, Garcia calls and says the fight is even at five rounds apiece. Two rounds are left. That's all. My whole life—our whole lives—coming down to six minutes.

"You got to take these last two rounds," I tell my fighter before the eleventh. "Move your hands, keep that left up, and back him up." I want TNT aggressive because Vegas judges like aggressiveness.

"This is it, son," Unc tells him. "The championship rounds are where champions are made."

And it is. The eleventh is savage. Two men going after the same goal: the right to be called the best, exchanging furiously in ring center. Time speeds by again.

For TNT, I'm sure, it stops, each minute seemingly hours, wondering no doubt when the bell will ring so his exhausted body can repair itself for one final charge.

A corkscrew right from Taylor. A sweeping hook from TNT. The crowd again on its feet. Me hearing, "Best fight I've seen in years," faintly, in the background.

Unc saying, "What courage. What courage these two sons of bitches have."

Sweat spraying from my fighter's head after being jolted with a Taylor jab. Taylor sneering through his closed eye, looking like a Cyclops, still trying to muster the punch that will finish my fighter for good.

The desert heat killing us all, drenching my open white shirt, pools of water running down my back, and me wondering what the hell the heat is doing to the fighters.

TNT slumping on the stool before the twelfth and final, spitting out his mouthpiece and me soaking it in bloody water, thinking about what Ali said after his brutal third fight with Joe Frazier— that it was the closest thing to death he'd ever felt.

Garcia calling, saying the count is now unofficially 6–5 for Taylor, but that a couple rounds could have been scored either way.

Me out of speeches, telling TNT that this round is for him, and for him only. Me telling him that I'm proud of him, that he's done something here tonight that people won't soon forget, that tonight he's gone and left himself a legacy.

Unc looking at me, saying nothing, but from the look on his face, I know he feels the exact same way.

Bodies spent but hearts still willing, the twelfth starts like a stack of dynamite being lit in a fuel truck.

Taylor's throwing bombs, obviously knowing he needs to make a final impression with the judges just as bad as TNT needs to. TNT's throwing back, the two men meeting together, hands flying, faces grotesque and nowhere near recognizable from eleven rounds ago.

A right from my fighter lands on the champ's jaw and he goes reeling across the ring. TNT pounces on him like a wildcat— hooking to the head twice. Taylor covers, then fires back with his own hook. TNT's mouthpiece almost flies out and Unc and I watch as the crowd builds into this deafening roar.

Midround, the pace slows. The two men have reached their limits, given all they have, every fiber of their souls. There's nothing left to give.

Both men jab—the punches are weak and slow for the first time in the fight. Neither man lands much. The crowd, which has been standing most of the fight, is still on its feet, waiting for a dramatic finish. But when a man's given so much of himself, when he's spent himself beyond what the human body can normally endure, what more do people want?

There's one last exchange. Both men trade—a hook from TNT, a jab from Taylor. Neither punch lands. Hands go up in the air from each fighter as the final bell sounds, proclaiming victory. No hugs, just a long look through swollen and sliced-up faces, men who have publicly been disfigured over the course of an hour, those disfigurements now physical badges of honor, gained in the ring.

"It's gonna be razor close," Unc tells me, clicking off the cell phone. "Garcia says they called it a draw on pay-per-view. Six rounds apiece."

"Holy shit, Unc. Could go either way, couldn't it?"

"Yep."

TNT hobbles over, spent. I grab my fighter by his shoulders and put my arms around him the best I can, his sweat and blood staining my shirt until I'm completely covered in both.

"What you did here tonight was important," I whisper to him. "Win, lose, draw, I don't ever want you to ever forget that."

"Thanks." He hugs me back and I think of how proud Sonny is of him right now.

Decisions in Vegas are never easy to predict—especially when you're going up against a champion. Some judges, they tend to vote for the defending champ in close rounds, thinking that the challenger has to "take the title" from him. Other judges just see two fighters as two fighters, regardless of the belts, and vote accordingly.

I've never known a fighter who was completely comfortable in the moments before a decision is announced. There's always this tremor of fear in a fighter before the verdict is read.

I honestly don't know, as TNT, Unc, and I stand in ring center, next to Taylor and his people, how the decision is gonna come out. It really could go either way. That's how close the fight was.

"Ladies and gentlemen, before we announce the decision, let's give a big, big round of applause for both fighters!" the announcer says. "This has undoubtedly been one of the greatest heavyweight fights in many years." The crowd responds with eardrum-popping cheers, and both fighters, through swollen lips, crack smiles.

Unc grabs my hand. I do the same thing with my fighter and here we are, the three of us, a human chain of boxing men, waiting for the decision to be read.

"We have the decision of the judges. Ladies and gentlemen, we have a unanimous decision."

I see Nylon getting the camera set up in one of the corners and he holds two fingers up—they're crossed for good luck. Taylor's trainer wipes his face with a wet cloth. I see Jack Nicholson in the front row, head raised, wondering who the hell is gonna be named the best fighter on the planet.

"Judge Tom Kasmarick scores it 115–114."

The Vegas lights are still bright, even outshining the stars.

"Judge Amy Logan scores the bout 114–113."

My fighter looks at me through his one good eye. His Adam's apple, I notice, moves just a bit. I squeeze his hand, and together, we wait.

"And Judge Richard Barnsworth scores the fight 115–113, for the winner by a unanimous decision . . ."

Still or *new*. Those are the only two words that matter right now. *Still* means Taylor wins. *New* means us.

"And *new* heavyweight champion of the world . . ."

TNT's jumping up and down and I'm hugging him fiercely. His heels are making a loud, thudding sound on the canvas. The ring is shaking and I notice a familiar gleam in TNT's eyes. It's that wild look, the look I've tried so hard to tame.

I make a quick mental list of who I'm gonna thank. Nylon is all smiles, no doubt ready to capture everything on camera. He'll be thanked. So will Unc. Maybe mention something about June. She'll get a big kick out of that. The sparring partners—can't forget them. All of these people I have to thank. And Sonny. Of course, Sonny.

It doesn't matter to me if people think that thanking a dead heavy-weight champion is crazy. Me and my fighter know what he's helped us do, and to me, that's all that matters.

The pay-per-view announcers are standing next to TNT. One of their guys is trying to keep his position between TNT and the camera and, through all the noise, is saying something, shoving the mike into TNT's face.

Oh, shit. TNT's still got that gleam in his eyes. I can't help but smile and shake my head as TNT starts to talk, his eyes getting bigger and bigger and bigger. There's no telling what that crazy bastard's going to say.

Round Twelve

Lately I've been seeing Sonny in my dreams.

He's in his fighting trunks when he comes to see me. They're a bright yellow or bold black. His shirt is off, gloves on, upper torso rippled with muscle and glistening sweat. "Let's work a few rounds," he says in a serious voice, and I'm intimidated, because he looks to be in fine shape, and I remember how big his fists were back in those days and how hard he could hit with them.

But I tell him yes, that sounds good, let's do that. And there I am, in a ring with Liston, gear on, ready to work, and when the bell sounds, we meet in the middle of the ring. Sonny puts out his left for me to touch, a gesture of respect, like him saying, "Good luck," or, "You all right, kid."

"Sonny?" I say to him.

"Yeah," he says, pulling his glove back when our fists touch, and he's bouncing on his toes, his gloves held high in the air, floating almost, toward heaven.

"Hey, man . . ." I forget what else to say.

His eyes get wide and they focus on mine. Not hard or hateful, but just kind of curious, like, finish what you was gonna say.

But I can't remember. I can never remember.

Being with him in the ring, though, only the two of us, somehow, it's enough.

He smiles at me and I smile back. I notice his gloves are still raised and I get mine in position, too, because I don't want to get cracked with one of his famous sledgehammer blows.

And I remember what was once said about him, that he was "somebody who reached for the sky above from the mud below." It always makes me sad when I remember that, like maybe Sonny never had a chance but he was always trying anyway.

Then there's another picture I see of him. It's from an old black-and-white tape I have. Sonny's shadowboxing in front of the camera. He's got a tight white T-shirt on and his arms are swelling like balloons, bursting out of the shirt. He's staring at the camera, not menacing or anything, just with a kind of sad look, like he's wondering what people are gonna do next to him.

But as Sonny starts punching, throwing lefts and rights with great speed, his face starts to loosen because he's doing what he loves.

Then me and Sonny are back in the ring. Sonny's got a smile on his face and I pivot around him, looking for an opening. He does the same. And we go on about our business inside the ring, working, working, always working, doing what we was both born to do.

ACKNOWLEDGMENTS

I would like to thank my parents, Greg and Pauline DeVido, for their years of support, love, and encouragement. Thanks also to my brother, Mark DeVido, his wife, Heather, and my sister, Kristen Seaman, and her husband, Dan. I am lucky to have such a terrific family.

John Kohler and Ann Clemency Kohler, thanks for helping shape my love of reading over the years. Thanks also to David and Beth.

Though my grandparents are no longer here, they are always with me in spirit: Lewis and Helen DeVido, and Peggy Kohler. You are thought of often.

Sarah Kelly, your faith in me and your love mean so much. Thank you.

My boxing coaches, Maynard Quesenberry and Dennis Kiernan, are good men both in and out of the ring.

Clyde Edgerton and Philip Gerard, thanks for your valuable contributions to this book.

Robert Lescher, my agent, believed in this book from the beginning. John Morefield, I appreciate the referral. Colin Dickerman and Panio Gianopoulos at Bloomsbury have been terrific to work with and have been committed to putting out the best book possible.

Thanks to my lifelong friends Allan Walters, Patrick Niehus, Mark Manetti, Andrew Zarechnak, and Elena. And to all my other friends who I don't have the space here to mention.

Since Sonny Liston passed away more than thirty years ago, my information on his life came primarily from outside sources. They include *Sports Illustrated* articles from Barbara La Fontaine and William Nack; Nack's article on Liston, "O Unlucky Man," should be required reading for anybody interested in Sonny's life. James Baldwin's article "The Fight: Patterson vs. Liston," in *Nugget*, was also helpful. The fantastic HBO Sports documentary "Sonny Liston: The Mysterious Life and Death of a Champion" contains a wealth of information, and the following books were also especially useful: *King of the World* by David Remnick, *The Devil and Sonny Liston* by Nick Tosches, *Sonny Boy* by Rob Steen, *In the Corner* by Dave Anderson, *Muhammad Ali: His Life and Times* by Thomas Hauser, and *Serenity: A Boxing Memoir* by Ralph Wiley.

A NOTE ON THE AUTHOR

Brian DeVido is a former Virginia Golden Gloves heavy-weight champion and two-time finalist. He received his M.F.A. from the University of North Carolina at Wilmington. His boxing fiction has appeared in *Words of Wisdom* and *Aethlon: The Journal of Sports Literature,* and he has been a sportswriter for the *San Antonio Express News* and the *Roanoke Times*. He currently lives in the Washington, D.C., area. *Every Time I Talk to Liston* is his first novel.

A NOTE ON THE TYPE

This old-style face is named after the Frenchman Robert Granjon, a sixteenth-century letter cutter whose italic types have often been used with the romans of Claude Garamond. The origins of this face, like those of Garamond, lie in the late-fifteenth-century types used by Aldus Manutius in Italy.